WE STARTED TO PUT IN THE IVs AND RIGHT AWAY RAN INTO DIFFICULTY....

With open heart surgery you want a large gauge needle so that blood or medication or both can be administered rapidly if needed. But the vessels were tortuous and tiny. Finally we were able to insert one small gauge needle.

Maureen gave as small doses of sedatives, tranquilizers, and muscle relaxants as she could, but even so the patient's blood pressure dropped precipitously. Then her heart stopped. A precordial thump—one bang on the chest over her heart—got her heart going again. The surgeon opened her chest quickly....

O.R.

BARRIE EVANS

A DELL BOOK

Published by
Dell Publishing Co., Inc.
1 Dag Hammarskjold Plaza
New York, New York 10017

Dell ® 681510, Dell Publishing Co., Inc.

ISBN: 0-440-17623-9

Printed in the United States of America
First printing—May 1982
Second printing—June 1982

Acknowledgments

Sam, who helped me to look at myself and like what I saw

Eleanor, who first motivated me to write

Lois, who helped me to write better

Thelma, who first published my magazine articles

Charlotte, who never ordered me to change professions but was damn glad when I did

B.J., who steered me on the path to anesthesia school

Ellen, my technical adviser, who dragged me through anesthesia school

Elaine, who bugged me to keep publishing

Jim, who inspired me to revise my last article on the beach at Baie Orientale

Lisa, who kept me in good shape and introduced me to Jeanne

Winnie, who insisted, "You've got it in you—now write it"

Jeanne, who had faith in my ability and motivation to do this book

Jane, who tried to provide me the experience I required

Judy and Pat, who encouraged me to be "their friend who wrote a book"

All my good friends, coworkers, and consultants in the anesthesia departments, in the operating rooms, and throughout the hospitals I've worked in

Diane and Jack, who listened breathlessly to every
word I read, on the beach at St. Anne
Joan, Bobbi, Edwina, Stephanie, and Jean,
who typed for me
Marie Anne, who provided an idyllic setting for
doing the "rewrites"
Last but not least—to my darling Arthur, whose
patience, faith, and love kept me going throughout,
and without whose constant interruptions this book
would have been three chapters longer

I

The overall effect was impressive, almost awesome. It was a large room. It seemed almost as big as a football field. It couldn't be that big. It was so white, so antiseptic, so impersonal. It could have been a temple of some kind, but it was filled with machines and people—doctors, nurses, and technicians.

There were lights recessed in the ceiling and riding on tracks—as much light as you wanted, anywhere in the room. The huge fixtures were moved silently along their tracks by merely pressing a button. The surgeon had a control, the circulating nurse did, too, and there was one attached to the side of the anesthesia machine.

Along the side wall stood a massive control board, almost like Mission Control. There were switches, lights, buzzers, and bells. There were large screens and small screens, readout ejection systems, and at the side of the entire apparatus, a generator. If power to the hospital was lost, this console would switch to its own generator in thirty seconds.

Over in a corner stood a long low machine with four round metal cylinders, two stationary, two revolving. Digital readouts appeared along the front.

It moved silently. Blood flowed into a large plastic ball off to one side and through thick clear plastic tubes. In time this machine would be the patient's life, the patient's heart, the patient's pump.

Large tables full of gleaming silver equipment stood in another corner. Great heavy instruments called retractors to pull large masses of tissue aside. Tiny curved instruments also called retractors to pull minute shreds of tissue aside. Big, thick needles and threads. Microscopic, delicate needles and threads. Each instrument had its assigned spot.

There was cacophony—the pump suction sucking, the respirator whooshing, the EKG monitor beeping. There was clicking, buzzing, whirring, and chugging. Each of the sounds meant something special to someone.

In an alcove stood emergency equipment: fibrillator, defibrillator, intra-aortic balloon pump. They were kept out of sight, but they would be used frequently.

Everyone in the room was busy. Technicians, specialists in biomedical engineering, worked the console. At the head of the operating table were three of us dressed in blue—two of us anesthetists, the other an anesthesiologist. On both sides of the table stood four hooded figures; paper helmets covered their hair, sideburns, and even beards if they had them. Blue and white masks covered their noses and mouths. All you could really see was their eyes. They were the cardiac surgeons—one attending, one fellow, one resident, one intern. Alongside the pump sat three perfusionists: two nurses, one technician. At the bottom of the table, hovering over the masses of instruments stood the two scrub nurses. Scurrying around in six places at the same time were the head nurse and the circulating nurse.

The patient's chest was open. A long metal instrument held the breastbone spread apart to show the heart, the lungs, the major vessels.

"Ventilate four times a minute now," the attending surgeon said.

"Yes, sir," I replied. I looked at the lungs expanding as I squeezed the bag. The two pinkish spongelike sacs had a coating of black specks on them—pollution.

"Ready?" he asked the perfusionist.

"Ready," she replied.

"Ready?" he asked the anesthesiologist standing behind me.

"Ready," he replied.

"Let's go on, then."

For a moment time hung suspended. Suddenly there was a loud report—like a crack. Everyone heard it; no one knew what it was.

"What's wrong?" the surgeon shouted. "The heart is getting smaller. Do something. Do something."

"What's wrong?" the anesthesiologist asked me. "The pressure is going."

"What's wrong?" the technicians muttered to each other. "The machinery is going crazy. Do something. Do something."

"What's wrong?" barked the perfusionist. "The pump is reversing. Do something. Do something."

"Look, look," the head nurse cried. A crack showed in the plastic bubble. Blood poured out as if from an open faucet.

"There's nothing in the heart," the surgeon shouted.

"There's no pressure at all," the technician muttered.

"The pump is stuck," the perfusionist shrieked. Blood covered the floor. It covered the attending's neat white shoes, the fellow's street shoes with shoe covers, the resident's clogs, the intern's bare feet. It covered the base of the respirator, the wheels of the anesthesia machine, the bottom of the instrument table. And still it came, more blood, bright red.

"Do something," shouted the surgeon.

"Do something?" asked the anesthesiologist. "What can we do?"

"Do something," muttered the technician.

"Do something," barked the perfusionist.

I moved forward. I woke up. I was sitting up in bed. Sweat poured from me. It was 5:27 A.M. In twenty minutes I would have to get up—get up and face my first day as a nurse anesthetist at Mid City General Hospital.

I lay back down. I had twenty minutes. I started to think of my new job, of my new career, of my new life. I was certainly looking forward to earning again—poverty was not my style and I'd just spent two years watching pennies.

And the work itself—it seemed to be just what I wanted. After all, I had studied anesthesia as a second career; an ulcer had almost forced me to. It hadn't been easy after twenty years of nursing—twelve of them spent doing administration with over four hundred employees in my charge—to go back to the classroom. But I had made it. I had really made it.

And now I would be doing the work I had prepared myself for in a place that seemed congenial.

I thought of all the pluses: it was near my home, the people seemed nice, the salary was good—not great, but good—they had all the latest monitoring devices and equipment, there was a good program of continuing education, and the on-call schedule seemed fair enough. Another good thing was that at MCG—that's what they called the place—I'd be able to work on all services: gyn, general surgery, neuro, ortho, vascular, ENT, pediatrics, eye, plastics, hand. I'd be able to keep up my skills—not get mired down just doing one kind of case, one type of anesthesia, one sort of patient. And that was another good thing at MCG—I'd get to do all patients, not only the ward patients the way they did at some hospitals: hospitals where the private patients were put to sleep by physicians—anesthesiologists—and the ward patients by anesthetists—nurses, like me. At MCG they practiced the anesthesia team concept: anesthetists put the patients to sleep and woke them up, while anesthesiologists acted as consultants—were there when you needed them. They used to joke about the team concept at school. "We do the work, you send the bill," they said.

I opened one eye and looked at the clock—5:33 A.M. Ah, well, why didn't I just go back to sleep? Why the nightmare? The sweat? The worry? Because MCG had an active open-heart surgery program? I tried not to think of it. During student days I had never felt secure in the heart room . . . not secure at all.

But it was no use spooking myself. I would think positively. I would do well. I would be happy. I

11

would be successful. And I would not think of the open hearts at all—at least not today.

Might as well get up. I leaped out of bed to meet the new day.

II

When I entered the building that May morning it was early—only 6:30 A.M. I didn't have to be there till seven but I wanted to be on time. I found my way to the operating room suite thanks to signs everywhere pointing the direction. I got off the elevator on the fourth floor and walked around the corner to the female lounge. It was almost deserted, but Vi, my new boss, was there, having a cigarette. "Hi, Barrie," she said. "Welcome aboard. We're glad to have you. I've got your locker for you and here are your uniforms. Take your time getting changed. I'll see you outside."

So far so good. I put on my new blue pants suit and matching jacket. That's what the anesthetists wore at Mid City General. I admired myself in the mirror: it certainly looked better than the baggy white outfit we'd worn as students. I put on my scrub cap—a cute little blue and white striped number, draped my stethoscope around my neck, and went outside. I was as ready as I'd ever be. I was walking toward the anesthesia office when suddenly someone said, "Barrie Evans—what are you doing here?" I looked up. A tall, good-looking man was smiling down at me. It was Marty, Marty Stevenson. We'd

Barrie Evans

both worked at a hospital downtown. I had been an assistant director of nursing, he an assistant attending obstetrician-gynecologist. I was glad to see a familiar face.

"I'm doing anesthesia now, Marty. I just joined the staff. As a matter of fact, today's my first day."

"Welcome to MCG. I'm on staff here. Maybe we'll be working together soon. I'll see you around."

"I hope so, Marty."

Vi was waiting as I entered the office. "You're doing orthopedics today, Barrie," she said. "I'm going to assign you to work with Maureen. She'll do the first case in your room and help you get acquainted. If you have any questions, just ask her."

Maureen was a tall young woman with lovely green eyes. They seemed intelligent and yet had a twinkle in them. I like to look at people's eyes—and hands. Hers were smooth, well groomed with long tapered fingers. A wisp of brown hair peeked out from under her cap. Maureen seemed to be okay.

We went to pick up our drugs: sodium pentothal, succinylcholine (a muscle relaxant), and our narcotics. Maureen asked the anesthetist giving out narcotics for five morphine and three Valium. I was pleased. Narcotic technique is one of my favorite methods of giving anesthesia. I like patients to wake up pain-free. Maureen and I would get along.

We went to our O.R. and set up. Maureen explained to me how the anesthesia cart was set up and showed me where things were kept. It seemed a very practical system. When we had everything ready, we returned to the preanesthesia room to meet our first patient.

"We have a routine here to get patients ready," Maureen explained. "Every patient has an intravenous started before going to the O.R. If it's going to be a small procedure, we use a small needle, a 20, for the IV; for long cases or where we expect blood loss, we use an 18. Open-heart patients get a 16, but you won't be doing those for a while yet."

I can wait, I thought to myself.

"We also put leads on each patient for cardiogram monitoring. We have the kind of EKG monitor that provides a readout. Did you have those?"

"No, we had the old type of EKG monitor—the kind that shows the cardiogram but gives no permanent record. I understand that with this type you push a button and a recording continues as long as you need it."

"Yes, that's right. This monitor has a memory of five minutes, so when you push the button it can go back and record permanently the rhythm for five minutes prior. It can let you see what the pattern was before the arrhythmia developed. It's neat."

I was impressed.

"Of course, we put a blood pressure cuff on all patients. We keep our special cuffs—the obese cuffs for the very fat patients and the leg cuffs for patients who cannot have blood pressures taken in the arm— here on this shelf in the preanesthesia room. That way you don't have to run around looking for one. The cuffs for the kids, the pediatric cuffs, are kept on the pediatric carts.

"The anesthesia records come down with the patient. They are written up, as much as possible, by the staff member who reviews the patients' charts the night before surgery. Each patient is also seen by one of the anesthesiologists prior to surgery. I like to ask my patient for the history too. I know that when they have lots of visitors the night before they may forget to tell us or the anesthesiologists something. Some of the staff laugh at me for asking the patient all the questions again as I'm getting him ready, but I'm compulsive."

"Sounds good to me, Maureen. I'm compulsive too. I feel you can't check too many times. I remember at school I had this guy assigned to me. He had a history of alcoholism, but he told everyone he hadn't had a drink in a year—swore it to the intern, the anesthesiologist, even his own doctor. Yet when I asked him again, just before putting him to sleep—I don't know if he got scared or what—he told me he had been drinking very heavily, a quart of vodka a day, for two weeks before coming to the hospital. I was glad he told me so at least we could be on the alert for the DTs postop."

The anesthesiologist came in. He was a fat little fellow, about five feet three, an East Indian whose turban was now covered by a helmet-type scrub cap.

"This is Dr. Subramanyan," said Maureen, "but no one can pronounce that, much less spell it, so we all call him by his first name, Rajah, or Raj for short."

He smiled and went directly to the patient. Then he came out and asked Maureen what anesthetic she planned on using.

"He's a young healthy guy, so I'm using morphine, Valium, and we'll prep awake."

She meant that the area from mid thigh to mid calf would be painted with an iodine preparation and the sterile towels and sheets put on before the patient was put to sleep. In orthopedics, the "prep" is long; it may take between ten and fifteen minutes; doing it awake cuts down on the anesthesia time for the patient. It is a safe method to use on those patients who are not in pain prior to their surgery. Maureen's patient was having his knee operated on for a sports injury—a torn ligament.

"Sounds good," Rajah said. "Call me when you're ready to put him to sleep."

Maureen would administer the anesthetic, but Rajah would be present when she put the patient to sleep and would be available throughout the procedure should she need him for consultation or assistance or both.

The patient was ready now. We were waiting for the surgical team: the attending (the patient's private doctor), the resident, and the intern. The attending came in in his street clothes to greet his patient. The intern arrived, and with Maureen at the head of the bed and the intern at the foot, we went into the O.R. Maureen had given the patient some Valium intravenously, so he was relaxed and somewhat sleepy. They placed his bed next to the O.R. table, and Maureen asked him to move over to the table and take his blanket along.

I tried to keep out of everyone's way. It would be easy to be helpful, to become involved—but I was here only to observe at this point. I stood to one side and watched.

As Maureen was connecting the EKG wires and checking the patient's blood pressure, the intern was placing a cotton pad around his ankle. The intern shaved the patient from mid thigh to mid calf. In orthopedics the shaving is done in the O.R. to cut down the chance of infection. Other patients are shaved the night before by the prep team.

The intern tied a length of gauze around the ankle and strung the leg up on an IV pole. She went outside to scrub her hands and when she returned she dried her hands on a sterile towel and put on sterile gloves. She scrubbed the patient's leg with the iodine soap and two scrub brushes for five minutes. Next she painted his leg with iodine solution three times.

"You like this kind of work, Doc?" the patient asked.

"It beats housework," she replied. "You're going to have the cleanest leg in New York City. This is the part we call instant suntan."

Sterile sheets and towels were placed under and around the leg and the leg was taken down from the IV pole and laid flat on the table with the foot wrapped in a sterile sheet. During the prepping Maureen gave the patient morphine through the IV.

It was now time to put him to sleep. The circulating nurse, the one who coordinates all activities in the room, pressed the intercom button to let Rajah know that Maureen was ready for him.

The three orthopedic surgeons were putting the last sheets and towels in place. Rajah came in and nodded at Maureen to go ahead. The patient was very drowsy now from the morphine and Valium. Maureen gave him his sleep dose of sodium pentothal, the amount based on his weight, age, and lifestyle. She touched his eyelid; he did not blink. Lost his lid, I thought to myself. He was ready to have the mask placed over his nose and mouth. She was giving him nitrous oxide and oxygen. She used 70 percent nitrous oxide and 30 percent oxygen. Ordinary air is approximately 21 percent oxygen. A person under anesthesia needs a higher concentration, so we use a minimum of 30 percent oxygen on a healthy patient, more on an older patient, an anemic one, or one with heart disease. The patient was breathing on his own, but Maureen was squeezing the bag to assist his respirations, making sure he was breathing often enough and deeply enough.

"May I start?" the attending physician asked.

"All set," Maureen said. The patient was breathing well. The surgeon made the incision. Raj left the room.

After a few moments, Maureen asked whether I'd like to take over the case. I knew there was no challenge in a case like this. Most of the work had been done at the beginning and Maureen had done it well, but she was now trying to assess my self-confidence. I agreed to take over while she had coffee.

Her coffee time extended for almost an hour. I'm sure this was deliberate on her part, and when she returned she asked me whether I would do the next case, also orthopedics. I was anxious to get started, so again I agreed.

The orderly pulled in a bed with a thin, tall, pale young man. He had his arm in a sling and seemed to be in pain. Maureen said, "He's all yours. I'll be right here if you need me."

I checked the name tag on his bed and asked him "Are you Bob?" When he said yes, I said, "Hi, I'm

Barrie. I'm your anesthetist. I'm going to be caring for you. What kind of anesthesia are you having?"

"What kind? What kinds are there?"

Oh, boy, I thought to myself, I left myself wide open for this, and on my first day, no less.

"Well, there's general, regional, and local standby anesthesia. With a general, you're put to sleep completely before surgery starts; with a regional, one part of your body, one region, is anesthetized—from the waist down, or an arm in your case, for example. Standby means that the surgeon injects a local anesthetic into the part he's going to operate on and then we give additional doses of tranquilizers and narcotics to blur your memory, relieve your pain, and let you nap during surgery—not too practical in an elbow injury. We try to choose the best anesthetic for you based on your age, the type of surgery you're having, length of the surgery, what kind of shape you're in, and what you and your doctor decide. In your case, Bob, you could have either a general or a regional, an axillary block—that's a needle under your arm to numb the arm."

"My doctor said I'd be put to sleep."

"Okay, great. Then that's what we'll do today. You'll have general anesthesia."

Bob was having an open reduction and internal fixation of his right elbow—they would have to cut him and set the bone by putting in pins or screws to fix it. When the ortho guys say *fix* they don't mean repair it—they mean keep it from moving.

I asked Bob what had happened. He looked at me a bit sheepishly and sighed. "Barrie, everyone asks me what happened and I feel so stupid . . ."

"Bob, if you'd rather not . . ."

"No, no it's not so bad. I might as well tell you—I told all those people in the emergency room yesterday. Do you know the new roller disco over by the park?"

"Yes."

"Well it's just getting started, you know; it's only been open for about a month. Well, anyhow, I was there with my girl, and well, Barrie, I *was* showing off. I had learned some new steps over the weekend, and ah, shit, to make a long story short, the place was crowded and I guess I zigged when I should have zagged. The next thing I knew I was on the floor. I guess I put my arm out to brace myself. I felt this homongous pain, in my elbow, you know, and then I couldn't move my arm. My girl and the cops brought me here. I tried to stop them but it was no use. Besides I couldn't move and the thing hurt like hell. When I got to see the doctor on duty he looked at me and asked, 'Okay, which is it, roller skates or skateboard?' It made me feel I was, well, you know, like on an assembly line."

"Bob, those two things—skates and skateboards—have provided a lot of patients for orthopedists—they won't let their own kids use them, many of them. Where I used to work we saw a lot of injuries."

"Worse than mine?"

"Much worse."

"Dr. Burke doesn't know how bad my arm is yet." He smiled nervously.

"You've got the best man for the job, Bob."

"Good. Thanks, Barrie. That makes me feel better."

"Listen, Bob, before I put you to sleep I've got to ask you some questions so I can take care of you in the best way I know how. Okay? Bob, when was the last time you had anything to eat or drink?"

"I had a hamburger at about ten and a couple of beers my girl sneaked in to me right before twelve—and that's it. They told me I couldn't have anything after midnight. What happens to you if you eat something, Barrie?"

"It's simple. We cancel the surgery." I smiled at him and then explained why. "After we put you to sleep, your reflexes relax and whatever food is in your stomach may come back up into your throat. From there it can easily slip into your trachea, or windpipe, and from there into your lungs. We call this aspiration, and aspiration can kill you. So we're not being mean by starving you—we're protecting you. After you've seen someone pull spaghetti out of a patient's lung you develop a healthy respect for an empty stomach. In an emergency we can, of course, put someone to sleep with a full stomach, but we have to know about it and then take special precautions."

"Boy, am I glad I didn't eat anything. What's next?"

"Have you had anesthesia before?"

"Yes. When I was a kid I fell out of a tree and broke my arm—the other one."

"Did you have any problems with that anesthetic?"

"Not that I remember."

"We'd like to know because if you did we could try to avoid whatever problems you had this time. Have you had any problems with your lungs—pneumonia, bronchitis, or asthma? Any heart condition? high blood pressure? problems with your kidneys? liver—have you ever had hepatitis or yellow jaundice? Have you ever had fits or seizures?"

"No, nothing. I'm a healthy guy, Barrie. I just have a bum elbow."

"Do you take any medication regularly at home?"

"Nope."

"Is there any medicine you are allergic to?"

"Yeah, I'm allergic to penicillin. I got a dose of the clap a while back and, man, did I ever get a rash from that stuff."

"That's good to know, Bob. Usually with your type of examination we put antibiotics into the IV to prevent infection. Don't worry, though—I won't be using penicillin. Bob, do you smoke—cigarettes?"

"Cigarettes, no. The other, yes."

"Well, I'm really only interested in the cigarettes. Cigarette smokers have five times as many problems with anesthesia as nonsmokers."

"I keep telling my mom that cigarettes and alcohol are no good."

"How about your teeth, Bob? Is there anything loose or that comes out?"

"Barrie, I'm a young guy. What's to come out?"

"We always ask about dentures, so we're sure they've been taken out, and/or loose teeth, so we're sure we *don't* take them out."

"Okay. What else do you need to know about me?"

Nothing. I could stop questioning him now—anything else I needed to find out would be on his chart.

I read his history and physical carefully. I read all

23

the laboratory values. I looked at the report of the chest X ray, the temperature, pulse, respirations, blood pressure, and weight. Everything was normal. He was indeed a healthy young man.

When the time came to start the IV in his good arm and I asked Bob to open and close his fist, he pumped his hand in a very professional way, and he hung it over the side of the bed to increase blood flow into the area. "Do you do any drugs?" I asked, automatically slipping into his kind of language.

"Well, in high school I did 'chip' for a while but I never got hooked and I don't do any now."

"Do you booze much?"

"Well, I used to get drunk all the time but now just some wine on the weekend is enough. I used to be a wild kid. I messed up quite a bit but that's all behind me. I have a good job now and I'm getting engaged soon. You should see my girl—she's beautiful."

"The one you were showing off for, huh? I'd love to. But first we've got to get you fixed up. Bob, when I was a student we had a little contest going for all the young guys on the ortho service. We called it the countdown contest. After I give you the sodium pentothal I'll ask you to count aloud backwards from 100 as far as you can before falling asleep. The record is 78. Want to try?"

"Seventy-eight? You bet I do. I'll get down to at least 50. What's the prize?"

"No prize—just to know you're the best."

Actually, the reason we used the countdown contest was to give the young fellows something to distract them, something positive to focus on, an area to compete in.

Raj the anesthesiologist came to check Bob out, and we were ready to go into the O.R. As soon as I had settled Bob on the O.R. table I planned to give him some intravenous morphine. He looked up at me fearfully as he saw the medication.

"I thought you said no more needles, Barrie."

"This injection is going right into your tubing. See, it's the painless kind." I wiped off a rubber nipple on the IV tubing and inserted the needle.

"Boy, why can't they all be like that?"

"Wouldn't that be great, Bob. Listen, if you get a 'rush' in your head or in your chest, a tight feeling, that's me, that's the morphine, okay?"

"Barrie, I know what a rush is, remember? Oh, boy, I'm getting it. I'm getting it."

"It'll go away in just a moment."

"Tell me about it, Barrie," he said jokingly. "I know, I know."

I watched him for a little while and checked his pulse and blood pressure. He didn't have much response—they remained the same. He seemed just as alert. I gave the other half of the dose.

"Well, that's it for now, Bob. That's all the 'stuff' I'm giving you before I put you completely to sleep. If you need more after you're under, I'll give it then. It's part of your anesthesia."

"What about the Pentothal, Barrie? Isn't that my anesthesia?"

"No. Pentothal puts you to sleep but that's all it does. If I gave you only Pentothal, you'd wake up again in three minutes. Your surgeon wouldn't like that and neither would you. So once we put you to sleep we give you things that keep you that way. Nitrous oxide and oxygen are our base, and we can add muscle relaxants, tranquilizers, narcotics, or inhalation agents—one or a combination, depending on what you need.

"Yours will be a fairly short procedure—a couple of hours or so—but you'll be in an awkward position. We want to make sure you have a good airway, so after we put you to sleep with the Pentothal, I'll give you a muscle relaxant, slip a plastic tube into your windpipe, and hook up the gases to that."

"I'll be asleep for that, right?"

"Right."

"It's funny. I thought you would just come in and give me a needle and I would go to sleep and then later on you would come back and give me another needle and I'd wake up."

"You're not alone, Bob. Most people have no idea at all about anesthesia. The important thing for you to know is that we never leave you, Bob. Not for a moment. You are monitored from the time we put you to sleep until we deliver you to the recovery room staff."

We were all set. Raj stood by my side as I put Bob to sleep. I knew I was being watched intently—after all, it was my first case at MCG. Not only Raj would be watching me but the three orthopedists—Dr. Burke, the attending, Bob's own doctor, the resident, and the intern. The O.R. nurses would be watching me too, and I knew that Maureen would be keeping

26

an eye on me as well. No one spoke for a moment as I slipped in the tube and then suddenly everything was a hubbub of activity.

"Did you put in the antibiotics?"

"Can I prep now?"

"What did you say you were using?"

I answered them all—one at a time—and as I finished listening to Bob's lungs to make sure that his breath sounds were good, the intern started to prep. Bob's arm was strung up by the wrist to a pole which hung from the ceiling. The intern prepped him from the wrist to his upper arm. When the iodine scrub and iodine paint were completed the nurse took the arm down from the pole and put Bob's hand in a sterile sheet. The hand was considered unsterile and had to be wrapped carefully to avoid contamination with bacteria. The three doctors took green sheets, towels, clips, and clamps from the scrub nurse, the one who handed the instruments, and soon had created a sterile field. Everything was covered with green except Bob's elbow.

Dr. Burke looked at me. "May we go ahead?"

"Yes."

He made the incision. My first operation at MCG was under way. So far so good. Once the bone was exposed things apparently didn't look so good. "A fracture dislocation of the elbow is one of the more complicated sports injuries," I heard Dr. Burke tell the intern. "Even with prompt repair and skillful handling there may be limitation of function."

Poor Bob, I thought. What a way to begin married life.

"How long do you keep them immobilized?" the intern wanted to know.

"Me, I try to get them moving as quickly as possible and hope for the best. These goddamned roller skates! Oh, don't get me started on that lecture."

Dr. Burke lined up the fragments of the broken bone, and soon the whirring of the drill could be heard. They put in a screw with treads—just like I have in my tool chest at home, I thought to myself. And there was the bone—in one piece again, sort of.

"Let's get the bleeders, boys. Hemostats, please."

"Give me some plain," requested the resident, referring to the type of catgut he wanted to tie off the tiny blood vessels.

"Suture scissors, please," demanded the intern.

"Bacitracin irrigation," said Dr. Burke. This was an antibiotic solution which he squirted into the wound, both to clear away debris like fat globules and old blood and also to prevent any contamination. After he irrigated he asked for a dry sponge—a piece of gauze to blot the area dry. One more look convinced him there was no bleeding.

He sighed. "Well, we've done the best we can now, boys. Only time will tell. Let's close."

It was time for me to think about waking Bob up. The procedure would soon be over. Maureen drifted into the room.

"Everything okay, Barrie?"

"Okay."

Yes, from our point of view it was. But would Bob be as good as new when this was over? Could he skate, or swim, or golf, or tennis, or whatever? Only time would tell.

O.R.

A sad way to start at MCG. A young man, happy, healthy—the world was his. But he zigged when he should have zagged. *I'll* never get on those god-damned skates, I thought to myself.

III

I had been assigned to only one case on Thursday morning, to be free to go to personnel for my picture and ID card.

When my case was over, I threw a white coat over my uniform. Might as well get going, I thought to myself. I knew my way to personnel by now. I walked quickly. As I turned the corner I almost fell over a young fellow. I had seen him before—it seemed that every time I set foot outside the O.R. I ran into him, literally or otherwise. He was slim and blond with an eagerness, an intensity, which piqued my curiosity. He was dressed in housekeeping blues. Every time I saw him, he was busy—cleaning, mopping, emptying garbage. He seemed quite dedicated. It was unusual. He held a piece of paper in his hand and was studying it intently.

"May I help you?" I asked.

He looked at me questioningly. I beckoned to him to show me the slip of paper. He smiled and handed it over. It was just like the one I had—for personnel.

"I'm going to personnel too," I said, taking my slip out of my pocket and showing it to him. "Maybe we can go together." I motioned to him and we started off.

"What's your name?" I figured that if I was going to keep running into him, I might as well know who he was.

"*Ich bin* . . . I be Lothar Hess. And you are Dr. Cerna, no? I have read it on your coat."

"Cerna? Who's Cerna? Oh, you mean C.R.N.A. That's not my name. It's what I do. My name is Barrie Evans. C.R.N.A., or Cerna, as you put it, means certified registered nurse anesthetist. That's my job. Do you understand?"

"Not so much. You are called, then, Mrs. Evans?"

"No, I'm called Miss Evans, but here we call people by their first names. My name is Barrie."

"*Ach,* yes, here it is so difficult. Hello, Barrie."

"And hello to you, Lothar. Well, here's personnel. Let's get our pictures and IDs done."

He looked at me questioningly. I wondered how much he really understood me.

A tall, impressive-looking black man came out, smartly dressed in a security guard's uniform.

"Hess, Evans, Williams, and De Leon, come with me, please."

He took us to a small room at the back of the Personnel Department. "Okay, we'll do the fingerprints first. De Leon." A small young woman in street clothes approached him. He began to take her fingerprints as the rest of us waited.

Something had happened to Lothar. His eyes opened wide, sweat stood out on his head, and he looked around the room wildly. "What's up?" I asked.

He looked at me blankly. *"Was ist los?"* I asked. He hardly realized that I was no longer speaking English.

He started telling me his story. I knew he'd never get to the point of what was bothering him before the guard called his name. "Lothar," I said, "we'll talk about whatever it is later. The man is going to take your fingerprints and your picture now. All new employees of the hospital have this done. It's not just for you. It's for everyone."

"You will have this also, Barrie?"

"Yes, I will."

"And after we are finished, you will me listen?"

"Yes. We can go and have coffee."

"Hess," the security guard called. Lothar looked at me desperately.

"Go on. It'll be okay."

He smiled but still looked terrified.

In a few moments I was called. I had my fingerprints done, picture taken, and then received my official Mid City General Hospital identification card.

Lothar was waiting for me. "We have a cup of coffee now, yes?"

"Let's go," I said. We went to the coffee shop.

"What was wrong back there, Lothar? Why were you so afraid to have your fingerprints taken? Have you got a record?"

"A record? What is this—a record?"

"A prison record. Have you been in jail?"

"Ach, no." He laughed. He started to sip his coffee and tell me his story.

Several weeks before he had come to this country as a member of the East German volleyball team. He had completed medical school the year before. As an athlete he was permitted to travel outside East Germany and he had planned carefully. He wanted to come to America. He had no friends, no family, no one in the United States, but he wanted to come, he wanted to be free. So he ran away after a game one night; away from his hotel, his team, and his previous life.

He shared a small apartment with two other men. It was an old place, a tenement on the fifth floor of an ancient building. When he opened the door he was in the kitchen; the bathtub was right there too. The toilet was in a corner of the room. Next came a tiny room—his—and after that the other room used as a bedroom by the other two men. It was poorly furnished, but he knew no one would bother him—it was his.

He had heard through his landlady, who was also German, that there was a job available in a hospital. It was only a cleaning job, but at least it would be in a hospital. He could work and he could dream.

The landlady was very kind. She went with him to apply for the job. She even filled out the application form. When they found out that he was a doctor, they didn't want to take him. They said he wouldn't stay in the job very long. The landlady was very convincing, though. They gave him the job. Actually, the thing he probably liked best about it was his uniform. He loved the dark blue outfit. It made him feel a part of something—like the volleyball team.

He would have talked all day, he was so happy to have someone to communicate with. "Lothar," I said finally, "we have to go back to work." He leaped out of his chair and ran to help me out of mine. I was hardly used to such good manners, but I loved them. We parted at the elevator.

"I'll see you," he proclaimed proudly, master of the American idiom.

"So long, Lothar. See you soon."

IV

It was my second week at MCG—Thursday—my first payday in two years. No longer would I have to live on ten dollars a day, no longer would I have to go to five supermarkets to see where my groceries were cheapest, no longer would I have to use circuitous means of transportation in order to save money, no longer would I have to wear the same clothes again and again—or buy only sale items. I could spend money once again. I could go out and eat whenever I felt like it. I could put up my hand and hail a cab, even to go to work. I could go to the theater, the ballet, even on a great vacation. I could buy new clothes, ones that fit—I had lost weight in school. The world was my oyster.

It was 6:40 A.M., a cold gray day. I was happy to get into the hospital. I greeted the security guard. "Hi, Carmine, are you going to go on the tour for new employees this afternoon?"

"Hell, no—I'm going home to bed," he replied.

I rushed inside. Damn, I thought, why did I pick such work? Most of the rest of the world is still asleep, and here I am already at the hospital. If I were still doing administration, I'd just be getting up.

I shook my head with disbelief and fatigue as I waited for the elevator. I hoped at least that today would be a short day.

On days when the schedule was light you could go home early; when it was heavy you had to stay late. Vi had explained that to me during my orientation.

A group of people were coming my way. That was unusual for this time of morning. I expected only the laundry workers, other personnel from the O.R., my coworkers from anesthesia, and the occasional visitor to a critically ill patient in one of the intensive care units.

Who were these people walking in back of the admitting clerk? They looked like a bunch of sleepwalkers. There were four couples, and three women alone—all with their eyes downcast. One couple was holding hands, one girl was chewing gum at a furious pace, another hastily put out her cigarette as the clerk pointed to the NO SMOKING sign. I looked them over speculatively and guessed who they were. If I was right, some of their lives would be in my hands over the next three hours.

They were TOPs—termination-of-pregnancy patients—here for an abortion. "You rape 'em, we scrape 'em," an orderly described the procedure.

I looked at the women now with professional interest. Fortunately, none of them was excessively fat. Bad as it is to be overweight, in anesthesia it's more than bad, it's dangerous, for fat takes up and absorbs large amounts of some of our gases. The result is that it takes a long time to get them out of the system. There are other problems; it's harder to maintain an airway on an obese person; healing is not as quick, and recovery is generally prolonged.

These women were not fat, and as far as I could tell from a quick peek, they were not unduly over-reactive or psychotic. But I wouldn't really be able to evaluate this without talking to them. I gave them another quick glance—they seemed okay. I got off at the fourth floor. They were going to seven. We'd meet again soon enough.

Not all of us "do" TOPs. It was one of the things they asked me about before they hired me for the job. Some of the anesthetists are against abortions for religious reasons. I myself wish the emphasis were placed on prevention rather than termination. If we were to stress sex education in grammar schools, if we were to make contraceptives known and really accessible to the young, and if teen-agers could find someone to discuss problems with when parents are absent, ignorant, or too formidable, we could cut down drastically on the number of pregnancies.

A day in "TOP City" is hard work—physically and mentally. I had already been there—in school—and I knew. It's difficult to remain objective. Some of the stories are poignant, some are disturbing, and some are unbelievable.

I set up my room. All the IVs were lined up in the hall, my pockets were chock full of drugs, I was ready to go, and the first patient wasn't here yet. I grabbed a cup of coffee, and when I came back there was a bed in the waiting area. The first patient had arrived.

She looked too young to be having a baby. She looked like a baby herself. She was propped up in her bed, reading her chart. I greeted her but got no response. She just stared at me. When I started to ask her the usual questions, she flared up. "Isn't all that written in my chart?" she demanded defiantly.

"Well, you should know, honey, you've read it, haven't you?" I challenged her back.

It worked. She started to get interested now. "What are you gonna do, huh? You're not gonna hurt me, are you?"

"Sylvia," I said, "calm down. I'm here to help you. I'm going to be putting you to sleep for your operation. Have you ever been put to sleep?"

"Yeah, I had an abortion last year, but they were in a hurry. They didn't explain anything to me."

"Last year?" I gasped. "Sylvia, how old are you?"

"I'm twelve."

I was dealing with a frightened child. She knew her way around and had lived more in her twelve years than most people have in fifty, but she was still a child. I had to let her know that I cared and that I knew she was afraid. And I had to be pretty cool about it or she would clam up and that would be that.

So I started off by chatting about the other abortion and how, this time, I would explain everything I was doing. "Sylvia," I told her, "you will hear nothing, see nothing, feel nothing, and know nothing from the time I put you to sleep until you are in the recovery room, okay? Is it a deal?"

"Yeah."

I put on the blood pressure cuff. She was familiar with it. "So what do you do when you're out on the street, Sylvia?"

"You really want to know? I hustle drunks. I hang out in this bar, see, and I watch the guys come in. When I see one who looks flush I wait till he's been drinking for a good little while and then I sit next to him. The bartender knows me. I don't drink but he gives me tea so it looks good. I'm sitting next to the guy and we're talking. I sort of bump him, so he reaches for his money. They all do that. They're checking to make sure their wallet is safe. So now I know where it is. Then all I have to do is wait till he's drunk enough. I got all night. When I think it's time I just take out my knife and zip, zip, I cut that wallet right out of his pocket. It's a snap. Sometimes I get very lucky. Once I got three hundred dollars off a guy. The other girls are stupid, the hookers. Not me, I don't go nowhere with those guys, I don't take no chances—zip, zip and it's all done. I make out."

"So, Sylvia, how come you're here now? What kind of contraceptive do you use?"

"Listen, my man don't like to use rubbers. I don't use anything. I never did. But I guess I should. This is the second time I got caught. I'll have to see, after, what to do."

We talked about going to the clinic for contraceptive counseling. She said she'd give it a try.

We were getting along well now. She seemed to trust me a little. Soon the anesthesiologist came along with her chart. He was Chinese. Sylvia was Chinese. She saw him and tensed. "Who's he?" she whispered. I told her.

"He looks like my father," she mumbled.

He asked her the usual questions; she muttered her

39

replies. "Sylvia Chin," he said. "Sylvia is not a Chinese name. You sure your name is Sylvia?"

"What's it to ya, huh, Doc? So maybe it's not Sylvia, maybe it's not Chin either. You like that name Chin? Chin is a Chinese name, isn't it?"

He was nervous now. She was upsetting his conviction that Chinese girls are "good" girls. I'd heard him on this subject before. "Where are you from, Sylvia?" he demanded.

"What's it to ya, Doc? Maybe I'm from the West Side, maybe I'm from Queens. So what?"

"No, no I mean, where were you born? You come from Hong Kong or Taiwan? Where are your mother and father?"

"What's it to ya, Doc? You're here to take care of me. Not my father. You make me sick. You're just like my old man. You even look like him."

He walked away, truly upset. "Things are so different over here," he said. "In Taiwan, a twelve-year-old is a child. Not like this one." He went into the office to try to control himself.

I tried again to establish rapport with Sylvia. I gave her some Valium to calm her down—and wished I could give him some.

At last it was time. We went into the operating room—the surgeon, Sylvia, and I. She was wide-eyed with fear now. She looked around the room. "Who are they?" She nodded her head toward the person waiting to put booties on her legs and another who was putting sterile gloves on the "field."

"They are the nurse and technician who will be caring for you."

"Is this all for me?" she asked. "The last time I was in a clinic. They didn't have all this stuff. What's it all for?" I showed her the tracing of her EKG on the little box right behind me. She was fascinated. "That's me, that's my heart on that TV screen? Well how do I look? Is my heart okay, huh?"

"Sylvia, your heart is definitely in the right place," I told her.

She smiled up at me. "Hey, you're okay. You make me laugh. I'm not so scared now, so if I don't wake up . . ." She was saying this as the Pentothal was going in.

I didn't have time to respond. This is what we're all afraid of, though, that we'll not wake up—we'll sleep forever. With surgery, patients fear pain; with anesthesia—death. Some people verbalize this fear like Sylvia, some ask a lot of questions around the issue, and some people deny it totally. The ones who deny are the hardest to put to sleep. Fears brought into the open can be dealt with; those buried deep inside do not make for a peaceful sleep.

Sylvia woke up very combative. She was cursing up a storm and throwing herself around in the bed. When I brought her into the recovery room I warned the nurses that she might give them a hard time. I told them, "She's a tough number, but she's only twelve. Try a little TLC—it worked for me."

I rushed back to TOP City—. My next patient was waiting for me. She was also young but at least over twelve. I introduced myself and asked the most important question: "When was the last time you had anything to eat or drink?"

This question is particularly important in TOP

City for two reasons. One is that the surgery here is basically elective. True, it has to be done, but it can be done tomorrow or the day after just as well if need be. The other reason is more complex.

Most women have resolved their ambivalence about abortion by the time they reach the hospital, but a small number still have not. In this particular group, many women solve the problem subconsciously by eating or drinking something on the morning of surgery. We did a lot of TOPs where I went to school. It was coming back to me now. I was beginning to be able to pick these women out as they were brought to the O.R. suite. These women eat because they want to have the decision about the surgery taken out of their hands. They want to have it canceled by us. In that way they're in the clear. Yet this is all subconscious. Consciously they may be resigned, even eager, to have their TOP.

"When did you eat last?"

"No habla inglés."

That didn't stump me. I can take a complete history in Spanish. It was a sad one this morning. Lourdes was a nineteen-year-old. She was married to Ramón, had three small children ages three, two, and eleven months, and here she was pregnant again. When did she eat last? She had a glass of juice just before leaving the house.

That was it. No anesthesia. I went to speak to the anesthesiologist and he agreed.

We waited for her gynecologist. Lourdes was weeping quietly in bed. "What can I do? I can't have this baby." This was another phenomenon I had discovered with Latin patients back in my OB (obstetrics)

42

O.R.

days. Few of them admit to speaking English initially, but when they decide to trust you or see that you are making an effort in their behalf, they do indeed speak English—a hell of a lot better than I speak Spanish.

When Lourdes's physician came in, she was very upset. She and Lourdes had had many conversations before the TOP was scheduled. They had agreed that for economic, social, and health reasons—Lourdes was anemic and always tired—the TOP was the only solution. I told the doctor that I would not be able to put Lourdes to sleep, but that if she wanted to put in a local anesthetic, a paracervical block, I'd stay with her and talk her through—a "vocal" anesthetic.

The discussion went back and forth. One moment Lourdes was ready to go into the operating room; the next moment she wanted to put on her clothes and go home. This was a decision she had to reach with her gynecologist. I went to set up the next patient. But soon Lourdes's doctor called me and asked me to give the help I had promised. The anesthesiologist came in and suggested that I give Lourdes a narcotic or tranquilizer just to dull her a bit. I refused; I had good rapport with her now and there was the chance that the drugs would make her wild, and then where would we be, since I couldn't put her to sleep without risk.

I told Lourdes that she would feel a great deal of cramping—like menstrual cramps only a bit worse. I said I'd tell her just when to expect it and that the whole procedure would be very quick. She seemed to quiet down and accept this. I sat at her side and spoke to her in a low, soothing voice.

"First of all," I said, "you will be washed off with an iodine solution. It will be cold."

She lay still and just listened to me—she understood English very well now. "Next you will feel the doctor examining you. She will put two needles inside you, one on each side. This will take away most of the pain."

She whimpered when the doctor started, but she did not move or pull away.

"Then you will feel a cold heavy instrument being put inside—on the bottom—that's so the doctor can see inside."

She seemed resigned now. "Tell me everything—don't leave out anything—hear?" she begged.

"Okay," I promised. "Lourdes, this part is going to be crampy. The doctor will first put in a small instrument to measure how big your womb is."

"Oh," she moaned. "I don't like it."

"Now will come the most uncomfortable part. She is putting in a bunch of instruments, one at a time, to open the neck of your womb. Each one is a little bit bigger and will cramp more."

"Stop, stop it, I can't take it! Ramón, get me out of here! Help! Help!" she shrieked. The doctor paused, and Lourdes cried, "You're killing my baby! Help! Help!"

The doctor said, "Very well, if you don't want it I'll stop the operation."

"No, no," poor Lourdes screamed. "I can't have the baby. I can't feed it. I can't take care of it. What would I do? Please, Doctor, I'm sorry, do the operation."

Now she lay quietly on the table. I stopped speaking and just held her hand and stroked her head until the procedure was over. We put her legs down and covered her with a blanket.

She sat bolt upright on the table. "Where is it now? I want to see the baby."

"You can't do that," said the gynecologist.

"Listen, you, you killed my baby. Now you show it to me."

"Lourdes . . ." she started to say.

Lourdes ignored her. "You," she demanded of the technician, "show me my baby. Show me my son that you all killed."

"I can't do that," the technician replied. "We're not allowed."

"You, God damn it"—she whirled on me—"show me my baby. I have a right to see it."

"What can it hurt?" I asked the gynecologist. "Show her the specimen. She's hysterical now. She can't be any worse than this."

"Maybe you're right. You show it to her."

I went over to the table which held the instruments used in the operation. I picked up the specimen bottle and brought it over to Lourdes. "Here you go," I said.

She sat up again. "What is that?" she demanded.

"That's what came out of you just now, Lourdes."

"But, but, but that's not a baby. That's not my son. That's just a bunch of bloody strings. Is that really what came out of me?"

The gynecologist turned, and together she and Lourdes examined the specimen. I tried to leave the room. "Hey," Lourdes called, "thanks for letting me see that thing. It wasn't a baby. It wasn't a son.

Maybe I wasn't even pregnant. It wasn't a sin, it wasn't a crime. It was all just a mistake—wasn't it?"

I was emotionally exhausted from this whole episode. Thank goodness it was time for coffee now and I could go out to the lounge and relax. One of the other anesthetists would do the next case. I felt as though I'd been sprung from a cage.

My next patient was ready for me when I returned. I scanned her chart and found nothing of great significance. She was thirty-three, married, with two children. She was in good health and had had anesthesia before. Then I happened to glance at the date of her last menstrual period. It was quite a while before. We were doing these abortions by suction curettage—and that method can be used safely only on women pregnant twelve weeks or less. I had to call it to the gynecologist's attention.

I decided not to give my patient any sedation until I knew we were going to proceed. I told her only that we were waiting for the doctor. I did not want to alarm her while she waited. She was a clinic patient—she might not have seen the doctor who would perform the operation. He would not be the one who had examined her last week in the clinic. I looked at the schedule to see who was assigned to the clinic or ward TOPs. It was always an attending physician.

The attending for today was Marty Stevenson. I smiled. Marty Stevenson was one good-looking man—good-looking without being pretty—tall and slim with a headful of curly black hair. He was in his late fifties but didn't look it. He reminded me of an Indian—quick and quiet.

"Barrie, how's it going?" he asked as he came in.

"Feeling comfortable at MCG yet? I'm glad we'll be working together today, but you look upset. What's up?"

"Marty, her dates are off. She may be too far along."

"Well, let's take her in and I'll examine her and see if I can go ahead and do her."

Marty explained the situation to the patient and we went into the operating room. They put her up in the stirrups—the straps and poles that hold the legs and feet. Marty put on a glove and did an internal examination with one hand, while with the other hand on her belly he felt how big the pregnancy was. He looked grave and preoccupied. "Take her down," he requested. He took off his glove and went out to wash his hands.

When he returned he told our patient that she was too far pregnant to be able to have a suction curettage. He was very gentle with her. She was listening carefully. He explained alternate methods, getting more and more technical. I was afraid she didn't understand what he was saying. He went on and on. Finally he asked her, "Any questions?"

"Did you say I'm too far gone to have this abortion?"

"Well, yes," he said, "but . . ."

"Never mind the 'but'; did you say it?"

"Yes."

"Oh, boy," she yelled. "You mean I don't have to have it? You mean I can't have it? That's great. Oh, boy, will he be mad. He'll go crazy."

"Who are you talking about?" Marty asked. "What's the matter?"

"The matter? Nothing's the matter. I didn't want an abortion. My husband made me come here. He wants it, not me. He said if I don't have this abortion that he'll leave me. He'll leave me and the kids. There's nothing he can do now, is there, Doc? You said it's too late, didn't you? Oh, thank you, thank you, God. You're letting me have my baby. Listen, Doctor, I'll see you upstairs in five months, right? Upstairs where they have the babies. Oh, boy, thank you, God, and listen, thanks to all of you."

Marty looked at me questioningly. "The older I get, the less I understand women, Barrie. Do you think you could help me on that subject?"

I smiled but did not answer. I would like to try, I thought to myself.

We wheeled the patient out into the hall so that the orderly could return her to her unit. She was so happy—a great contrast to the other patient who was waiting.

The next patient was lying in bed with the sheet pulled up over her head. This can mean one of two things; a depression or denial syndrome or, more commonly, that the patient has taken out her false teeth and feels embarrassed. I said "Good morning" to the sheet. I heard a response but the sheet did not move. I proceeded as though there were nothing strange about conversing with a sheet. Little by little the sheet was lowered. I went on as if nothing were happening.

Finally I was conversing with the woman rather than with the sheet. She was beautiful—really breath-taking—tall and slim with lovely skin and hair. She wore no makeup yet looked exquisite.

As if she had made up her mind about something she suddenly looked up and asked me, "Do you know Dr. Brown?"

"Yes."

"What do you think of him? Do you think he's a good doctor?"

"I haven't been here long, but I hear he's one of the best men on the staff—as is the doctor who's caring for you."

"I'm pleased to hear you say that. I agree with you. Or, I should say, I did agree. Now my feelings are somewhat different." She heaved a great sigh and turned to me.

"I might as well tell you what brought me here. I have been married for nine years to a wonderful man. During the early part of our marriage we did not want any children. Travis was too busy getting ahead in the company. We traveled around quite a bit and entertained almost constantly. His career went straight up, and when about three years ago he got the position and location he wanted, we decided it was time to start our family. We're both Catholic and there are many children on both sides of the family. For the first year we were not too concerned when I didn't get pregnant. Since then, however, it's been a different story.

"Both Trav and I have gone through extensive work-ups. I never knew there were so many tests for infertility. They found nothing wrong with either of us. Did you see the show *Ashes*? I felt just like the girl in the play. We made love at all times of the day and night and kept charts. It really got to the point where lovemaking became a chore—for both of us.

"This particular day was the right day according to the chart. Travis had come in late the night before from a business trip and was staying in town that night after meeting a client from overseas. What to do? Well, Trav has a sofa in his office so I came into town and while the secretary was at lunch we made love in Trav's office. It was crazy, but I didn't want to miss another month. We really enjoyed it—it was different. And as luck would have it, this was the day I conceived.

"I was so excited when I missed my period. I called the doctor and he took the pregnancy test. The results were positive and we were ecstatic. Travis told everyone at the firm. I asked him to wait a bit, but he said such good news was there to be shared. I asked the doctor if there was anything I should do. He said, 'No, just relax and enjoy it.' That's what he said about everything.

"It didn't seem to matter to him that I had never had German measles. He knew that. Last week I came down with it. You know what the chances are for birth defects; one out of two if you have the disease in the first three months. I can't take that chance. I can't wait for nine years to conceive and then give birth to a monster.

"My doctor could have given me the rubella vaccine, he should have given it to me. He knew I never had German measles. He doesn't even know I'm here. I just picked out another doctor. I'm glad to hear you say he's a good one. In another hour the life within me, which I waited so long for, will be sucked out and thrown away. Oh, I'll survive. I'm made of strong stuff, but don't you think it's ironic, after all I've done, that this is where I should end up?"

I sedated her well and put her to sleep as soon as we entered the O.R. I cautioned the O.R. nurse against any conversation in the room. I wanted to make it as easy as possible. In the recovery room I placed my patient in a corner—away from the other patients—and told the head nurse a bit of the story. I asked her to send her back the moment she was fully reacted, and then I left.

The morning was going quickly; it was now 10:15 A.M. We still had three more patients on the schedule. I went out to speak to the next one, an attractive young woman lying in bed. She seemed rather cheerful, certainly by comparison to the others. Preparations went smoothly and she seemed so composed that I did not feel it necessary to give her either tranquilizers or narcotics prior to going into the O.R. She was a dancer, twenty-three years old, married, with no children. Her husband was unemployed so they felt this was not the time to start a family. He had escorted her to the O.R. and then left. He'd left word for the doctor that he'd be back by noon.

When she was completely set, we went into the O.R. Everything began as usual. I put her to sleep without a problem. Surgery started. Her gynecologist was a cheerful fellow who hummed during surgery. He wasn't humming a tune—just humming. I was busy at the head of the table doing all the many things we do after we put someone to sleep: assisting with the breathing, taking the blood pressure, watching the EKG screen, adjusting the flow of the agents we use to keep the patient asleep, listening to the chest for heart and breath sounds, giving additional tranquilizers, barbiturates or narcotics as needed, adding medication to the IV bottle to help the uterus contract, adjusting the position of the operating room table to assist the doctor in performing the operation, calculating the correct amount of IV fluids, and charting all this on the patient's record.

Everything was moving along when two things simultaneously caught my attention. The gynecologist had stopped humming. He was no longer sitting on his stool but was standing over the patient with an instrument in his hand and muttering to himself. At the same time, I heard the heart rate go up rapidly. I counted; it was 120 beats per minute—normal is between 70 and 90. "Doctor," I asked sharply, "what's the matter?" In the midst of all his muttering, I heard the word *perforate*. Had he put an instrument through the wall of the uterus?

"Doctor," I asked once again, "do you have a perforation? Her heart rate's 120 and now her pressure's dropping."

"I need a consultation," the doctor told the O.R. nurse. "Call the chief and ask him to come down here stat"—immediately. "I think I've perforated," he said to me. "I'm afraid I'll have to go in and explore."

I had already turned off the nitrous oxide and was giving her 100 percent oxygen. I asked the nurse to get the anesthesiologist, but she told me he was in the next room with a sick child and could not come. He had sent word to go ahead.

I was on my own. And I would have to make use of the emergency equipment we always set up in TOP City and so seldom used.

I gave a muscle relaxant and after visualizing her vocal cords, I swiftly passed a breathing tube into her windpipe. If the doctor had to explore her belly to see where the hole was, he would need good relaxation of the abdominal muscles. After I passed the tube, I put some air into the balloon at the end of the breathing tube. This would make a tight seal so that no secretions could get into the lungs. As soon as this was done, I hooked the breathing tube up to the anesthesia circuit. She could not breathe on her own now because I was using muscle relaxants. I took my stethoscope and listened all over both sides of the chest for breath sounds. I wanted to be sure that the tube really was in the windpipe and not in the esophagus and also that it had not slipped down too far—if it had, only one lung would be ventilated.

All was in order; I breathed a sigh of relief and hooked the patient's breathing circuit up to a ventilator—the machine that would breathe for her. I regulated the number of breaths per minute, how much air would go in with each breath, and the concentration of oxygen I wanted to deliver. I put a plastic airway in her mouth next to the tube to prevent her from biting down on the tube and cutting off her airway. Then I secured the tube in place by wrapping translucent tape around it and fixing the tape to the patient's face. I taped her eyes shut to prevent dirt or foreign matter from getting into them.

The chief arrived and scrubbed his hands. The

O.R. nurse rushed in with a large table full of instruments for the exploratory operation.

My anesthesiologist yelled in from the next room, "Everything okay, Barrie?"

"Yes, I've tubed her and so far so good."

I ordered two units of blood to be crossmatched in case she needed a transfusion. I was running her fluids in quickly now. She was still in shock, and I tilted the O.R. table so that she was lying on a slant, head down. This would improve her blood pressure, but only temporarily. I started a second IV. If she needed transfusions I would need one line for blood and the other for fluids.

I was set now and so was the surgeon. After a quick prepping and draping he made the incision. The chief and a senior resident assisted him. He entered the abdomen quickly—there was no humming now. He examined the uterus; sure enough, there was a ragged tear. One blood vessel was bleeding profusely—a pumper, we call it.

She was lucky, this patient. They were able to control the bleeding, to repair the tear and still preserve her uterus. She would be able to become pregnant again. Once the bleeding was under control the chief dropped out, leaving the attending and the resident to close.

"Pete, how about the family? Is there anyone you want me to speak to now?" the chief asked the attending gynecologist.

"No, the husband isn't coming back until noon."

We hadn't needed his consent to operate, not in a life-threatening emergency.

We finished the case. She was sleepy but breathing well. I was able to take out the breathing tube. We got ready to take her to the recovery room. As we were wheeling her down the hall the elevator door opened and her husband stepped out.

"Hi, Doc," he called. "Came back just in time, right? How's my doll doing? Can I see her now?"

"Wait for me there a moment," the doctor answered. He left me in the recovery room with the patient and went to tell the husband what had happened.

I've had enough excitement, I thought to myself as I went back to the O.R. to get ready for the next case. Please don't let it be another mess. But I didn't get my wish. My new patient, who had come in the day before, was accompanied by an aide. That's a bad sign—it usually means a problem.

I approached the patient and started to introduce myself. She answered me with shrieks of fear—piercing sounds—but no words. She was rocking back and forth in the bed at a furious pace. It was clear I would get nothing from her.

I turned to the aide and asked her what the story was. Fay was twenty-nine years old and had been in the state mental hospital since early childhood. Her mental age was about six and under normal circumstances she could help herself minimally. She was toilet-trained and could feed and dress herself, but not much more. The aide was unable to tell me either the circumstances surrounding her pregnancy or how it was discovered.

Now she was in unfamiliar surroundings and frightened. Trying to reason with her was pointless. The premedication they had given her upstairs had had absolutely no effect at all.

I tried to approach her again and she shrieked so loudly that people ran from all over the O.R. suite to see what the trouble was. There was no way to take a history, no way to start an IV. I decided on a gentle touch—a mere laying on of the hands. That worked until I tried to *do* anything. As soon as I attempted to put on the blood pressure cuff or to look at her teeth, the shrieking began again. I thought about using Ketamine, an anesthetic sometimes used on frightened children. It can be given into the muscle as well as through the IV and so will work on patients who will not allow an intravenous to be started. But it has a disadvantage: it may cause psychological disturbances. It has been known to give patients terrible nightmares, some of them recurrent. Still, what was the alternative? To force Fay to have the IV? Get four or five people just to hold her down? That's not the way I like to do anesthesia.

The anesthesiologist came into the corridor. Once again Fay shrieked. He was as unprepared for her reaction as I had been. We went into the office and reviewed her chart together. We decided to induce Fay with Ketamine and to give her Valium, which would cut down the possibility of hallucinations.

The anesthesiologist asked the aide to get into an O.R. scrub outfit so she could stay with Fay as we put her to sleep. We wheeled the bed into the operating room and Fay shrieked again until she saw the aide. I asked the aide to turn Fay on her side so that I could inject the Ketamine into her buttock. Fay was rocking back and forth wildly now and the shrieks were pitiful—like those of a wounded animal. The anesthesiologist turned aside.

Soon, however, the Ketamine took over and Fay started to snore. The orderlies were standing by to help us move her to the O.R. table. We got her there without a problem. I started the nitrous oxide and oxygen, adding a small amount of narcotic, the Valium, and a drying agent, atropine. One of the side effects of Ketamine is that secretions are increased; we wanted Fay to have a clear airway.

All was finally in order and the anesthesiologist left.

The surgeon performed the abortion. It was merciful. It was hard to imagine what kind of baby Fay would produce—and what kind of animal had produced it with her. Was it a staff member or a fellow patient?

When the procedure was over, the aide was waiting. She came with us to the recovery room. The recovery room nurse was glad to have her there; they were not equipped to deal with this kind of patient. I left Fay sleeping quietly now—looking just like any other patient in there.

One more case, I thought to myself, and then my morning in TOP City will be over.

She turned out to be small and beautiful, with a mole over her left eyelid—an Oriental doll. The man with her should never have gotten into the O.R.

suite; visitors are not permitted. But no one was about to argue with *him*. He was about six feet five, 250 pounds, and scowled at anyone who ventured near her.

When I came to take the history, he answered every question for her.

"When did you eat last?" I asked.

"She didn't eat nothing today," he replied.

"Do you smoke cigarettes?" I asked.

"No, she don't," he answered.

She smiled and remained quiet.

"Do you understand me?" I asked her.

She nodded.

It was only when I asked for her previous anesthetic history that she spoke. He stood by and scowled.

Every time I approached her, he asked, "What are you doing to her?" before I ever got a chance to explain. He touched everything, he fingered the EKG leads, read the label on the IV. Finally we were ready to go into the O.R., and still he showed no signs of leaving.

I said, "Okay, you can say good-bye now and go to the waiting room."

He made no move.

The doctor stood waiting. "Uh—Mr.—uh, Kim, you'll have to leave. We're taking her into the operating room now."

"Kim, who you calling Kim? Do I look like a Kim? I ain't no gook, God damn it," he yelled.

She turned her head to one side and covered her face with the sheet, as her nameless friend finally left.

We went in. I put her to sleep. The doctor terminated the pregnancy. She woke up. She moved into bed. She went to the recovery room. At last, my morning was over. I breathed a sigh of relief and went to lunch.

When I got back things looked quiet. There were a couple of ways to see what was doing. The easiest was just to check the hall. When we brought our patients into the operating room they came in large, comfortable O.R. stretchers which waited outside until the patient's surgery was completed. If the hall was full of stretchers the O.R.'s were full of patients.

You could also check the schedule—that mammoth piece of paper that was the game plan of the day in the O.R.—but I hadn't gotten the hang of it yet. It was simpler to check the hall.

Vi was coming toward me. "Had lunch yet, Barrie?"

"Yup. Boy, what a day in TOP City."

"How many?"

"Gee, I don't even remember. Let me see—six or seven, by God. That's a lot of work, Vi."

"Yes, I'm sorry. I hated to put you in there by yourself, but we're short-staffed today. How did it go? I heard you had a perforation."

"Yes we did, Vi. It was my first."

"Well, good thing you've got it behind you. You know what they say—you do enough TOPS, you'll get a perforation. Sad but true."

"Well, I've had mine now. I hope that's it for me."

"Listen, Barrie, you've had a rough day—go home."

"Gee, Vi, thanks, that's great. I'm going out tonight. I can take a nap now."

"No problem—see you in the A.M."

"Ciao."

We were coming home from the theater that night by subway, my date and I. A young Oriental couple got on the train with us. She sat next to me and he stood over her. He was small and thin and looked down at her fondly. There wasn't too much room but we moved over so he could sit down. She nodded. "Thank you," she murmured. I nodded back.

At our stop they, too, stood to get off the train. She nodded again. I nodded back. I turned away and then suddenly I looked back; she seemed familiar. She was small and beautiful with a mole over her left eyelid. We got off the train. She moved ahead rapidly; her man was very protective. We came through the turnstile together. "Hey," I said, "don't I know you from somewhere?" A look of panic distorted her face and disappeared again in an instant. I remembered the morning and how I knew her. What was she doing on the subway at this point? I wondered.

My date moved forward. "Are you a nurse?" he asked.

"No, a patient." She laughed nervously.

I tried to distract him before he embarrassed her.

"Oh," he tried again, "did she put you to sleep?"

She nodded. She looked at me pleadingly and yet resigned. I winked at her trying to tell her not to worry.

She bowed and turned to the man. "My husband, Mr. Kim," she said.

"Hi, glad to meet you. Have a nice evening," I muttered.

"Who was that?" my date asked me. "She doesn't look sick at all."

"Oh, her—well I guess she's Mrs. Kim."

V

I was doing okay at MCG. I was starting to feel a part of the group. No longer did I dread coming to work, wondering what would face me. I now knew—and mostly I was able to handle it. The bad days would come as long as I was an anesthetist. Everyone has them. It's just that when you deal with people's lives the bad days are really bad.

I liked my coworkers, most of them. The ones I didn't care for, I stayed away from. The rest, I enjoyed chatting with over a break, a cup of coffee, or lunch. That was it, though. I tried to keep my hospital life and my personal life apart. The people I saw socially knew nothing about MCG and usually nothing about the medical field.

I had been burned once—that was enough. When I was an administrator, I got involved with one of the pediatricians, a married guy. It was a game for us both, an exciting game with high stakes. We both had a lot to lose. I remember one night I was at a dinner at the Waldorf—one of those boring fund raisers. All the administrators had to go, and after the speeches and dinner I knew my boss would invite us down to the Bull and Bear to continue our evening.

O.R.

This particular evening I had arranged with Greg, the pediatrician, that he would meet me in the Waldorf lobby at nine. He had a meeting at the New York Academy of Medicine and was leaving it early. My problem was getting away from my group. But it was seldom that Greg could be free for an entire evening. It was worth it to me to try.

The formalities were over by 8:45, and as usual my boss suggested we retire to the Bull and Bear. I had worked out a plan. I had spent all the time the speeches were going on devising it. I was definitely ready.

At 8:55, as I politely sipped my drink with one hand, I furtively set off my beeper with the other. At first no one heard it but me. Soon, however, all the guys looked up. "You on call tonight, Barrie?" my boss asked.

"Yup—I better go see what's doing." I left the table as if to go to the phone. When I returned they were waiting to see what the emergency was. After all, they worked there too.

"Ah—it's not fair," I grumbled to them. "I'm on call once a week as an administrator and every night as director of nursing. I get called both ways. Got to go, guys. See you in the A.M." I ran out to meet Greg—the night was ours.

When the fling with Greg was over, though, it was hard for both of us. It was not easy to see him every day, sit on the same committees, make rounds on his service. I didn't want to get burned again. I'd stay away from the people at MCG. Or would I? What if Marty Stevenson decided to get friendly? He still intrigued me, but so far the only thing he'd done was buy me lunch in the hospital cafeteria.

I soon had more important things to worry about.

Maureen came up to me as I was walking down the hall toward the O.R. "Barrie," she said, "I've been looking for you. You've been here about two and a half months now and tomorrow will be your first day in the heart room. I'm assigned to help you. Let's go get started."

The day I had been dreading had arrived.

Each of us in anesthesia seemed to have his or her own particular fear. I would face any kind of a case but open-heart surgery. I have a friend who feels the same way about anesthetizing children.

A beautiful blond eight-year-old child came to surgery one day when my friend was assigned to pediatrics. The child was gravely ill with a large malignant mass in her neck. The surgery took hours, but the doctors had been able to get almost all of the tumor so far. If they could get it all, perhaps she could live. They dissected very carefully and were almost home free. Suddenly the child's blood pressure disappeared, showers of blood covered everyone. The patient had a cardiac arrest. A major blood vessel had torn. Everyone ran. They got blood, they got fluids, they got a vascular specialist, a defibrillator, more emergency equipment. But it was too late. Within moments the child bled out—the small life was extinguished.

My friend had cried. She said she never wanted to anesthetize another child. This had been her second bad experience. Later that week she was making a preop visit to pediatrics. The nurses were still talking about the blond child who had died. "Did you know," they asked my friend, "that before she went to surgery she came around and said good-bye to each of us. She put all her dolls in plastic bags and kissed them farewell. She told her small roommate she would not be coming back."

My friend still shivered when she thought of it.

It was open-heart surgery that made me shiver from the first time I encountered it in my student days. Part of it is that there's such a ritual, a mystique, a solemnity, about it, much more than for any other kind of surgery. And unfortunately, my student days in the heart room had been fraught with disaster. Just thinking about it made my palms get wet, my heart start to pound. . . .

My first open-heart patient came in as an emergency one evening when I was on call. He had been transferred to our hospital from an institution without an open-heart program. I was a senior student but had not yet had my six-week affiliation in the heart room. The staff anesthetist who was working with me and supervising me tried to be kind, but she could not realize how terrified I was. She tried to settle me by having me read the manual on how to set up for open-heart anesthesia. The words jumped around on the page. It was 5:00 P.M.; the patient was scheduled for surgery at 7:00. We set up together and went over to the surgical intensive care unit to see the patient. They had told us he had come to the hospital unconscious and with a breathing tube in place. Wrong—and wrong again! As we entered the unit a tall, handsome, bluish-looking fellow sat up in bed gasping for air—surrounded by a very concerned family. He was gravely ill. The chances were one in ten that he would survive the operation, but without it he would surely die—and soon.

We took him into the operating room with a portable tank of oxygen and a portable EKG monitor. We put him to sleep without incident and the surgery began. But there was even more wrong than they had thought. His left ventricle had thinned out so much that it might rupture at any time. This had to be corrected and the surgeons tried everything. They tried to sew tissue to tissue, but it didn't hold; the tissues were too damaged. They tried to put a felt patch in, but again the whole thing crumbled and gave way. For hours they tried one thing after another—to no avail. It was long past midnight when they pronounced the patient dead.

They wanted to send me out of the room and finish the case by themselves. The anesthesiologist told the staff anesthetist, "It's not good for a student to have to go through this for the first heart case." But I refused to leave. After all, I had put him to sleep. I had said to him, as I've said to all my patients since, "Just take a deep breath. You're going to sleep now—quickly and pleasantly. And when you wake up, you'll be in the recovery room." I had made my patient a promise of life, but I hadn't been able to keep it. It was my first death on the table.

I saw it through till the end, staying long after I was needed. I helped the O.R. nurses clean up the body. I removed tubes, the IVs and the catheters that had been inserted at every available place. I even helped them wheel him into a room off the O.R. suite and prop him up in bed so his wife could see him. And then I collapsed. I went off by myself and cried and had nightmares the rest of the night. Thank goodness I was not called out for any other emergencies.

The trauma of that first case had done something to me—left me with an uneasiness, a vulnerability. Open-heart surgery was so exact, so precise. The anesthesia was so complex, so adaptable—it changed from minute to minute. Late in my senior year, when I started my rotation in the heart room, I wondered whether I'd be able to meet the challenge. I wanted to do well.

I was happy—I should say proud—and yet anxious when I discovered that my patient was a lawyer whose name appeared often enough in *The New York Times* to become a household word. When I say "my patient" I do not mean to imply that I would care for him alone. In the open-heart room there are always three members of the anesthesia care team: two anesthetists—one who does the case and one who assists—and the anesthesiologist. The plan of care is shared responsibility.

It was with excitement tinged with fear that I went up to the Gold Coast—the private floor of the hospital—to make my preoperative visit.

I knocked and then entered a bright, sunny room filled with flowers and plants (and he hadn't even had his surgery). A distinguished-looking man in dark blue silk pajamas sat up in bed looking at me with piercing blue eyes. At his side sat a beautifully made-up, beautifully dressed blonde. I introduced myself and started the interview. I was already familiar with his history after reviewing his chart and all his lab work. He was in his early sixties—a big-time smoker and drinker—and he had had that squeezing chest pain diagnosed as angina, indicating coronary artery disease, for many years. Within the last year, however, it had become much more severe. Merely to go out in the cold brought it on, walking for more than a block also activated it, and golf was just out of the question. He was coming in for a coronary artery bypass graft (CABG: we called it cabbage) so that his doctors could increase the blood supply to his heart. There's a lot of controversy about whether or not a CABG actually increases life expectancy, but it generally increases the quality of the patient's life.

As I proceeded to tell my patient and his wife about what anesthesia we planned to use on him, they seemed well-informed indeed. He knew what his odds were and he was prepared to take his chances.

As I started out of the room at the end of the interview, his wife called me aside. "He's all I've got," she said. "My children are grown and live far away. I've got a wonderful grandson named after him. Our life together is just really beginning again, now. Please take good care of him. I need him so."

I reassured her and said a cheery good-bye.

He arrived in the O.R. the next morning at 7:00 well sedated and comfortable. He had even had a good night's sleep.

All the lines went in easily: the two intravenous lines, the arterial line, and the central venous pressure. I had been told this was a good omen, that if the lines go in easily, the case will go well. I put

him to sleep smoothly with none of the awful varia-
tion in blood pressure that can often occur when
anesthesia is induced.

Surgery went well. He went on the pump without
any trouble; he had good veins in his legs to use for
the grafts; he came off the pump without a problem.
Pump time was short, and this was to his advantage.
The longer the time on the pump, the greater the
problems with blood clotting. Almost before we knew
it, it was 12:30 P.M., the chest was closed, and we were
ready to leave the operating room.

Our caravan started down the hall. At the foot of
the bed was the senior surgical resident. In the bed
our patient was hooked up to a portable EKG monitor: an indwelling catheter was keeping his bladder
empty of urine; the four lines we had put in at the
start of the case were still in place with six bottles of
blood and fluids swinging on IV poles; chest tubes
provided a means of drainage. The breathing tube in
his windpipe was hooked up to a portable cylinder of
oxygen. We were breathing for him now and would
do so for the next few hours with a mechanical respirator. The breathing tube would stay in until the
next morning to assure safety and consistency of ventilation in the immediate postoperative period. I
walked at the head of the bed, breathing for him
with one hand and pushing the bed along with the
other. The anesthesiologist walked along with me.

In the surgical intensive care unit, the head nurse,
two staff nurses, and a technician from medical electronics were waiting for us. I told them about him:
how he tolerated the procedure, how much blood he

had received, how much fluid he had received, how much urine he had passed, how much anesthesia he had been given. They in turn told me his vital signs, his blood pressure, temperature, and pulse. We connected him to the respirator and I could stop breathing for him as it took over.

So far so good. But when I finished for the day at 3:00 P.M., I stopped by to look at him. I knew the anesthetic course was not considered over for at least forty-eight hours—he had a couple of hard days ahead before he would be out of the woods.

The next morning before I even set up for my cases I went in to see him. He was looking great, sitting up. He was gesturing to me that he wanted the breathing tube out. I did a blood gas—a lab test which tells how well he is ventilating, how much oxygen is in his blood, how much carbon dioxide. When the result came it looked good. I got the anesthesiologist to come in. Yes, the tube could come out. And as soon as I took it out he asked to shave. That was a good sign indeed.

The next day he left the surgical I.C.U. and returned to his room. On the fifth day I went up to visit. He was looking great, his wife was beaming. There were so many flowers that they were almost falling out of the room.

"Sit down, won't you?" he asked. "Let me tell you, Barrie, you're one of the reasons I came through this so well. Your experience, your self-confidence, your calm manner. They made me feel I was in good hands. I owe you my life. Thank you."

I wondered if he knew how anxious I had been,

how inexperienced I had been, how hard I'd tried, how proud I . . . silly—of course he didn't know.

Tomorrow would tell the tale for me now. It was my first open heart at MCG. Of course I'd have Maureen to help me. Would I do as good a job as I wanted? Impossible. I was too hard on myself. But would I ever feel the surge of confidence I felt with other kinds of cases?

Maureen and I set up together. I knew the basics. What I needed to know was just how open-heart surgery was done here at MCG. I was happy that Maureen would be with me tomorrow. She's an even-tempered woman who knows how to handle stress.

There's no doubt about it. Anesthesia work *is* stressful. The responsibility for another human being's life is awesome. Each of us has to find ways to deal with it. My way is not too good—I have insomnia and nightmares—but it is much less self-destructive than that of others I know. I've heard about anesthesia people who drink—to excess. And some who turn to narcotics for escape. They start out easy, just a pop here and there to relieve the tensions of the day. But the work we do produces tension every day, and pretty soon it takes more and more to mellow out. And once the slide starts, it's the beginning of the end: users will steal, cheat, plot—first to get high and then to stay that way. High is their only way to face life, and soon that life is over. One day, one night, one long weekend, there is no dope—and the withdrawal sets in. And they know they're hooked—just like any junkie in the street. Usually it means an end to their profession either by their own or the hierarchy's hand. They are accused, they are warned, they are watched, and finally they are discharged. They lose their friends, they lose their profession, they lose their self-respect, and in some cases they lose their life.

Better to have insomnia and nightmares, I have decided. I can deal with them. After all, I'm not going to be doing the heart room every day.

"Once every week or two" is what I was told when I was hired. At MCG they did two hearts a day—one in the morning and another in the afternoon. Whoever worked from noon to 8:00 P.M. did the afternoon hearts and the rest of us rotated on the morning ones.

I was getting myself psyched up now. I reminded myself I wouldn't even be doing tomorrow's heart. It would be Maureen's case. I'd just help out.

I went to my locker to check that my antiembolism stockings were there. I'd need them tomorrow. When I stand for more than an hour I get leg cramps. I've been hospitalized three times with phlebitis. I don't want that again.

The last time was the worst. When I was ready to go home, my doctor told me I'd have to wear a support up to my waist, a body stocking he called it. It sounded sexy.

A week before discharge a woman came in and measured me. She put up my legs—one at a time, the bad one first—on something that looked like a skewer. Then she used a tape measure every two inches right up my legs—and later on my hips and waist. This took almost an hour. When she left I was exhausted. "This is nothing," she had told me. "Just wait till you

72

put on the garment." The way she said *garment* gave me a premonition that it might not be so sexy after all.

When the garment arrived, I could go home, my doctor had said. Each day I eagerly awaited the mail. Finally it came. It took me thirty minutes and half a can of talcum powder to get into the damn thing—and of course sitting was out of the question. If I tried to sit it was like a knife in my crotch—and I had enough problems with the leg. But I had to live with it for three months.

So nowadays I wear antiem stockings on long cases—and always in the heart room.

Maureen and I finished setting up, gathered the anesthesia records and lab slips we needed, and headed for the elevator. We were going to make our preop visit.

Ah Loo was a Korean woman living on borrowed time and seemed to show it. That worried us. A patient's attitude is one of the most important factors in his or her recovery. All of us in hospital life have seen patients who have overcome almost insurmountable odds because they wanted to live—needed to live, for reasons of their own or to care for someone else: an invalid wife, an aged parent, a psychotic child. But the converse is also true: a person who prepares himself for death all too often dies. We did not know if that was the case with Ah Loo because we could not communicate with her. She spoke no English, Maureen spoke no Korean, and mine was limited to "Take a deep breath," *Soomul kipi shi sae yeo*.

She was alone in her room. An elderly, wrinkled

woman dressed in black pajamas. We smiled at one another, but that was all, since no interpreter was available.

Maureen took me to the desk and showed me how to retrieve our patient's chart from the chart rack. As we were sitting reviewing it, one of our Korean-speaking anesthesiologists came by. He had been requested by Ah Loo's surgeon both because he spoke Korean and because he was very good. We all went back into the room together to speak to her. She told the anesthesiologist that she had had symptoms for years in Korea but hadn't done anything about them. Finally her family had persuaded her to come to the States, and she now lived with a daughter in Queens. She was a poor historian. Many things we needed to know she had forgotten. Maureen and I sat quietly by while the doctor and patient conversed in Korean.

The next morning as Maureen and I were walking down the hall toward the open-heart room, I saw the orderly wheeling Ah Loo in our direction. She was fast asleep: she did not even respond when Maureen called her name. Usually Oriental patients require a great deal less anesthesia than Occidentals: smaller doses of tranquilizers, narcotics, and muscle relaxants. Perhaps it is because they seem to have a higher pain threshold. Perhaps it is because they are usually small and we give drugs based on the patient's weight. In any event, we see time and time again that Oriental patients are totally sedated by what we consider a light premedication. That was certainly the case with Ah Loo.

As Maureen prepared the many test tubes for last-minute blood tests I tried to let Ah Loo know that I would be starting her intravenous. I gently took her arm. It felt awfully warm. I put my hand to her head. Hot. I looked at her chart and found that prior to coming to the O.R. her temperature had been 100.4°F: high, something to watch, but not enough to cancel the case. Maureen called the floor to ask the nurse what the story was. The nurse said that she had paged the surgical intern but that the orderly had come for the patient before he answered and she had sent her.

Maureen asked me to recheck the temperature. We use a thermometer which gives an electronic readout. It starts at 94°, and the readings climb until a buzzer sounds and a dot appears; the dot indicates the patient's temperature. I used a rectal probe since it's more accurate. Besides, Ah Loo was snoring now, lying on her back with her mouth open—no candidate for an oral thermometer.

Maureen helped me turn our patient, and I inserted the thermometer. The numbers went higher and higher 94.0, 94.2, 94.4, 94.6, 98.0, 98.6, 98.8, 99.0, 100.0, 100.8, 101.0, 101.2, 101.4. Would it never stop? What was wrong with our poor Korean lady? 102.0, 102.2, 102.4, 102.6. Finally it buzzed and the dot showed 102.6. A high fever for an adult. Maureen called Ah Loo's surgeon and he came to look at her. Before he even examined her he told the fifteen or so waiting people that the surgery was canceled.

The surgeon and the resident examined the almost comatose woman, but it was difficult because she was so unresponsive.

It was dangerous to return her to her room because she was so sedated that she needed constant observation. Yet she could not go to the recovery room because she had not had surgery and was possibly infectious. Maureen decided we should take her to the surgical I.C.U. That is where she would have gone postoperatively, but the nurses were very surprised to see an open-heart patient at 8:30 in the morning. We explained to them that they would have to keep her until her premedication wore off, then call for an interpreter to explain to poor Ah Loo why she had not yet had her surgery.

The diagnosis was meningitis. The surgeon started her on a rigorous course of antibiotics and hoped to operate on her at a future date.

It was eighteen days later when Ah Loo once again appeared on the O.R. schedule. Maureen and I were again assigned to her with the same anesthesiologist. I was superstitious. I felt that the events of the previous time did not augur well for our Korean lady. How right I was!

We had saved her records, put them in the delayed-surgery file to give us a head start next time.

Again, the day before the operation Maureen and I set up our equipment while all the others were doing the same.

The nurses were setting out all the instruments, needles, valves of various sizes—in case this should be a valve-replacement—and all of the hundreds of little items necessary for the operation. The nurses who work in the heart room are a special team, led by a very quiet, efficient, and experienced head nurse—one with a conscience. There is no room for doubt here. Sterility can never be in doubt: the motto "If in doubt throw it out" applies in spades in the heart room. Availability can never be in doubt: if you think you'll need one of anything, you bring three. Whether things will work perfectly can never be in doubt: any flaw in any instrument must be detected now and that instrument sent out for repair.

The pump team—two nurses and a technician—were busy too. All of them have had extensive training and experience in how to run the pump: more formally, the SARNS heart and lung machine. The pump is vital because all the time the surgeons are working in the heart itself—replacing a valve, repairing an aneurysm, an outpouching in the wall of the heart, replacing the blood supply to the heart with pieces of veins from the legs—it *is* the patient's heart. Without it the patient could not live. Keeping the pump's many parts in order is essential. After every use, or run, it is taken completely apart, cleaned thoroughly, its many disposable components discarded, and then readied from scratch for the next patient.

Then there are the boys from medical electronics. At MCG this department concerns itself with all machines and equipment with electrical components. This includes a computer that can give us results of the blood work done on our patients from the pre-operative period right through the day. That large screen that shows the EKG, the arterial wave form, the arterial and venous pressure and the temperature works from a console, a bank of buttons and dials located in the gallery next to the heart room. Here the boys tune us up and tune us in; they provide the electronic aspect of what we are going to do.

The patient gets many professional visitors the day before surgery. The cardiologist, cardiac surgeon, resident, intern, anesthesiologist, anesthetist, pump technician, I.C.U. nurse, and chaplain will all be there to do their best to convince the patient and themselves that everything will be all right.

The morning of the operation, I couldn't sleep. I was at the hospital at 6:00 A.M. Maureen came at 6:45.

When Ah Loo came down this time she was sleepy but not unresponsive as she had been before. No longer did she have toxins and fever to produce coma. Her temperature was normal and she looked all right.

We started to put in the IVs and right away ran into difficulty. There were many valves, which prevented us from advancing the needles: the vessels were tortuous and tiny. Finally, after trying several times, we were able to insert one small gauge needle. With open-heart surgery, where you may need to pour blood or medication or both in rapidly, you want a large gauge needle in place so the fluid will enter the patient's body more quickly. Yet it was impossible to insert either a central venous pressure line or an arterial line. We would have to ask the surgeons to do so by using central lines—major blood vessels from the surgical field.

We wanted to insert a Swan-Ganz catheter, a special line we use for very sick patients to measure pulmonary artery pressure. But though our anesthesiologist tried several times, the catheter could not be passed.

Maureen gave Ah Loo as small doses of sedatives, tranquilizers, and muscle relaxants as she could, but even with these minimal amounts and the skillful insertion of the endotracheal tube, her blood pressure dropped precipitously and her heart stopped. A precordial thump—one bang on the chest over her heart—by her surgeon got the heart going again. He opened the chest quickly and Ah Loo was put on the pump in very short order.

Her blood pressure was all over the lot. When it fell we gave her a tiny dose of a vasopressor to make it go up. Up it went: it shot through the roof. We had to give other drugs to make it come down. Clearly Ah Loo was going to present an anesthetic challenge.

The suregon had passed off a central venous and arterial line for our monitoring, but the blood vessels in Ah Loo's legs—which would be used to create new circulation for her heart—were in poor shape too. Nothing was going to be easy.

While she was on the pump she did not put out enough urine, so we had to give her medicine to make her urinate more. We had to give so much that she was losing too much potassium, so we started replacing that also.

Usually the time on the pump is a relatively safe one from an anesthesia standpoint, but not with our lady. We were busy the entire time, giving this, checking that, while the surgeons worked to provide new circulation for the Korean lady's ailing heart.

Barrie Evans

The room was quiet, the only talking that of the surgeon: "Cross-clamping now. How many minutes? Pump suction on."

We were sure by now that when she came off the pump there would be further problems. Usually the way you go on is the way you come off. This case had been a challenge all along—there was no reason to think it was going to get easier.

The intricate part of the surgery was over. With many people, when the work on the heart is completed, the heartbeat resumes a normal pattern. With other patients it is necessary to shock or fibrillate the heart into beating once again. Needless to say, Ah Loo's heart did not resume its regular rhythm on its own. More than that, it would not respond to the shocking it got. Each time the paddles were placed and the current turned on, a few beats occurred—then nothing. The surgeons tried massaging the heart—to no avail. Each shock was given with increasing voltage on the fibrillator. Finally, with the fifth attempt, the heart started to beat—erratically at first and then in a regular rhythm. We all sighed with relief.

Now came the usual problems of coming off the pump: the heartbeat was too slow, the heartbeat was too fast, the blood pressure was too low, the blood pressure was too high. The output was too low, the potassium was too high, the bleeding was too great. All of us, all the teams, were working at a frenzied pace trying to keep up as one after another problem faced us. We felt as though we were being tested by demons.

Yet we seemed to be making headway. One by one

the problems were solved. Ah Loo came off the pump; we gave her some fresh frozen plasma to improve her blood-clotting mechanism; fresh blood with all the clotting factors in it came up from the blood bank, donated by family and friends. This would help her too.

The chest was closed. The operation was over. The patient's bed was brought into the room in preparation for moving her off the O.R. table.

Suddenly, the EKG monitor showed some very rapid, awful-looking complexes. As quickly as they came, they went. We looked again, and there was only a straight line: a cardiac arrest. We did all we could—we used every drug we had, the surgeons pounded on her chest and shocked her. But it was an exercise in futility. Ah Loo was dead.

The surgeon went to the phone to call the family. The medical electronics technician shut off his console. The O.R. nurses went out to get the shroud pack to wrap her in. Someone came in with her dentures. They had to be put in before rigor mortis set in. I opened her mouth, put in her teeth, closed her mouth. I looked at her face. Ah Loo seemed to be smiling. She was at peace at last.

When we were finally finished, Maureen and I went for a smoke. "Barrie, you look like a ghost," she said. "What's up? Want to talk about it?"

Did I! It poured out of me. I told her of my fears of being in on heart surgery—that I seemed to dread each case more than the one before. That I felt so small, so totally inadequate—and it seemed to get worse and worse. I could not handle the deaths. I was beginning to feel that I was the jinx.

Maureen knew what I was going through, knew what it was like to feel so terribly inadequate—how humbling and awful it is. "First of all," she said, "you know what the odds are in the heart room. No matter what the patients have going for them, the best we usually give is fifty-fifty. Now add to that Ah Loo's age, mental outlook, physical disability, and all the other factors like nutritional status—and then figure out her odds. They were really lousy.

"You've got to try not to get so wound up in the role you play. You are one of twenty people. We all tried hard, but her number was up today. Come on, Barrie, it's time to go home. Forget about today."

I started to get dressed. I knew she was right. I had to put my work out of my mind. I had to—or it would destroy me.

I went to my health club. That always changes my outlook, even though the topics of discussion I overhear never seem to vary—new fashions, new places to eat, drink, and play, new movies, new shows, and men. . . .

"I met him at the beach. Do you think he'll call me?"

"I met him at a party. Do you think he'll call me?"

"I met him at a disco. Do you think he'll call me?"

"I haven't heard from him in a week. Do you think I should call him?"

"I've been calling and calling him and I always get his machine. What should I do?"

I took a relaxing yoga class, then retired to the sauna. There too the conversations soothed me. They were so predictable—as were their outcomes—not like work, not like open-heart surgery, not like Ah Loo.

"Let's go out and have a bite," I said to one of my friends. "I'll meet you upstairs in half an hour."

I was relaxed, clean, open, able now to enjoy my evening.

VI

I used to be a nursing administrator and a workaholic. I was always on call one way or the other: as an assistant hospital administrator I took call with the other assistants one night in seven and one weekend in seven. As director of nursing I was always on call for acute emergencies within the department. In our hospital, as in every other, nursing was the largest department. It was seldom that they called—but when they did, you can believe it *was* an emergency. The son of a prominent figure was in the E.R., high on God knows what, and the reporters were hot on the trail; a nurse had taken an overdose in her hospital apartment and was critically ill in the I.C.U. Things like that, difficult things.

At that time in my life I loved the work, the challenge, the stress, the razzle, dazzle, hassle of my day-to-day existence. I ate it up. The hospital was my life, almost my whole life. When I went on vacation, one of the guys from work drove me to the plane. When I returned, he was waiting for me. When I needed my hems turned up or turned down, the hospital seamstress did it for me. There was a great apartment for me on the premises, rent free. I was smart enough to turn that one down, but I lived in a hospital cocoon and for a long time it was very pleasant.

The men in my life fitted around my work—and when I was tired of them, I used work as an excuse. I wasn't looking for a permanent relationship; it didn't fit in with my plans. I couldn't handle it. A motto I had read stuck in my head: "Men are like streetcars; if you miss one, another will be along in three minutes." I indulged in a wonderful trans-Atlantic love affair. I'd go to England a few times a year; he'd come to New York once a month on business. It was a treat for us both: a couple of workaholics spending our free time together. We worked in different fields, so we could talk to one another about what we loved: our work. Time stood still.

Of course, I didn't realize how all-consuming my work really was. One day, however, I found out, and the discovery was to change my life permanently. My work had consumed my stomach lining. I had a gastric ulcer—and a hemorrhage, a bad one. I went to the hospital and had the whole bit—blood transfusions, private-duty nurses, milk and cream, no alcohol, no cigarettes, no coffee, no tea, no spices, no citrus fruits, no visitors, no work. No work. *No work at all.* It brought me up short—I was no longer in control—my body had betrayed me.

I spent three weeks in the hospital. One of the surgeons who came to visit me warned me that with a second bleed they'd operate, take out most of my stomach. My father had died at an early age of cancer of the stomach. He had started with an ulcer too. These were very sobering things. I was depressed, severely depressed. My life as I knew it was crumbling. I went to Palm Beach to recuperate. It was off-season. There was little to do—a good thing for me, since there was little I could do. I couldn't swim, or walk, or eat what I wanted, or concentrate, or read, or be pleasant with other people. I was no longer in control—my body had betrayed me.

I stayed for three weeks. When I returned I was tanned, fat (from all that milk, cream, custard, junket, and ice cream) and fit—I thought. I was ready for work. My doctor had suggested I return to work for two hours a day the first week, then four hours for a week, and after that, full time. I thought she was crazy but I complied. I was overjoyed to be back—to be returning to my world. I planned to work from 8:30 to 10:30. By ten o'clock the first morning I thought I'd die. As soon as I could I left. I rushed home and went to bed. I was depressed, severely depressed. I was no longer in control—my body had betrayed me.

In the afternoon one day that week I went to the park. I sat on a bench. The nannies were out with their charges. The derelicts were out with their wine bottles. The tourists were out with their cameras. I had some heavy thinking to do. I realized I could not do it alone. I went for help and worked through my problems. Finally I could see how self-destructive I was. I could see that all my work, all my efforts, all my charging around was just an avoidance pattern, a copout on life. It was time to grow up, grow up and change, grow up and live.

With no definite goal in mind I resigned my job. People said I was crazy to give up such a great job, such status, such money, such responsibility. But it was killing me—I was killing myself. This hemorrhage had been a warning. The next time I'd not get off so easy.

I looked around for new fields—ones with challenge, where I could use my intellect and my judgment, where I could deal with people instead of pieces of paper, where I could see results in minutes rather than months. I went all over the country. I looked, I interviewed. I wrote. I talked. I weighed and balanced and finally decided on anesthesia.

For four months after I made that decision I did not work. I did not set the alarm. I did not have meetings. I did not write reports. I did not worry if the phone rang. I disciplined only myself. I was learning to grow, to change, to live.

I was hoping also to change in my relationships with men. Men are like streetcars, but there are no more streetcars in New York.

I couldn't react the way I had previously. I'd eat myself up. I had to find a coping mechanism. After all, people in the medical field see tragedy every day. We are not gods (even if some of us think we are).

I had learned to adapt, to cope, to live.

It was a nice day about two weeks after my day with Maureen and Ah Loo. I had come to work singing. I got off the elevator, said good morning to a few people, and checked the schedule.

My name did not appear anywhere. I had no assignment. I went into the office to see what was wanted of me. "Barrie," my boss started. "I want you to go and help Maureen. She has . . ."

"The heart room," I said mournfully. "That's it,

isn't it? You're going to put me in there again, aren't you?"

"Well, no, I'm not going to *put* you in there. I just want you to help Maureen. She was off yesterday and someone else set up for her. Just go down there, make sure that everything is in order, help her to get the patient ready, and once that's done, come out here. I have a delayed case for you to do."

Who could argue about that? Wasn't Maureen my friend? Hadn't she oriented me when I first came to MCG? I started down the hall. The patient had arrived, and Maureen was getting last-minute things ready. I told her I had been sent down to give her a hand. She glanced at the patient and raised her eyebrows. She was a woman of indeterminate age, sitting bolt upright in her bed, trying to breathe. It looked like it was very hard for her.

"Barrie, before you get any of the lines in, let's get some oxygen for her," Maureen said.

It seemed like a damn good idea to me. The lady's lips were blue, a deep purple to be exact. Sweat was pouring from her and she seemed very tired. She was an addict, had gotten an infection of the inner lining of her heart, probably from a dirty needle, and subsequently the function of one of her valves had become impaired. She was here today for a valve replacement. She looked awful to me.

I went into the room and looked for the transport oxygen. The scrub nurse looked up from her instrument count. "What's up, Barrie? Oxygen so early? Doesn't look good, does it?"

Don't think about it, don't think about it, I cautioned myself. None of the heart patients look good when they're out there getting ready. I couldn't understand why they did all the preparations in the hall anyhow. Where I came from we did them right in the room. . . .

"Listen, I'll talk to you later." I grabbed the oxygen tank and returned to the patient.

Usually when we give the open-heart patients oxygen in the hall, their color improves immediately. Not so today. I had started by giving her oxygen via two small prongs into her nostrils. Now I switched to a mask, since more oxygen would get to her that way. I encouraged her to take deep breaths. Her color remained the same. The priest came. He smiled at us—we knew him quite well: the church was just two blocks away. He seemed to know the patient. He spoke to her quietly and soothingly about her surgery, about her children, and about God.

"If I'm in the way, miss," he said to Maureen, "just let me know. I'll leave and you can go on with the preparations."

"Father," Maureen whispered, "surely at this point you're doing more for her than we are."

The anesthesiologist appeared. She nodded to me, took her equipment, and started putting in the arterial line.

The surgeons appeared. Maureen opened the door halfway and called, "May we come in?"

"Please do," the head nurse replied.

"Okay, Barrie," said Maureen. "Thanks for your help. I know you have a case to do."

I was very glad to get out of there.

* * *

Patients with fractured hips come to the O.R. in their own beds, so that they do not have to be moved unnecessarily and also so that when the operation is over they can be properly positioned in their own bed. Since these beds do not fit into the preanesthesia room, they are left in the corridor and patients are set up there. Everyone who passes by can see your patient before surgery and if it looks bad, everyone commiserates with you. There was plenty to commiserate about with me today.

The bed was filled with pillows, traction equipment, and pieces of foam to cushion bony prominences; somewhere in the midst of it all lay Sadie Schwartz. Although patients generally respond better to their first names, we call senior citizens by their last names as a sign of respect. "Mrs. Schwartz," I called.

No response.

I called again, louder this time. Nothing. "Sadie," I shouted.

"What?" she responded.

She looked drawn and tired. I looked at her chart. She had had no medication prior to coming to surgery.

Sadie was ninety-six years old and looked every day of it. She was just a bundle of bones—and one of them broken. I worked very gently with her. I used paper adhesive tape on her fragile skin: cloth tape sometimes causes old skin to come right off. And as I worked, I tried to explain what I was doing.

But Sadie didn't seem to care. "What's the matter with you, miss? Why don't you let me die? I'm an old woman. I lived my life. What do you want from me?"

"We're here to fix your hip, Sadie. I'm going to give you the anesthesia, put you to sleep."

"You'll do me a big favor? You won't wake me up. My life is over. Let me die. Without my husband why should I suffer? Why should I live?"

I told the anesthesiologist I had bad vibes. I didn't want to do this case. She agreed, but Sadie had signed her consent for surgery, and there was no reason to cancel the operation. You can't cancel surgery for bad vibes.

The anesthesiologist said she'd do a spinal. Sadie would tolerate that better than a general anesthetic.

Before she started the anesthesia, I gave Sadie a *minute* dose of Valium, since the elderly are very sensitive to all drugs, but most particularly to depressants.

In the O.R., things were not quite ready. They were setting up the table for use with the image—an X-ray machine which looks like a TV screen but which shows what you are doing. It is invaluable for setting hips and putting in screws, pins, and nails, because you can see if the fracture is properly reduced and whether the pins or whatever are being properly placed.

Three people were getting things ready—an X-ray technician, a nurse, and another technician who worked in that room. The mattress for the O.R. table had been taken off and a large, sturdy board substituted. They were busy securing the board and fixing up last-minute things on the table. I opened the door a crack. "May we come in?" I asked the nurse.

"Might as well," she replied.

The intern and I wheeled in the bed. Sadie slept

peacefully as she was gently lifted onto the O.R. table. She slept peacefully as we turned her on her side with the fractured side down so that the anesthesia would reach there predominantly. She slept as the anesthesiologist painted her back with iodine, palpated for landmarks, and put in the local anesthetic.

Sadie had scoliosis—a curvature of the spine—which made it exceedingly difficult to do a spinal anesthesia. The anesthesiologist tried several times without success. Finally she decided a general anesthetic would be easier on this particular patient.

Sadie had had some changes on her EKG, but her old chart, which was very thick—Sadie had been in the hospital many times—indicated that they were old changes. As I anesthetized her, the anesthesiologist was putting in a CVP line to let us know Sadie's fluid status—whether we were over- or under-hydrating her. It is important in elderly patients not to give too much fluid. Old hearts cannot take it as well as young hearts; sometimes, just a little too much fluid added to an old system can result in heart failure. The elderly have little reserve.

Sadie was somewhat anemic, and the procedure she was to undergo was a bloody one. For this reason I started her transfusion early. I warmed all her fluids and her blood: cold blood can cause a cardiac arrest.

The EKG showed the same type of pattern she had had preop. The intern came in from the scrub room ready to prep the patient. "Bad vibes," she said. "I do not like this patient's attitude."

The procedure was long and difficult. Her bones were very soft, and only by using great skill was the orthopedist able to bring the pieces of bone back together again. Sadie lost quite a bit of blood: we gave her two units, using packed cells instead of whole blood to give as little volume as possible.

As the case was coming to a close, I asked the circulating nurse to call the recovery room and set up an EKG monitor, heated humidified oxygen, and a heating blanket.

At the end of the case I took Sadie off the ventilator that had been breathing for her. She had not had any muscle relaxants for two hours; I had switched to an inhalation agent early, and she was breathing well on her own.

I called to Sadie loudly, and she opened her eyes. I told her I was going to take out her breathing tube if she could take deep breaths. She immediately did so, and I extubated her.

In the recovery room she was alert and looked around. The nurse put the oxygen mask over her face and she breathed well. Her vital signs as the nurse reported them to me were good.

"Let's put her on a monitor," I said. "She has a history of some ST elevations"—signs of some heart damage. "Nothing new. No changes throughout the case. I'm just being careful—hell, she's ninety-six."

But as soon as the leads were attached and the EKG monitor turned on, we saw an EKG we did not like. There were changes indicating a left bundle branch block—a defect in the conduction system of the heart—changes indicating that Sadie might have had a silent heart attack. Bad vibes.

I called the intern and the anesthesiologist. They

looked at the tracing and called for a medical consult. They drew bloods for tests to determine whether she had indeed had a heart attack.

They sent the blood work to the lab. The medical resident came and looked at the patient, looked at the EKG, listened to Sadie's heart and lungs—and left. He'd let us know—later—what he thought. Surgical and anesthesia types like us are always in a hurry. Medical types have plenty of time to come to conclusions on their patients: weeks, months. In surgery it's hours. In anesthesia it's minutes.

The enzymes came back very elevated: a positive sign of a heart attack. Damn! The intern and I discussed Sadie. She said, "I'm going to see if there's a bed for her in C.C.U."—coronary care unit. I'd been thinking the same thing. She called. There was a bed available. Sadie was on her way.

The next forty-eight hours would tell the tale. We were depressed. We knew that spark, that will to live, was not in Sadie. Could she make it without it?

I came out into the hall and glanced toward the heart room. The oxygen tank I had used for Maureen's patient was sitting in the middle of the corridor. They would need it when they transferred the patient to the I.C.U. I walked down the hall briskly. As I went to pick up the tank, I thought about the patient, her color, her attitude, her prognosis. She'll never need this oxygen, I said to myself. She'll never get off the table. Why should I bother lifting this tank and tying it onto the bed?

I sighed and lifted the cylinder of oxygen. At the base of its holder were two prongs. I fixed them onto a railing at the head of Maureen's patient's bed and tied the cylinder firmly to the bed. I checked to see that there was enough gas left in the cylinder. I sighed again. The odds on open-heart surgery were poor enough, but some of the patients they selected to do here at MCG made them impossible. No other hospital would take them. Some people thought it was cruel to operate on such seemingly hopeless cases. I had talked to one of the cardiac surgeons about it.

"Look at it this way, Barrie," he had said. "Without the surgery they will die—that is certain. They will live with pain and die with pain. They are really not even living now—just existing. So what does surgery offer them, these patients no one else will do? It offers them a chance, a straw to grasp. They know that they are dying now. We offer them odds—very long odds to be sure—that they might live. Who is to say? It's an individual decision. I'd take the chance if it were me—and I bet you would too."

He was probably right. I *would* take the chance. I'm a gambler.

At 2:30 P.M. I had just brought some narcotics into one of the O.R.'s. I was singing: the day was almost over. I passed the bed in the hall outside the heart room. Funny, I thought to myself, it's taking an awfully long time in there today.

"Hey, Barrie."

I turned. The O.R. supervisor was calling me.

"Ummm?"

"Listen, you want to get that O_2 tank off that bed for me, please. We need to get the bed out of the corridor."

"The bed out of the corridor? What for? What's the problem?"

"Didn't you hear? The patient cooled. Take the tank down. We'll need it for tomorrow's case."

I started toward the bed, then heard the phone ringing in the anesthesia office. I went to grab it. I was looking for a distraction—any distraction.

It was the emergency room. "Come down right away. A patient needs intubation."

I looked at the clock; it was ten minutes to three. Ten minutes before my day was supposed to end. I sighed and started to run.

I rounded the corner and flew down the short flight of steps to the E.R.

When they called it the pits they weren't kidding. The one at MCG was quite spacious for an emergency room—you could probably treat between fifty and seventy-five people there without its even looking crowded. It was the patients who made it so depressing. They say that if you work there long enough you'll have seen it all, and they're probably right.

The waiting room looked like a set for a B movie. The chairs were the same kind they used in the waiting room of the ASPCA—the kind that are cold in the winter and hot and sticky in the summer. There was poor lighting and no ventilation. If one person was drunk (and there were many), if a person threw up (and there were many), or if a person needed a bath, a change of clothes, and a deodorant (and there were very many), the entire waiting room reeked. As for the poor other people, the only way they could escape was to be called inside.

Everything we needed to work with is at hand. There is a large trauma room where at least two and at times three seriously injured people can be treated simultaneously. It has all sorts of sophisticated equipment, and when we are called to the E.R. for a Code Red (cardiac arrest) or an intubation, we head like homing pigeons to the cardiac room.

A handful of people were huddled around the patient.

"Oh, boy. I'm glad to see someone from anesthesia," said Benny, the resident on for neurosurgery. "This is a head injury, a bad one. We need her intubated immediately."

She was a young girl and starting already to get into respiratory trouble: a bad sign.

"Be very careful with her neck," Benny cautioned. "It may be broken."

The girl was snorting loudly through one nostril: a bad sign. Her hands were curled up in a spastic movement as were her feet: a bad sign.

Benny said she was already decerebrate, had no brain function: a very bad sign.

Her mouth was clenched shut. There was no way I could get in my laryngoscope to visualize the vocal cords. I would have to do a blind nasal intubation. I would try to pass the breathing tube into her nostril; if I were lucky, she would inhale the tube through her vocal cords.

I was not lucky. The tube did not go through the cords; it went into the stomach instead. I pulled back the tube and tried again. No go. To get the right angle to get the tube into the trachea I needed to be able to bend her head forward. I couldn't do that. I couldn't move her neck: it might be broken. But time was running out. I asked the nurse for some succinylcholine, a muscle relaxant, and gave it immediately. I had to paralyze the girl in order to open her mouth and pass the tube, which was in her nostril, down through the vocal cords.

I looked at my patient. The girl who was pink when I arrived was now purple. Her heart rate was going down—rapidly. I had no more time. I opened her mouth, inserted the laryngoscope, and called for a suction catheter, needed to suck out secretions. I saw the vocal cords. I looked up. I needed help. Six terror-stricken faces were looking at me. I chose the nearest one—a medical student. "When I say shove," I said to him, "push the tube down. Get it?"

"Got it," he replied.

I guided the tube to the vocal cords with the forceps. I could feel my hand shaking. "Shove," I said. I could see the tube going through the cords. We had an airway. I hooked her up to some oxygen and started to breathe for her. We wanted to decrease the brain size by decreasing her CO_2, her carbon dioxide. I could do this by breathing rapidly—hyperventilating—for her: the CO_2 would be blown off. She was turning pink again now. I checked the chest. Her breath sounds were good and equal on both sides, indicating that the tube was not down too far and thereby aerating only one lung. I wiped my forehead.

"Now," I asked Benny, "what's the story here?"

"Well, Tammy and her boyfriend were riding their bikes in Central Park. Somehow he cut in front of her. They collided. She was thrown off hers and fell on her head. He fell off his and bruised his hip. He'll be okay. But she shows signs of brain stem damage, bad signs. We'll take her to X ray now and get an arteriogram. Maybe there's something operable. I don't think so, though. The brain has swelled to a tremendous size from the impact of the fall. We are trying steroids and diuretics to get the swelling down. It's so massive, though, that there's almost no hope. Our only chance is if there's a subdural or epidural."

He was hoping that she had a collection of blood which could be released by drilling burr holes in her head.

"Benny, everyone's tied up in the O.R. There are no anesthesia people free. I'll go with you to X ray. We can put her on a ventilator there while they do the films."

He called ahead. They told him to come right up.

Everyone looked at us as we passed through the hall. The girl was beautiful. Red curly hair, long eyelashes. I could see the question in everyone's eyes. "What could be wrong with *her*?"

As we entered the doorway to the X-ray department, the orthopedic intern appeared. "Barrie," she started, then stopped herself. "What's this?" she asked. We told her. "Let me help you," she said.

We moved the girl onto a special X-ray table. The muscle relaxant had worn off. She was making all those jerking, random movements again. Gently, they restrained her wrists and put a canvas tape around her forehead, tying her down to the table. "Watch her neck," I cautioned the technician.

The inhalation therapist came. He set up his respirator: it would breathe for her now. The radiologist came. He passed a small tube through a needle in her neck—a needle in her carotid artery.

There was nothing to do but wait now. I went outside to let Vi know what was happening. "Do you want me to stay—in case they do her?"

"Would you? There's no one else."

I went back to X ray. Benny and I waited outside while they did the films. All around me the work of the department went on. A radiologist was dictating the report of a gall bladder series, another one was reporting myelogram results, a student X-ray technician was being reprimanded for leaving a confused patient alone. Benny's beeper went off continuously. "No, no, I have this girl, bike accident. I can't come," he said repeatedly. Time stood still. The attending neurosurgeon called.

"What's with the girl?"

"Nothing yet," Benny answered.

Finally, what seemed hours later, the door opened. The radiologist came out, a scowl on his face. He and Benny looked at the films. No good. Nothing operable. Just that unbelievable swelling: no collection of blood. No surgery, no anesthesia, no hope, no future. Just a bed in the intensive care unit.

What was her future? Pneumonia? Tracheostomy? Bedsores? Death? Or life as a vegetable? How could this be—this was a beautiful girl out on a summer day, riding her bike with her boyfriend. Now her life was over.

I went outside. There was the stretcher on which

100

we had brought her. There was the board on which the police had put her in the ambulance. There were her jeans—they were white once. Now they lay cut up the middle in a heap. Her red T-shirt there too. Memories of a former life. A young life changed in an instant. And what could we do about it? Nothing Nothing Nothing.

I changed my clothes and went home. It was five o'clock. Two hours of overtime, and not even a feeling of accomplishment. What a way to make a living.

I thought about the two women I had cared for today. An old woman who wanted to die—and would probably live. A young girl who wanted to live—and would probably die.

I tried to put them out of my mind, but I found I couldn't. Sadie wasn't the problem. I had come to adopt a *che sarà, sarà* attitude about the elderly, but it was not so easy with the young girl.

I crossed the street. It was a lovely evening. Lots of people were out bike riding. I wanted to tell them, "Take care. Watch out." I walked through the park. I stopped off at the zoo. I looked at the people watching the monkeys. I looked at the monkeys watching the people. I smiled. I sat on a bench and watched people strolling by. So few looked happy. Every once in a while I'd see a couple looking at each other lovingly. Occasionally I'd see a father beaming down at his son. I saw a little girl run proudly to her nanny. "Look look," she urged as she jumped rope.

I wanted to stop them all. I wanted to tell them about the old lady, the young girl, the senseless tragedy. The ironies of life. I thought about what would happen if I tried. They'd call the cops and take me away. I'd end up in Bellevue.

I stood up and stretched. I started for home.

This would be a hard day to forget.

VII

I had been at MCG, it seemed, forever, but it was really only twelve weeks. I no longer felt like an outsider. I knew the hospital, the staff, and my fellow employees well. I was ready to go on call. How different would it be now from my student days? It had been awesome enough then—awesome just to hear about. I remember how during my first six months as a student I used to sit in the cafeteria with students who were a year ahead of me and listen to their horror stories of what happened to them when they were on call. Being on call meant that for a twenty-four-hour period on a weekend and a twenty-one-hour period during the week they were on tap for any emergencies. It meant they had to stay within the hospital itself but in a building far away from the patient areas. They slept in a room with a falling ceiling and no ventilation: the air conditioner did not work and the window could not be opened. They shared the room with roaches, water beetles, and often bedbugs, dust so thick they could write in it, dim lights, and the constant threat of the telephone. They were permitted to move around, since they carried a beeper, but it usually went off either when they were in the bathroom or far away from any phone.

When I was assigned to call—first with a faculty member, later with a staff anesthetist and, during the last six months, with only the anesthesiologist—I learned that they were not exaggerating. I looked on being on call as a rite of passage. On the one hand, it meant that I had advanced to a certain point. On the other, I questioned my ability to withstand the onslaught—doubted my capacity to function under emergency conditions. I knew that the people who came to the O.R. in the middle of the night or during the weekend were not the usual run-of-the-mill healthy patients. If they were, they could wait until the next day to have their surgery. The fact that we were caring for them in these off hours generally meant either that their situation had worsened to the point where it would be dangerous to wait any longer or that they had come in off the street with a condition requiring immediate attention.

And I knew they would not come to the hospital the way scheduled patients do. Many times they would still be wearing all or some of their clothes. There is no time for undressing them when their life is hanging in the balance. Often they would not be clean: they might not have had a bath or shampoo in weeks or months. Many times they would come into the hospital drunk: we say they are AOB (alcohol on breath). People who are drunk sometimes require more anesthesia than usual, sometimes less. I had to try to gauge this in advance. Most of the patients who come in as emergencies must be considered "full stomachs," because even though they may not have eaten within the previous six hours, such things as bleeding, pain, or stress delay the emptying time of the stomach. I had to be careful not to trigger vomiting and possible aspiration of stomach contents into the lungs.

There might not be time to ask the usual questions, and even if there were, the patient might not be able to respond.

But I had lived through call in my student days. Now it was time to find out what it was like at MCG. I had come to work at the regular time—7:00 A.M.—and been given a light assignment so that I would be finished by 11:30 A.M. and could go on "rest break" until 3:00. It might be the last rest I'd have until call ended at seven o'clock the next morning.

My morning went well. I had two cases—a hernia and a gallbladder, and the second patient was in the recovery room by 11:10.

Benita and I were on call together—she for OB and I for surgery. We decided to treat ourselves to a very good lunch. By the time we had finished, it was almost two o'clock and we were stuffed. We went to the call room where we would spend whatever part of the night we were not working, and we rested for an hour. At 2:50 P.M. we were back in the O.R.—ready to work.

From three until six we completed the cases that were going on in the O.R. Call officially starts at six. If we had had no cases to finish we could have set out our emergency equipment early. As it was, we did it later. We dragged out every piece of equipment we might possibly use during the night: cooling blankets, blood warmers, blood plasma, defibrillators, arterial lines, humidifiers, and transport oxygen tanks. We had to have these things at hand: during the night there would be no one to go and get them for us.

I had learned as a student that when you're on call you revert to childhood behavior. The most important things are food and sleep (and in that order). As soon as we finished our afternoon cases, we conferred about dinner. We had lots of options: the Chinese takeout place, an Italian restaurant, the greasy spoon on the corner, Philly Mignon, or something exotic, such as Thai or Cuban food. We had a great choice. We were located in a busy area.

I volunteered to go out to pick up the food. As I signed out to Benita, I felt like an animal released from a cage—away from the smell of the gases and the terrible stress of never knowing what would happen next. I walked along the street pretending I was just like everyone else—that I didn't have to go back there. I took deep breaths. Of course I was breathing soot and car exhaust fumes but I made believe I was in the park breathing fresh air. It was a great game, escape from reality, and for the few moments that I was outside I loved it.

By 6:30 I was back with the food. So far we were in luck: no cases in the wings yet. We set out our feast in the lounge. I had brought Italian food, and we were in the midst of our antipasto when Benita's beeper went off. She went to the phone: it was a stat cesarean section. She was off. I put her food away. Luckily I was able to finish my meal without interruption, but I was just cleaning up when *my* beeper went off. Here we go, I thought.

*   *   *

It was one of the pediatric surgeons. He had an emergency appendectomy on a twelve-year-old. He wanted to start at 7:30. Great! I was ready. I'd rather have a case now during waking hours than in the middle of the night.

I went outside to look up the anesthesiologist's number. I wanted him to know that a case was coming up, so he could make himself available. I already knew some details from the surgeon: the patient was a small, thin twelve-year-old, a full stomach, in good health except for her appendicitis.

I had put out equipment for an adult. I had to change all of it now to meet the needs of this child: a smaller mask, breathing tubes of assorted small sizes, a smaller breathing bag, smaller suction catheters. We usually use halothane, an inhalation agent, on children, so I checked my machine once again to make sure I had filled my halothane vaporizer. I'd checked it before, but it never hurts to do it again. I'm compulsive about anesthesia; most of us are.

I went out into the hall, and within moments the emergency room orderly arrived with a stretcher. A pale, thin, dark-haired youngster was lying there with her right leg pulled up close to her chest. She was obviously in pain and trying to guard against any more.

The orderly told me that the patient spoke only German. We were in luck. I can make my way in German.

I asked her her name and explained in halting German that I could understand her if she spoke slowly. She smiled, her whole face lit up. She told me that her name was Brigitte, she was from Stuttgart, and she was here in America with her mother and father for a visit. They had arrived two days before and were planning to tour the United States by bus. She had learned English at school but now she was too nervous to use it.

I told her we were going to do just fine. It was rather a circus for me to try to explain things to her. But I had to do it. I didn't want her to be more afraid. After all, here she was with bad abdominal pain in a strange country with a strange language. It was not easy for the child. Yet she was interested in everything I was telling her despite the language barrier.

We went through the whole routine. I was able to start the IV easily: I used a little local anesthetic so that it would hurt less. Children are frightened by all needles, but they respond less traumatically to the tiny needle used for the local than they do to the larger one used for starting the IV. When the anesthesiologist came, he was unable to communicate at all with Brigitte so he wrote down exactly the information I obtained.

We put her to sleep and the surgeon took out her appendix—it was a hot one, large and very inflamed. They did a lovely skin closure: Brigitte would be able to wear a bikini.

The operation was over. She was breathing easily, although it would be a while before she was fully reacted from the halothane. I took out the breathing tube and we gently lifted her into the bed and took her into the recovery room. *"Tief atmen"* (Take a deep breath) I said to Brigitte.

"I know what that means," quipped Benita, who

had just come back from doing the cesarean section. "I just don't know what language it is."

The surgeon came into the recovery room with Brigitte's parents. They would be spending their vacation in New York instead of traveling. They were happy, though. Their daughter had come through the surgery okay. She was stirring now. *"Mutti,"* she called out. Her mother went to her. She was okay. I left.

It was 8:15. I gathered up all my belongings to take with me to the call room: my nightgown, some fruit, a couple of magazines, my pocketbook, and some clean linen in case the maid hadn't made the bed. (Benita had warned me this happened frequently.) Before I left the operating room I clipped a slip of paper with my name and telephone extension to the O.R. schedule in the office so that anyone could find me in a hurry instead of going through the operator.

As I was doing this, my beeper went off. I called the operator and found that one of the GYN residents was looking for me. A woman in the emergency room was bleeding heavily: she was having a miscarriage. What we call an incomplete abortion. I put away my things and went back to the O.R. to check once again that everything was in order. At the end of every case we discard all the dirty equipment and set up again with clean things so that all will be in readiness.

As I was in the hall chatting with the O.R. nurse the elevator opened and the orderly wheeled out our patient. She was a short, stout woman, very pale and obviously frightened. I started to speak to her, but a look of total noncomprehension came over her face.

Damn, I thought, can't anyone speak English who comes in here at night? I asked her where she was from. She was Greek. I knew no Greek. We would have to do the best we could. I spoke slowly and clearly and finally I was able to get a history.

She was thirty years old, had been in good health, no false teeth, no allergies, no medications. She had had a cup of tea at 3:00 P.M.; it was eight o'clock now. Sounded okay, no problem: tea without milk should be out of the stomach in four hours or so. The chief resident came and asked her the same questions I asked and got the same story. I paged the anesthesiologist. As he started to question the poor woman for the third time, the chief resident asked him please not to go through it again. He told him what we had both elicited.

The anesthesiologist left to continue making preoperative visits; he had three more patients to see and told me to go ahead with this one. We took her into the O.R. Everything seemed okay—her blood pressure was normal, the EKG looked fine. The GYN resident was ready to go.

I told the patient I was going to put her to sleep. I administered the Pentothal and put the mask over her face. The airway was good, she was exchanging well: anesthetic gas and oxygen were going in and out. They put her legs up in stirrups and started to wash her off with iodine solution. But as soon as I placed her in Trendelenberg position—head down, bottom up—I found it very difficult to ventilate her. I reversed the bed, quickly took off the mask and slipped a plastic airway into her mouth. It didn't help. I gave a short-acting muscle relaxant in case she was having a spasm due to secretions in the back of her throat. Immediately thereafter, I went into her throat with the suction catheter and sucked out some clear mucous. It did not help. I was still unable to ventilate her. I asked them to find the anesthesiologist immediately. Time was of the essence now. No oxygen was getting to this woman's lungs or brain. She was cyanotic—turning blue. I prepared to slip a tube down through her trachea. I was sweating now, my heart was pounding. This was a real anesthetic emergency.

The anesthesiologist came to the doorway of the O.R. "Barrie, what's the matter?" he asked.

"I can't ventilate her. Come, give me a hand quick."

"Did you give her some Sux (succinylcholine, the muscle relaxant)?"

"Yes, but it didn't help. She's cyanotic and I'm getting some EKG changes."

Then I lost my cool. The patient was going to die in moments unless I got a hand here. I wanted to intubate her, but I needed help. "God damn it, don't stand there and quiz me. Get in here and do something. This lady is going. Hurry up, for God's sake!" I was screaming.

He started to tell me he was not in a scrub outfit but he thought better of it. He ran in, and together, with great difficulty, we got the tube in. I turned on an inhalation agent and we gave various drugs. Finally I was able to ventilate her well. She was pink, the EKG was normal, and all looked okay.

My hands were shaking. It had been a close call.

Now the anesthesiologist started to grill me. When did I first encounter the problem in ventilation? How much Sux had I given? Did I give it in a dilute or concentrated form? How many minutes was the patient in trouble? I answered all his questions. I felt I had been careful, had used my best skill and judgment.

At the end of the case the patient woke up fully alert and we removed the breathing tube. We took her to the recovery room and I ordered oxygen for her just as an extra safety measure. An hour later she vomited: meat, noodles, and green vegetable. The food was still formed, indicating she had eaten it recently. We questioned her. I asked her about what she had vomited and what she had said about tea at 3:00 P.M.

"Oh, yes," she said. "I have supper with my husband at six. But he says if I tell you that, you will not put me asleep."

"You are right. You see all that you vomited. If that went into your lungs you would be dead now. Do you understand me?" I asked.

"Yah, Greeks strong. No problem."

No problem! Oh, well, ignorance is definitely bliss.

It was 9:30. I returned to the O.R. again to put the room in order. Each evening two operating rooms are designated as call rooms, set up and prepared for any case from an anesthesia standpoint. One room is reserved for short or "dirty" cases: abscesses, patients with communicable diseases, or septic cases. All other cases are done in one of our larger O.R.'s, one with all sorts of sophisticated monitoring devices.

The porter had mopped the floor; all was in readiness. I took one more look, gave a sigh, and shut off the lights. I felt I would soon return. But I didn't realize how soon. As I passed the O.R. office, the evening nurse called me: "Barrie, we've got another emergency—neurosurgery. This lady . . ."

As she was speaking, my beeper went off. It was the neurosurgery resident. We had to get going as soon as possible. He had an old lady with a depressed skull fracture. She was in the intensive care unit. "As soon as you're ready," he said, "page me and I'll bring her over with you."

"I'm ready now, Ed."

Usually patients are brought to the O.R. by orderlies, but when they are critically ill, professional staff accompany them to insure safety.

I went down to the intensive care unit in the next building. I hated to go there. The staff was quite unfriendly and we people from anesthesia were definitely made to feel like strangers.

But tonight was an exception. As I came through the door the nurse pounced on me. "Anesthesia," she said. (They never address us by name.) "We need you badly . . ."

I interrupted her and said, "Yes, I know all about the old lady on the neuro service."

"Oh, no, not *her*. We have a guy here in severe respiratory distress. He needs to be tubed."

I went over to his bed and was she ever right. The man was blue, sweat was pouring out of him and he was struggling for his breath—for his life, really. He was semiconscious.

I asked them for the intubation equipment. As usual, half was missing. I don't like to start until I have everything at hand that I might need. The nurse was surly and uncooperative. She told me how busy she was, how many patients she had to care for. I tried to ignore her. I was checking my equipment quickly. I didn't have too much time. The laryngoscope did not light properly. I asked for fresh batteries.

"I thought you were going to do a blind nasal"—passing the tube through the nose and having the patient suck it in. "What do you need a laryngoscope for?"

"Honey, you do your job and let me do mine. Get me the batteries, okay?"

She got them. The equipment now worked.

"Let me have an airway," I asked. More grumbling, but it also appeared.

"Now how about a syringe, and while you at it, give me a clamp and some benzoin." Each thing I asked for drew a comment, usually an unpleasant one, from the nurse. During the time I was assembling my equipment the inhalation therapist was helping the patient breathe.

I was now ready. In those patients we expect to leave intubated, we prefer to pass the tube through the nose rather than the mouth: it is more comfortable. We also use a soft-cuffed tube, meaning that the balloon is made of a softer plastic—which means less trauma to the vocal cords. We try to do these patients blind (without inserting the laryngoscope), since they are usually awake and frequently uncooperative, due to fear, lack of oxygen, and sometimes disorientation. If we can't do a nasal, though, we do an oral intubation—so I needed the laryngoscope just in case.

I sucked out the patient's secretions from his nose and throat. I lubricated the breathing tube. "Sir," I said, "I'm going to pass a tube through your nose. It will help you breathe better." I put the tube into his nostril. He started to struggle. I continued to advance the tube. It was hovering above his cords now. With one movement I tilted his head forward, he took a deep breath, and I shoved the tube down further. A big sputtering of secretions came through the tube—usually a sign that it's in place.

I took a sterile suction catheter and sucked out the secretions. I hooked him up to some oxygen and he breathed on his own. I listened to the chest after inflating the balloon. It was in—success! He was looking better already. The whole episode had taken five minutes.

Just as I was about to put on the benzoin before taping the tube to his face, I was called again. I was needed for the old lady. I asked the nurse to tape the tube for me.

I rushed over to the next bed, grabbing the chart on my way. An old lady was lying there with a bandage around her head: she had an IV, an EKG monitor, and a very worried niece. She had arrived in the I.C.U. only a short time before; her chart was not yet complete. I greeted the patient and tried to take the history from the niece. The only clear thing I could get from her was what I already knew.

The woman had been in a taxi, going to the opera.

A car had cut the taxi off and the driver had had to stop short. As a result, she had been thrown forward off the back seat and had hit her forehead on the metal partition which protects the driver.

I could not tell whether her confusion had preceded the accident or was a result of it. Her terrible frontal headache most probably was directly related to the blow to her head, as was the double vision. Whenever I asked a question, both aunt and niece offered a comment, but neither was very helpful.

"Do you take any medication at home?" elicited "Yes, a heart pill" from the niece and "Yes, a blood pressure pill" from the aunt.

"Do you have any allergies to medicines?" got me "Yes, that little pink pill makes her break out" from the niece and "I get sick to my stomach from codeine" from the aunt. I gave up.

Together with Ed, who had now finished the chart, I brought her to the O.R. The procedure would be rather short. She had a depressed skull fracture. The place where she hit her head had caved in like a Ping-Pong ball. The surgery would consist of putting an instrument under the indented piece and popping it back out.

I put the old lady to sleep. There were no problems with anesthesia or surgery. I kept the anesthesia fairly light, since I knew we would soon be finished. A neurosurgeon likes to be able to test his patient, if possible, soon after surgery. In some cases, he wants to make certain that reflexes remain intact; in others, he wants to know whether or not the confusion, the headache, or the stupor has cleared. I used "walking and talking" anesthesia: instant asleep, instant awake. The patient was old and thin so I gave minimal amounts of drugs.

In the recovery room, she opened her eyes and looked around. She had a huge bandage around her head: she looked like a war casualty. I called to her and she responded.

"How are you?" I asked.

"I'm well, thank you."

"Does anything hurt you?"

"No, should it?"

"No, of course not. Do you know where you are?"

"Well, young woman, I really don't. The last thing I know clearly is that I was on my way to the opera. Pavarotti was singing. Do you like him? He's one of my favorites. He's doing *Tosca* tonight. Well, I'm certainly not at the Metropolitan. My goodness, what place is this? It looks like a hospital."

"It is, my dear. You had a little accident, but you're okay now. I'll get your doctor for you." I put in a call for the attending neurosurgeon and once again left the recovery room.

It was midnight. Once again I gathered my things and headed for the call room. Once over there I called the operator to let her know where I was, took off my clothes, and hopped into the shower for a quick bit of relaxation. Benita was in the next bed sleeping soundly.

I got into bed and was sure I hadn't slept at all when the phone rang. As I was reaching for it I peeked at the digital clock: it was 1:13. The operator told me it was a Code Red in the emergency room. A cardiac arrest.

This was a rush, no questions asked. My role here would be to put in the breathing tube. Without an airway, there's not much that can be done for a patient. As I got dressed, I thought back to the code I had attended recently. An old, old man had had a cardiac arrest. He looked to be about a hundred. I ran into the ward and took my place at the head of the bed. One doctor was breathing for him with positive pressure oxygen, another was pumping up and down on his chest: they were doing CPR, cardiopulmonary resuscitation.

Chester, one of the surgical residents, was preparing to intubate the patient. (Surgical house staff spend a month on anesthesia to learn to intubate for just such emergencies.) A big smile came over his face as he saw me. "Thank God you're here. Take over."

When I had all my equipment ready I said, "Okay, stop." For those few moments it would take me to suck out the secretions and put in the breathing tube, they would have to stop the closed chest massage.

One young intern was assigned to start an IV in the old man's neck. He decided this was a good time to do it. "Stop that," I ordered him. He started to tell me how vital his function was. How if the patient did not have a line they couldn't give drugs. How it was unfair for me to monopolize the area he needed to work in. He went on and on.

I never stopped what I was doing. When it was over and the tube was in and hooked up to a respirator, I looked up. "Honey," I said, "if I don't do my job, none of you need bother doing yours. Without an adequate airway, your patient would be dead." I laughed now, thinking about it, but there had been no time for laughing then.

I kicked open the door to the emergency room. Although it was 1:25 A.M., the place was jumping. In one room a woman moaned in pain. A drunk was trying to attack the X-ray technician, a resident was running with a syringe in his hand, a mother tried to comfort her crying child. In the hall one of the orthopedic residents was showing a set of X rays to the senior resident. I hoped it was not another case for the O.R. But where was my Code Red? It should be in the cardiac room. I ran in, but it was strange. The group around the table were all pediatricians. That was very unusual. Children were generally treated in another section. I made my way through the group. A tiny baby lay on the table, so small she could hardly be seen, and so white—white as the sheet on which she lay. At her head stood the chief pediatric resident, breathing for the baby. A tiny endotracheal tube was in her windpipe, and he was ventilating her. Without his help she could not breathe at all. The rest of the pediatricians were busy too. One was trying to get a blood gas from one of the baby's tiny arteries, another tried unsuccessfully to start an IV. Huddled by the door stood a young couple looking utterly terrified—the parents.

What did they want from me here? The baby was intubated. There was no cardiac arrest. There was plenty of help. I looked from one person to another but could determine only that this case, this baby, was my supposed cardiac arrest.

119

Finally I asked the chief resident, "Sam, did you call me for something? I got a page for a code here."

"Yes, Barrie. I need an anesthesia consult. I have an oral tube in this baby and I want to replace it. I want her to have a nasal tube, but her condition is so poor that I'm afraid to compromise her airway even for the few moments it will take to change tubes. I need advice."

"Well, if you want my opinion, leave the oral tube in until the baby's condition stabilizes. But Sam, you know you should be speaking to the anesthesiologist, not me, when you need a consult. I'll call him for you."

I went outside to telephone. The anesthesiologist was sleeping in the on-call room in another building. I dialed, and on the third ring he answered with a brief "Yes?"

I explained the situation to him and asked him to come immediately.

"Put the resident on the phone," he demanded.

"I can't do that. He's with the baby now and can't leave. Please come over. He needs you now."

He muttered something and banged the phone down. I went back into the cardiac room to let Sam know that he was coming. I'd have let him know a lot more—like why did he have them wake me at this ungodly hour when it was the anesthesiologist he needed? What's the point, I thought to myself, he's got enough to contend with.

While I was waiting for the anesthesiologist, I asked the E.R. nurse what had happened to this baby. She told me that she was five weeks old, born at another hospital, a normal spontaneous delivery, and had done well until noon of the day before. Then the baby had become fretful, refused to eat, cried continuously, and had fever.

The mother had called her cousin, who was a pediatrician, but he had made light of it. He had told her it was probably a virus or maybe the baby was just colicky. But the baby had seemed to deteriorate; she had become pale and listless. About midnight, when the mother was again able to speak to her cousin, he still seemed unconcerned; he told her she was an overanxious parent and finally said that if she and her husband wanted to, they could take the baby to a hospital emergency room and have her checked out.

They were very young, the parents, but they knew this was something serious. They had set out immediately for the hospital, but they no sooner hit the front door than their little daughter stopped breathing. By the time they got into the cardiac room she was blue.

"No one really knows what's wrong with the baby," the nurse concluded. "It's a pity isn't it? So much time wasted."

When the anesthesiologist arrived, I gave him a quick history and then we both went to the cardiac room. Things were unchanged. He checked the position of the breathing tube and found it to be okay. "Sam," he said, "you have a gravely ill infant and you don't know what's wrong. You have an excellent airway now. It would be foolhardy to tamper with it to put in a nasal tube. If the baby survives, we can always put in a nasal tube, tomorrow or whenever. The baby certainly doesn't need any more trouble now."

As he was consulting with the resident, I was asking the nurse for a lamp to warm the baby. She was lying fully exposed on the table. It was quite cool in the E.R. and the baby couldn't afford to lose body heat. I also asked for some bandages to wrap her arms and legs to help retain body heat. I took a piece of tube gauze—a stretchable bandage—and made a little hat for her. Poor thing, she looked like a war victim. But I had to try to help her, try to keep her alive.

Then there was nothing more for me to do. I returned to the call room to try to sleep. It was hard enough—I kept thinking of the young parents, the baby, the little old lady . . . It was after two before I drifted off.

The phone rang. It was 3:30 A.M. I grabbed the phone and swung myself out of bed with one movement. Benita turned and sighed in her sleep.

The surgical chief resident was on the phone. "Barrie, it's a young guy, gunshot wound of the neck. It's a bad one—hurry."

I was on my way in another minute, running through the corridors.

I was lucky. I arrived before the patient. I quickly grabbed the narcotic keys and slipped a plastic package of morphine into my breast pocket. The package contained prefilled syringes of morphine—we called it a six pack. I rang the anesthesiologist. He started to ask me a lot of questions.

"I told you all I know. Young guy, bad gunshot wound of the neck."

"Well, if he isn't even there yet, call me when he comes."

Less than two minutes later, I heard an awful clatter in the hall. The patients who come to us from the

E.R. have their IVs started with solutions in glass bottles. (In the O.R. we use plastic—it can't break, it stores more easily, and it's quiet.) We can tell by the amount of noise just how sick our patient is: very sick—lots of IV solutions—lots of noise. This one sounded bad.

"Bring him into the O.R.," I said to the intern and the orderly. "We can put him to sleep right away." As they were moving him into the room I rushed to the phone on the wall. I dialed. As soon as the anesthesiologist answered I yelled "Hurry" and hung up. I got to the patient just as the stretcher was being pushed next to the O.R. table.

"Don't let me die. Don't let me die," he begged. I tried to comfort him, but I could see I was not getting through. First of all he was dead drunk; secondly, he was scared to death. We asked him to help us move him over to the O.R. table.

"Don't let me die. Don't let me die."

We shouted to him, "Harry, we're trying to move you."

"I can't feel my legs, I can't move," he moaned. "Don't let me die, don't let me die."

We lifted him onto the O.R. table—four residents and I. While I was putting oxygen on him they were testing him neurologically. He felt nothing below the waist on either side; he could not move. I checked his blood pressure and quickly pressed on the EKG leads.

All we knew was that it was a serious injury—we did not know exactly what damage had been done. The bullet might have severed a major blood vessel.

Time was of the essence, but I wanted to wait for the anesthesiologist because the wound probably would cause some deviation in the man's anatomy. A gunshot wound to the neck often means a difficult intubation.

Suddenly, I saw he was having difficulty breathing. He was whispering hoarsely with his last energy, his last spontaneous breath, "Don't let me die. Don't let me die."

I pulled up on his lower jaw and hoped to improve his airway mechanically but it didn't work. I tried to assist him in breathing but I couldn't get any air through. I couldn't put in a plastic airway; he was still alert and struggling.

"Tim," I said to the chief resident on surgery A, "I can't wait. He's turning cyanotic. I'm putting him to sleep now."

"Hurry," was his only reply.

I had started thinking out my dilemma as soon as I had heard "gunshot wound of the neck." There were three approaches to the problem of getting this type of patient intubated, but two of them required time and I felt we didn't have any.

I decided to give him my "best shot"—a sleep dose of Pentothal—paralyze him, look in with my scope, suck out any blood and secretions, and try to get the tube in.

I quickly injected the drugs and inserted my laryngoscope. The back of the throat was full of blood. I sucked it out and looked again—more blood. I could recognize nothing. Obviously the bullet had really distorted his anatomy. The heart rate was now becoming irregular. Time was running out.

"Tim, I can't see a damn thing. There's no way I can tube him. You'll have to do a trach." In a case like this, a tracheostomy set (for inserting a breathing tube into a patient's windpipe) is always part of the equipment set out by the O.R. staff. But when I looked up, nothing was happening. I asked the technician, "What's wrong? Why don't you give him a knife?"

"I'm sterile, and the nurse hasn't given me a knife blade," he answered.

"Fuck sterility!" I yelled. "This guy is going to die. Break scrub and get the damn blade. Hurry up!"

As I was saying this, Harry's heart stopped beating. Quickly, I gave him a thump on the chest and it started again.

The technician had picked up the blade and given the knife to Tim. He quickly made the cut and inserted the tube. I hooked the trach tube up to the oxygen after inflating the balloon and quickly breathed for the patient. His heart rate picked up. His color was improving. I put him on the respirator. It would breathe for him now. *I* breathed—a sigh of relief.

He was not going to die just yet. The anesthesiologist came into the room and I quickly told him what had happened so far.

Now I needed to give the muscle relaxant so that surgery could proceed, but Harry couldn't tolerate any more anesthetic right now. He had no blood pressure.

As I was checking his vital signs the anesthesiologist was doing a blood gas to see how well we were doing with his ventilation. Luckily, we had a line in. You can't hit an artery without a blood pressure. I took out the spirometer—a device to measure the rate and volume of breathing—and hooked it into the system. It showed us that we had the correct volume for his estimated weight and were giving ten breaths a minute. I drew a small sample of blood from his finger to see whether or not he had lost a great deal of blood. I put my sample into two little glass tubes. The anesthesiologist took them outside, to a machine which spins them for five minutes. At the end of that time we would know what percentage of the blood was plasma and what percentage red blood cells. The normal percentage of red cells is 35-45. We call this test a hematocrit—or crit for short. Harry's crit was 40—at least blood loss was not a problem—not yet.

I rechecked his blood pressure. He had one now—high, sky high. We had corrected the previous problem of too little oxygen. We were giving only oxygen at this point—oxygen and a muscle relaxant. I dialed in the nitrous oxide and gave him some morphine. His urine output seemed a little on the light side. We decided to give a small dose of a diuretic. Soon his output was good. Now, at last, he was stabilizing: his blood gas was within normal limits, his ventilation good, vital signs good. The anesthesiologist took over for a few minutes.

I went out to the lounge for a cigarette and an apple. I thought about Harry—where he was going. My guess was he wasn't going far, not with an inability to feel or move below the waist. I started to wonder if I had done the right thing. What kind of life would he have? He was a young vital man. What would he be now? I shook my head. I was not here to play God—just to put him to sleep and wake him up again.

I returned to the O.R. and once again took over the case. "Tim, what's doing?" I asked at a quiet moment.

"Barrie, there's nothing much we can do for this guy. The bullet shattered his trachea. I'm just controlling bleeding and cleaning up the mess. He was shot at point-blank range. Look at the powder burns. The bullet came out posteriorly, just grazing the spinal cord. There's no telling now if the injury to the spinal cord is just edema or if it's permanent. Poor guy. What's the story, Joe?" Joe was the intern who had admitted the patient.

"The guy was picked up in one of those all-night topless places about an hour ago. Who in his right mind would be out there at that hour? We never found out who shot him—had to be a pimp or a hooker. Someone definitely did not like him. He's here with a convention—he's a lawyer from the Coast. Poor devil—he'll never walk into a courtroom again. He's married and has five kids. What a bummer."

It was 6:45 A.M. We were through. We were taking him to the I.C.U. He'd require intensive care for many days now. All in all, he was in pretty good shape—if you could say that with what he had.

I finished my chart and looked up at the clock. It was time to go home. I'd slept maybe an hour the entire night. I was off today but it would be a lost day. I'd go home, walk my dog, take a bath, and go to bed.

I thought about my night and the people I'd helped. The old lady with the skull fracture, the baby, the man turning blue in the intensive care unit, the Greek lady. . . . And I thought of Harry—who would probably never walk, might never talk again. What to wish for him? A short life, a long life, no life at all? It was out of my hands. All I could do now was go home.

VIII

People say you can't remember what happened to you at age two, but I don't agree. One of my earliest and least pleasant memories concerns an event that took place then. I remember having a stomachache. The pain was awful, and since I had just eaten some fruit I wasn't supposed to, I waited for quite a while before telling my mother, waited until I could hardly stand the pain.

My next memory is of lying on a huge white slab—I thought it was an ironing board. From somewhere in back and over me a gigantic figure, all in white, was trying to come at me with a large black object shaped like an iron. I was sure I was going to be pressed to death. "Don't iron me, don't iron me," I cried, but to no avail. Reinforcements came; now they were holding me. Once again I begged them, "Don't iron me."

No one spoke to me and with one last frantic burst of strength I kicked free. This time there were five of them—one on each arm and leg and, of course, the first one, the one with the iron. The iron came closer and closer, it loomed larger and larger. "Don't iron

. . ." and I was gone. Such was my introduction to anesthesia. I guess a psychiatrist would have a good time with why I am doing anesthesia today.

I love children, and as often as possible I do pediatric anesthesia. Thankfully our service has a very positive attitude toward anesthetizing children. We never hurry the child—if the surgeons have to wait for us they simply have to wait. Parents always accompany children preoperatively, as much for our sake as for the child's. In pediatric anesthesia we must depend upon a third party for the history. It is seldom that we can get the information we need from the child. If we are fortunate, one or both parents will be visiting the child the day before surgery, when the anesthesiologist makes his visit.

The preparation of equipment for pediatric cases depends on the age and weight of the child and the length of the procedure. Temperature regulation and prevention of heat loss are extremely important in caring for infants and children under anesthesia. Infants have, in proportion to their weight, a much larger surface area than adults, and they lack the protective subcutaneous tissue to prevent heat loss.

So we preheat the O.R. to seventy-five or eighty degrees, dropping the temperature as the operation progresses if the child is maintaining an adequate temperature. We place a heating mattress under the sheet on which the child lies. And we wrap up small infants with bandages on their heads, arm, and legs during surgery and have a heated form of transport waiting outside the O.R. door to return them to recovery or the nursery. For longer cases we heat and humidify the gases the child breathes. All these measures help to keep up the temperature in a not too stable heat regulation system—the system of a child. Children are not small adults, infants are not small children. Their systems are not miniaturized adult systems. They are systems which are only partially mature.

Oral rehab. Rehabilitating the mouth? Yes. Parents abuse their children's mouths. We rehabilitate them. The problem is threefold. First, many parents prop their babies' bottles, particularly at night. The residue of the milk gets on the developing teeth and rots them. As children get older, parents give them other things that rot the teeth: Soda, candy, and other sweets. These are the two main reasons that we see these young patients. The third is a matter of neglect: not brushing the teeth at all. We seldom see this in normal children, but we see it all too frequently in retarded children who have never been taught to brush. If you can picture an underdeveloped child of five who has had every tooth pulled from his mouth and who comes in for a fitting for false teeth—yes, false teeth at the age of five, before permanent teeth have even come—you will understand the magnitude of the problem.

Ignorance and neglect crosses all socioeconomic lines. Money makes no difference—except perhaps that more money means more junk food.

*   *   *

The ward service was working. The dental technician who would help on the procedure had arrived. I asked her what she knew about our patient. She did not remember the child, knew only that he was retarded. I called the pediatric floor to get an age and weight so I could set up. They told me he was eleven years old and weighed forty-four pounds—he was very small for his age. I was ready by the time he arrived.

His mother was with him. When I spoke to her she smiled nervously. He was her firstborn. She had four others, all normal. But she had contracted German measles during that first pregnancy, and he was the result. He was deaf as well as retarded. He lived at home with her. How did she take care of four normal children and Bobbie too? "I manage," she said.

Bobbie was a very thin, handsome boy. He smiled at me—his mother's smile. He was cute and quiet. He let me approach him. I made sure to let him touch first. I let him hold the blood pressure cuff before I put it on him; the same with the EKG leads. I showed him a cold circular object—the precordial stethoscope—and taped it onto his left chest. I would attach a length of tubing to the bell and plug a specially made plastic earpiece into my ear when I put Bobbie to sleep. It would help me to monitor his every heart beat.

I wondered how he would respond to the IV. All children—and most adults—hate needles. With normal children of five years or older, we let them decide whether they would like to go to sleep by needle or by mask. It is much easier for older children to go to sleep with Pentothal, but some of them are so terrified of injections that they prefer breathing an un-

132

pleasant gas. If they are undecided, we tell them we prefer the IV.

Bobbie could not make decisions. I had to make them for him. I asked his mother to help me when I started the IV. She was very good with him. It went in without a problem. It had taken about fifteen minutes and we were ready to go. It was time well spent. We had a quiet, cooperative child who should now go to sleep easily. When children cry and become hysterical, they increase the secretions in their nose and throat and thereby become more difficult to put to sleep. We were helping ourselves as well as the child by keeping him calm.

Bobbie started to doze as his premedication took over. He turned on his side and curled up. His mother said that was how he slept at home. But this was no normal sleep. Bobbie was being subjected to the hazard of general anesthesia just to get his mouth fixed.

Bobbie's mom left now as we prepared to take him into the O.R. She had four other children to worry about. She would return at two o'clock to take Bobbie home. She kissed him gently and waved to me. Bobbie was very sleepy as we lifted him onto the table. We hooked up all our equipment. The dentist needed free access to the entire mouth. We tried not to get in each other's way, so we planned to insert the endotracheal tube through the nose rather than through the mouth as we usually do.

I lubricated the tube, and as soon as Bobbie was asleep and relaxed, I inserted it into his nostril. I pushed it downward and backward gently. Then I

opened his mouth and looked in with the laryngoscope at the tube and Bobbie's vocal cords. I picked
up a Magill forceps and guided the tube toward the
cords.

"Ready?" the anesthesiologist asked.

"Go," I replied.

He pushed the tube as I was guiding it. It went
through the cords and we were all set. I inflated the
cuff, hooked Bobbie up, turned on the Halothane,
taped the tube to the face, taped his eyes shut, listened to the chest before relying on the monitoring of
my precordial, positioned the tube so that it would
not lean on Bobbie's nostril, and ventilated him all
the while. All of us in the anesthesia game learn early
how to make two hands seem like three.

Bobbie got a thorough cleaning first. The dentist
was upset. "I brush my dog's teeth," he said. "Why
can't parents do it for their kids? This kid has probably never had his teeth brushed in his life."

When he began, the teeth were yellowish brown.
By the time he was through, Bobbie had lovely white
teeth. "What's the use?" he asked himself aloud.
"They won't get brushed again until the next time he
has this done."

After the cleaning it was time to do the fillings.
Bobbie had lots of cavities. The procedure took one
and a half hours. The dentist said, "This boy has
more wrong with his mouth in eleven years than I
have had in fifty. What can we do? Over and over we
are called upon to handle things that could have
been prevented with a little time, a little effort, and a
lot of education."

I took the tube out at the end of the case. Bobbie was breathing well, but the premedication and anesthetic would keep him asleep for a good little while yet. I told the recovery room people about the deafness and his retardation.

I asked for some heated humidified oxygen. It was 12:30. By the time he was alert, his mother should be back in the hospital. They would ask her to stay with him until he was discharged from recovery. He would be comforted by her presence. He was handsome lying there in his bed, but I wondered what the future could hold for a boy like Bobbie.

I was still preoccupied with his case when I went to get my check. Vi was sitting in her office.

"Check your assignment for tomorrow, Barrie. You've got a pediatric heart."

My nemesis—and this time it was a child with a birth defect in her heart. The anesthesiologist and I went up to the pediatric floor to make our preoperative visit. There she was sitting crosslegged in her bed: a little black doll. She was three years old but looked only half that age. Her hair was carefully combed into braids and she was eating her lunch. Boy, could she eat. She was a tiny child unable to grow properly because of her heart problem but she was enjoying that lunch. Sitting next to her was her doll.

When Antonia arrived in the operating room the next day, her eyelids struggled to open but she was not aware of what was going on. The case started well. There was no problem with the anesthesia or the surgery, and the defect, even though more compli-

135

cated than originally anticipated, was repaired with
relative ease.

The problem came when it was time for her to
come off the pump. Her blood pressure was sky high,
her heart beat erratic, and not enough urine was
being produced. We were finally able to stabilize her,
but we could not make the urine output pick up: a
bad sign. We went with her to the surgical I.C.U. As
we lifted her into her bed, we saw that amidst all the
bottles and machinery was her doll, dressed in a cap
and mask.

When I stopped in later in the day Antonia was
about the same. Her urine output had not picked up
but I told myself it was still early, it was bound to get
better. Still I had an uneasy feeling: was this tiny doll
of a child going to survive?

The next morning when I came to work I stopped
short in the hall. The lounge where we changed our
clothes was directly opposite the pediatric I.C.U. Standing outside the I.C.U. unit was an empty crib—empty,
that is, except for a pink sheet and a doll, a doll with
a cap and mask.

Oh, no, I thought to myself, she can't have died
too. She hasn't had a chance at life. She's only a baby.
I flung open the door to the pediatric I.C.U. I was still
in my street clothes. I was not allowed in there
dressed the way I was. But I could see in. She was not
there.

Later I asked the cardiac surgeons what happened.
Her kidneys had never really opened up. She was
never able to excrete the wastes that built up. Her
lungs and her little heart had given out. They had

worked on her all through the evening and night. But at 3:00 A.M. her heart had stopped. Damn, damn!

For every anesthetized patient who dies either on the operating room table or within forty-eight hours of the time of surgery, a form must be filled out. It is to alert the director of the anesthesia department of all deaths which occur. The form includes a history of the patient, the type of surgery, type of anesthesia, and what happened to the patient. If the death is considered an anesthesia death, the director will proceed to investigate further; if not, the form is merely kept on file.

Already in my short stay at MCG, I had become all too expert at filling out these forms. I knew I had yet another to do now.

I went into the anesthesia office for my form. All the phones were busy. The secretaries were typing away furiously. One looked up and asked me what I wanted. I requested the form.

"What happened, Barrie? Knocked off another one, huh?"

It was more than I could take. It was a silly remark at best but with all my sadness at the events in the heart room, I felt as if I had been stabbed. I went into one of the offices—deserted at this time of day—and started to fill out the form. The picture of the empty crib and doll came to me. I started to go over the case in my mind—every procedure, every drug—and I could find nothing wrong. If we had it to do again tomorrow, we'd do it the same way. I saw the little girl as she had been when we made our preop visit: a cardiac cripple but alive. I saw the empty crib and the doll. Maybe I should do some other kind of work. Maybe tomorrow would be better. I went to the locker room to dress. Everyone had left. I was alone. Thank God. I left the hospital with a heavy heart—and a splitting headache.

IX

The next day I resolved to start with a clean slate—to put yesterday's death behind me. I'd have to get used to death somehow if anesthesia was to be my profession. I would have to accept that not all my patients could live. It was so hard, though, when it was a child.

At least today I'd be starting a new service—one I'd never been exposed to as a student. Students were never assigned to either hand surgery or plastic surgery. The surgery was of such a delicate nature that no student anesthetist could be allowed to do these cases. The slightest movement by the patient before the surgery was over was taboo. But I was no longer a student, and I was scheduled for the plastics room.

Vi always made certain we never started on a new service by ourselves. Today she had assigned Joan, one of the older anesthetists, to help me get acquainted. Joan had told me in no uncertain terms that talking in the plastics room was a no-no. "If you have any questions," she told me, "save them for later. Write them down if you have to, but once the attending is in the room, mum's the word."

Patients who are not having a general anesthetic do

not go into the preanesthesia room. They are prepared for anesthesia in a special room directly adjacent to their O.R. Joan and I prepared the patient in the usual manner: IV, EKG leads, blood pressure cuff, and history. Taking the history was quite difficult since the patients who have plastic surgery under local anesthesia or local Brevital, another short-acting barbiturate, generally receive twice as much premedication as other patients. The reason for this is that they must lie perfectly still on the O.R. table for one to four hours. The heavy premed allows them to catnap or even to be totally zonked. Each person reacts differently to medication, and nowhere is this more evident than in the plastic surgery room. We give medication by body weight, age, and the amount of the patient's normal activity, but it is more complicated than that. A young, active 170-pound woman can sleep peacefully from her premedication while a seventy-year-old, 96-pound woman, whose greatest morning activity is to go to her front door to pick up her *New York Times*, can sit up in bed waiting for me to do something to make her sleep.

We are familiar with one reason for this: what we call white-collar addiction. It takes a skillful questioner and a knowledge of what to look for. "Do you regularly take any medications at home?" is guaranteed to get you a negative response. "Are you taking any drugs at home?" is even worse. The best technique seems to be to assume they take some medication and then try to find out what it is.

I was told that a positive approach—"What medicines do you take at home regularly?"—will sometimes get a good history, but that more often than not the answer will be "I don't take any medicine *regularly*." The trick is not to be put off, to go on to ask, "And what medicines do you take occasionally?" This elicits something like, "Oh, I don't know" or "I really can't remember, dear" or "A little white pill, I don't know what it is, I've been taking it for years." The direct approach might be best. Simply to ask in a very soothing manner (especially if the premed has had no effect on the patient), "Do you take any of the tranquilizers—Valium, Librium, anything like that? What do you take to get you going in the morning? What does your doctor suggest for you when you're tense and need something? What helps you get to sleep at night? If anything bothers you, a headache or a bad back, what medicine makes it feel better?" It seems that most people are afraid to lie outright, even if they are fearful of confessing the medication merry-go-round that constitutes their day.

Most days, Joan told me, the patients in the plastics room are women. Today, however, we had a fifty-year-old male model, Tracy. He was a handsome fellow: tall, slim, and with a great suntan. As I got close and peeped at him, I could see those telltale scars around the eyes and at the hairline along the temples and behind the ears: he'd been here before. His chart showed that he'd had his eyelids done once before and his face lifted twice.

Plastic surgery falls into three broad categories. First, there are people like Tracy who look great to the rest of the world but have a small defect they feel will change their life. Second are the people who have been mutilated by birth, surgery, or accident and who need reconstruction, often in stages. Third are some of the more modern plastic repairs: bellies to be tightened, thighs and arms reduced, breast implants following mastectomy.

The two most common procedures at MCG were the ones we were doing this morning: eyelids and facelifts. Many of the patients were being done a second time, either because of a poor result from another surgeon or because time had taken its toll: they were sagging again and had returned to their own surgeon. Unfortunately, it is frequently harder to undo a poor job than it is to start from scratch.

As soon as the surgeon appeared in the O.R. suite we moved Tracy into the room. The team in this room always works together—not much conversation is needed here.

For the last week there had been a new member of the team. Lothar had been promoted to scrub technician. He'd told me the good news a couple of days before.

Sure enough, there he was at the scrub sink. He was soaping his hands and arms in a ritualistic manner. What memories it must have brought back to him. Memories of his former life. He was standing erect. He looked so important, so competent, so happy. I peeked at him and returned to what I was doing. I didn't want to interrupt his dream.

It was a good thing not much conversation was needed, because Joan told me that when Dr. Palmer comes into the room, "Good morning" is all that is permissible. All was in readiness when he opened the door to the plastics O.R. The patient was lying on the table, the IV running, the EKG beeping away, a

142

knee strap across the patient's knees to prevent him from moving around much. Next to where Dr. Palmer stood were two photographs of the patient: a frontal view and a side view. Special photographers take these pictures, and from the looks of the photos they must try to make the patient look particularly ugly before surgery so that the result will look truly stunning.

All the instruments were laid out by the technician who scrubs here daily. For Dr. Palmer, all is regimented, all is ritual, and as long as there is no break in the routine, all is well. As Joan put it, to work with him is to feel a part of a symphony orchestra—with him as the great conductor. He certainly didn't look like a great anything to me. He was tiny and thin, the sort of person you'd never look at even once in the street, but here it was obviously different. Patients, I am told, look at him as though he's ten feet tall, and he loves it. I was warned that he had a fearful temper; "Just let any part of his ritual be altered and you will hear it—not just in the O.R. but outside at the scrub sinks. Everyone tries to keep him happy— it's so much easier that way," Joan said.

The first thing he did when he came into the room was scrub Tracy with an antiseptic soap. He started at the forehead and worked his way down the face. He used two pieces of gauze, one in each hand, and worked symmetrically. Then he took two larger pieces of gauze and shampooed Tracy's hair. Joan said he must tell the patients he is going to do that beforehand, because they never complain—even the fancy ones. He left the shampoo on and went outside to scrub again. The two technicians—Lothar, who would assist him with the operation, and the one who would pass the instruments—covered Tracy's head with sterile sheets and towels. Another sheet was placed over the abdomen so that the only uncovered part was the face. Lothar saw me and winked.

When Dr. Palmer returned, he slowly and methodically dried his hands while prowling around the room. He reviewed Tracy's films, went over to the instruments and asked a question or two, made sure the new electrocautery machine was on hand to stop bleeding, checked the EKG monitor to make sure the rate was okay. The room was as silent as a chapel. No one was allowed to talk unless he was asked a question, not even the patient. "You've had weeks to talk to me about all that," he interrupted when Tracy tried to ask him something. "Now it's time for silence."

He was ready to draw the lines indicating where he would make his incisions. I was fascinated. It was like watching a great painter. He picked up a little wooden stick sharpened to a point on one end. Lothar held a small glass with some blue dye in it. Dr. Palmer dipped the tip of the stick into the dye and then made a series of dots as his outline. When he was satisfied with it, he traced a solid line of dye.

Now he was ready for Joan and me, but he himself would inject the local anesthesia. I gasped involuntarily when I saw the length of the needle. Our job was to give the Brevital so that Tracy would not feel the needles going in. It was tricky because we were not right next to our patient. Dr. Palmer and Lothar were on either side of the head; Joan and I were relegated to a position on Tracy's side. If anything happened to interfere with the airway, either we must ask Dr. Palmer to handle it, or we must contaminate his whole surgical field and handle it ourselves. If we gave too little of the drug, Tracy would not go to sleep; if we gave too much he might obstruct or not breathe well. No wonder they didn't let me do this type of anesthesia early on.

Once Dr. Palmer had injected the first side we kept checking vital signs until Tracy was alert again.

The Brevital was in. Dr. Palmer ran a finger across Tracy's eyelid. The eyelid did not twitch. Tracy was ready. Dr. Palmer injected the local, then called the patient's name a few times. Tracy responded to his call; his blood pressure and pulse were stable; we could relax a bit. Our patient was once again responsive.

Unlike most surgeons, Dr. Palmer was quite knowledgeable about anesthesia. He'd done a year of anesthesia as a part of his residency program. He kept looking at Tracy's EKG and asking us about his condition.

Dr. Palmer injected and worked on one side at a time. By the time he got to the second side we had some experience with drug dosage. We knew now how Tracy reacted initially. We could adjust our dose appropriately.

It was fascinating to watch what Dr. Palmer did. He cut along Tracy's hairline from the base of the ear to the temple. Then he made another incision around the back of the ear. He lifted the skin and pushed away the tissue below. He was finding a plane in which to work. Gradually he peeled away Tracy's excess skin from the underlying tissue much as I

145

would peel an orange—only he was much more skill-ful. All the time he was doing this, he was controlling bleeding by cauterization with an instrument that looked like a small flashlight. He pressed a button along the side and a spark came out of tiny wires at the top. Sometimes he used a pencillike instrument hooked up to a large machine—also a cautery. He held the edge of the skin with a forceps or clamp. As he continued, the piece of skin he was holding got bigger and bigger. Finally he had loosened as much as he wanted. He cut away all the excess and placed the remaining skin against Tracy's face. *Voilà*, a new, smooth, young face.

Now he stitched it together again. He used very fine suture material on a tiny needle. Each stitch was minuscule and buried under the skin where it could not be seen. When the stitching was over he checked again. Everyone leaned forward to look. It was amazing. Tracy looked ten years younger. When he finished the second side, he gently washed Tracy's face, put on a dressing, and wrapped him in gauze. By the time he was finished Tracy looked like a battle casualty, but underneath it all was a new, young Tracy.

I could see why they came to Dr. Palmer from all over the world—he *is* a genius.

Joan took Tracy to the recovery room. "Go to lunch," she told me.

I slipped into a white coat and went across the street to a greasy spoon that might just as well have been an annex of the hospital. Half the patrons were hospital employees. I looked for a place to sit. A couple of surgical house staff members were in one of the booths. "Come join us, Barrie," called Jeremy, one of the chief residents. They were in the midst of a story about one of the attending surgeons. Jeremy was telling about a case he'd been in on the day before. "So all of a sudden the patient began to tach"—have a very rapid heart rate—"off the wall. He was doing this old lady, a bronch"—looking into the lungs with a bronchoscope. "The patient wasn't blue—hell, she was black. The anesthesia people told him they couldn't ventilate her. He just kept right on doing his bit, totally oblivious. The anesthesiologist looked at me in desperation. I just had to shove S.R. aside and pull out the scope. The anesthesia people got a tube down just as she started throwing multifocal PVCs"—cardiogram changes from lack of oxygen. "We almost lost the patient. Barrie, have you met S.R. yet?"

"I sure have. Day before yesterday they sent me in to do a case with him. It was 2:25 P.M. I didn't want to do the case because I had to leave promptly at three for a dentist appointment. 'Don't worry,' they told me, 'You'll get out.'

"I said that it was impossible. The patient had a left breast mass and a fatty tumor on her back. 'Don't worry,' they insisted, 'you will be out by three.'

"I put the lady to sleep. As soon as I said she was ready, S.R. called for a knife, clamp, knife, suture. Before I could blink an eye he finished with the breast lesion. Then he wanted her turned on her side so he could do the back. He went through the same routine: knife, clamp, knife, suture. I never saw anything like it. But we were finished with the procedure at ten to three and in the recovery room before three."

*　　*　　*

It was 12:30 now. Joan was in the lounge. Our boss was there also, eating lunch. "I'd love a chance to look in on Sadie and Tammy," I said to Joan. "I haven't seen them since that terrible day I told you about."

"Ask Vi. If she hasn't assigned you to an afternoon case, I think I'll let you."

In some hospitals the anesthetists visit the patients after their surgery to see how they are doing from an anesthesia standpoint—to get an ongoing picture of the patient. But Maureen had told me the first day we were together that at MCG these visits were made by anesthesiologists, not by nurse anesthetists. She did not know why the system was set up in this manner: she thought it had something to do with billing. The only patients seen by anesthetists preop and postop, she had told me, were the open-heart patients—and the less I saw of them the happier I'd be.

I asked Vi. She said that since my first afternoon case was at 1:30, I could go. First I went to the coronary care unit, which was in another building. It was brand new and had the latest in gadgetry: all those machines, all those consoles measuring parameters of the patient. And it had almost a whole hospital staff in itself. Each two patients had a nurse assigned to them. The medical and surgical service each had a full-time intern and resident. In addition, there was a raft of attendings, fellows (doctors who had completed a residency in a specialty but wanted to learn still more) and residents making rounds or taking care of something in the unit. A nurse clinician, an expert in coronary care, gave classes and demonstrations to the nurses. She rotated her hours so that she could teach the evening and night nurses too. Each shift had a head nurse, an assistant head nurse, staff nurses, aides, orderlies, and a clerk. Housekeeping provided a maid and a porter whose job it was to keep the unit immaculate.

It was very quiet. For people who have had heart attacks, noise can be detrimental. Excitement of any kind is to be avoided whenever possible; for this reason radio and TV are forbidden: more than one myocardial infarction has been caused by watching an exciting Ranger game. There is piped-in music, but so bland that it is really piped in nonmusic. Rest and tranquillity are an integral part of the recovery process.

I looked around, and there was Sadie over by the window. It was a beautiful day, and sunlight streamed into the room. She was sleeping, an oxygen mask over her face, her EKG monitor beeping away in a regular rhythm. But the ST changes remained, clear evidence of her recent damage.

I went to the desk. "How is she?" I asked the nurse.

"Hard to tell."

"Her enzymes?" The blood tests.

"Inconclusive, all of them."

"Thanks."

I left. Well, I said to myself, at least she's still alive. I took the elevator to the intensive care unit. The I.C.U. has two wings, one for surgical patients, the other for medical patients. I was headed for the surgical side.

"What's up?" the head nurse asked. "We didn't call anesthesia."

"No, no," I reassured her quickly. "I'm not here

for a code"—a cardiac arrest was our usual reason for coming to I.C.U. if we were not bringing in a patient—"I'm here to see a patient who came in last week. You know, the girl from the bike accident. I intubated her in the E.R."

"Oh, you mean Tammy. There's no change—no change at all. She's over in bed three. Her boyfriend is with her."

Bed three was right next to the desk. I strolled over and looked at her chart. I hesitated to go directly to the patient. What could I say to the young man? I looked at her. She was just the same, it appeared. She was lying in bed with the head of the bed cranked up to a 60° angle. She still had her tube in, the one I had passed with such difficulty. She was hooked up to the respirator, which was breathing for her. Two IVs were running.

Bent over her was the boy—and he *was* a boy. He had blond curly hair and looked like an angel. He was talking to her. She did not respond. He stroked her hair tenderly. She did not respond. He took her hand. She did not respond. They were so young, the two of them, and the situation looked so hopeless. How must he feel, what terror, what guilt—I wondered if he was actually able to digest the whole thing yet.

I sighed and turned back. I had difficulty handling this and I wasn't even involved. What must he be going through?

I returned to the O.R. My assignment for the afternoon was in urology.

I came out to the preanesthesia room not knowing

what I'd find. Earlier, I had been told that the next case would be a transsexual having his/her testicles removed. Orchiectomies—the medical term for this procedure—are performed not infrequently, but not for *this* reason. Usually they are done for cancer of the testicles and it is a procedure associated with great emotional trauma, especially when the man is young. Plastic implants of varying sizes can be inserted to make the man look normal. Furthermore, the cancer usually attacks only one testicle, so that the man is still both potent and fertile. Nevertheless, the assault to the psyche is hard for these young men to deal with.

But that should definitely not be the case today.

There was no one in the preanesthesia room when I went in to check, but as I was leaving, the orderly wheeled in a young blond woman. I went into the lounge for a cup of coffee, and as soon as I sat down a call came over the intercom: my patient was here. I returned and found that only one of the ten spaces in the preanesthesia room was occupied: by the blonde. Somebody goofed, I thought, and idly looked at the tag at the bottom of her bed. It read "Jean Thompson." Jean Thompson *was* the name of my patient, but this couldn't be. I went outside to check the schedule again. Yes, Jean was indeed scheduled to have an orchiectomy. Oh, well, I thought, maybe somehow the tags got mixed up on the beds.

I went back into the little room to check it out. The patient was a beautiful woman with the translucent skin so many blondes and redheads have. Her eyelashes were long and lustrous, her ears tiny and delicate, her hands small, her fingers tapered, her long nails carefully manicured.

"Hi," I said, "I'm Barrie Evans. What's your name?"

"I'm Jean, Jean Thompson," she answered in a melodious, high-pitched voice. I took her wrist and checked her identification tag. She was Jean Thompson. There was no doubt about that.

"Jean, I'm your anesthetist. What are you having done this morning?"

She gave me a calculating look—she was trying to size me up. "Well," she said, "I might as well say it in plain English. I'm having my balls cut off. In my heart I'm a woman but somewhere along the line God made a terrible mistake, in making me. Have you ever met anyone like me before, Barrie?"

"Yes, I have. I used to work with a woman like you at another hospital. She had had surgery too, to change her from male to female. I knew her for a couple of years first when she was a guy and then later on as a woman."

"I'm glad you at least know about this kind of operation," she said. "Many people have never even heard of it. They think we're freaks and call us all kinds of dirty names."

She was very nervous. She started to shake as I started her IV. I thought that maybe by talking I could distract her a bit. Besides, I was curious to hear her story. "Tell me about yourself, Jean," was all I needed to say. She was off and running.

"Barrie, I've always known I was a girl—from my earliest childhood. You know how kids play? Well, I was never interested in trains or guns. I always wanted to play with dolls, to dress up pretty like the girls did. They never let me, though. I come from a small town in the Midwest. My father is a minister: my family is looked up to in the community.

"From the start I knew something was wrong with me. I didn't want to do the things my father liked—fishing, canoeing, or baseball—but he insisted. I was his son, I had to act like a man. My mother was a plain person; she knew I was unhappy, but she didn't know how to handle me. So she ignored things, hoping it would all straighten out in time. My greatest thrill was going into her room and trying on her clothes and hats. I would stand in front of the mirror for hours, pretending to be a famous actress, a singer, a dancer, anyone—but always a female.

"One day my father caught me—I was about nine at the time. Barrie, he beat the shit out of me and sent me away to military school. 'That will make a man out of you, by golly,' he said. Of course, it did nothing of the sort. The only thing it did was to make my misery more acute, my sense of being different greater and greater. The boys called me names—faggot, *maricon*—I didn't even know what they meant at the time.

"I ran away when I was ten. I didn't know what to do or where to go, but I headed east. I thought that if I could ever find a life for myself it would be in New York. I had no money. I knew no one. I started to steal—shit, I had to eat. The first things I stole were clothes. I was a woman, I wanted to look like one. I was tall for my age and started to let my hair grow. Damn that military school anyhow. . . ."

Jean stopped because the O.R. supervisor had

come into the room. "Barrie, there's going to be a delay in your room. Your surgeon has an emergency in his office. Is *this* your patient?" She looked as startled as I guess I had, just a few minutes earlier. She left.

"We have lots of time, Jean. Tell me what happened in New York."

"I began stealing all the time. I worked the dressing rooms in a couple of exclusive department stores. You'd be surprised at how careless women are when they're trying on clothes. They leave their pocketbooks on the floor while they're busy admiring themselves in the mirror. I had a routine. I got good at it. I was able to survive.

"One night in a coffee shop I was picked up by a guy. He took me home. When he found I was a guy, too, I thought he'd kill me, but he made love to me instead. It was my first experience with a man. I loved it. I wanted more. I started haunting the gay bars. I couldn't get enough sex, but I hated the gay scene. I felt it was not for me. I wasn't gay—I was a woman.

"A fight broke out in a bar I was in. It got out of hand and someone called the cops. It took them a good little while to break it up. They put us all in the van and hauled us off to jail. They made us all strip down. They were looking for drugs. There was a young cop there. When I got undressed he got crazy. He put me in a separate room from the rest of the group. First he punched me, but not where it would show: on my body not on my face. He kept mumbling to himself, 'Faggot, fucking queer.' He had a funny look on his face. When he had punched me enough he unzipped his pants and took out his cock. 'Bend over, faggot, so I can fuck you up the ass.' Why is it that the same people who claim to hate what you are use you? That night I was beaten and fucked repeatedly. I vowed never to go to jail again. That's one vow I've kept—about the only one.

"I kept up that life more or less for years. I stole, I hustled, I drank, I smoked dope. I found out more about New York in a few years than many people do who have lived here all their lives.

"Last September I met Stephan. It was funny how we met. It was on a Sunday. I was over at Carl Schurz Park—you know, over on the East Side. I was just taking the sun, watching the tugboats go by on the river, sitting on a bench and relaxing when a guy came by and asked if he could share the bench—a straight guy, a decent guy. We started to talk. We liked each other right away. We went out that night. Nothing happened, you know. He was shy and I was terrorized he'd find out. By the time we got together for the second time I figured there was no way out but to tell him the truth. We sat down and drank a little wine. He was feeling mellow. I was freaking out. When I told him, he couldn't believe it. He didn't know what to do. He said he felt comfortable with me but as a man to a woman; he had never been with a man. We talked and talked and finally we, you know, had sex. It was kind of strange for both of us—we were so anxious. But it worked out. Not great, but not a turn off.

"Since then—that was last November—I've moved in with Stephan. I work as a waitress and he's an auto mechanic. We're saving our money so I can have all the operations—this is just the first, you know. After that we'll get married, adopt a couple of kids, a boy and a girl. I'm a very sentimental person. I want to lead a normal life. We live in Astoria in a two-family house. No one knows about me—not even the downstairs neighbors. I'm really looking forward to my operation. The only thing is, I'm afraid to go to sleep. Is there any way it can be done without putting me out?"

"Certainly. I can give you some tranquilizers and narcotics and your surgeon can put in a local anesthetic. It's a short procedure and you should have no problems."

At this point the urologist who would do the operation came into the room. We discussed the anesthetic, he was amenable, and we went into the O.R.

Once inside I could feel the tension. This just was not the kind of surgery we usually perform. The scrub technician was a man, as was the circulating nurse. They looked at Jean with wonderment and dismay. I put up a drape so that she did not have to watch as they washed off her genitals with the iodine solution. The urologist methodically prepped and draped. I gave Jean some Valium; she was napping. The urologist told her he was going to inject the local anesthetic. She hardly stirred. I gave her a little morphine intravenously, and soon she was sleeping soundly. The operation went on without incident.

But as they placed a clamp at the base of the testicle and closed it, the men in the room—the technician, the nurse, and the assistant resident—all drew in their breath. They were identifying with this mutilation.

The testicles were gone and the final skin suture

was put in. Jean still had a penis. That would be removed at a future time, the inside gutted out and an opening made in her bottom. Through this opening they would turn the skin of the penis inside out, making a vagina for Jean.

The hormones she had been receiving had already given her great-looking breasts. But the penis was long and thick even in its dormant state. The technician shook his head slowly from side to side. "What a waste," he muttered.

The resident put a suspensory on Jean and we returned her to her bed. In the recovery room the nurse assigned to her knew the case.

"Don't forget to call Stephan at work," Jean called out to the resident. "Barrie, I loved the anesthesia. I was afraid to go to sleep and this was just wonderful. Do come up and visit me in my room. I want you to meet Stephan."

I'd like that. I was anxious to meet him.

X

I was in at the crack of dawn. It was one of those cold, raw, November-like mornings, but it was only October fifth. I was lucky: I'd had a ride into work. Last night when I was walking my dog I'd met Phil, one of the GYN residents, walking his. I'd asked him if he was going into the hospital in the morning and he'd said, "Yes—but very early. Meet me at 5:50 on your corner and I'll pick you up. If I don't see you, I'll just go ahead."

I hated to go to work by bus. I had to take two buses, and inevitably I missed the second one. I didn't mind in the warm weather but on a day like today I'd use any excuse to put up my hand and hail a cab. So a ride to work was always welcome.

I was waiting as Phil drove up. There was no traffic at this hour, and in seven minutes we were in front of MCG. I hopped out as Phil went off to garage the car.

It was so early I hardly knew what to with myself. I'll set up my room first, I thought, and then I can just hang out. I love to watch people; this would give me a chance to be a spectator instead of a participant for a change. There was no other way for me to spend my time. There was no coffee at this hour—the cafeteria wasn't even open—and no one had a newspaper. I could move at a leisurely pace instead of my usual rush.

It was 6:25 A.M., and it was quiet in the PAR, the preanesthesia room. No one was there yet. The drama would begin in about twenty minutes and continue all day and perhaps half the night, but for now all was peaceful. Each of the ten little rooms was empty of patients. There was a small portable anesthesia machine, a supply of IV fluids, the sticky leads for the EKGs, and a supply of medications, syringes, and needles in each one. At the side of the room was the narcotic-supply locker. It was an impressive-looking piece of equipment. As soon as even one of its two locks was opened, a red light went on and a loud buzzer went off. It was usually kept double-locked. There were indirect lights over each of the ten rooms so we could see exactly what we were doing when setting up a patient. Now only one of the overhead lights was on.

I leaned on a chair. I thought about Jean Thompson. What would she be doing at this hour? Sleeping, most likely. What would her future be? Where would she ever find the money for all her remaining surgery? And where would she have it? That kind of surgery was not done at MCG. She'd have to go elsewhere to have her penis removed.

I idly watched the scene in the PAR. I knew it by heart now. The characters changed daily but in essence it was always the same.

At 6:45 the chief anesthetist, Vi, and the anesthetist assigned to give out narcotics for the day arrived.

"Barrie, what are you doing here at this hour?" Vi exclaimed in astonishment.

"Morning, Vi. Hi, Joan. I got a lift with Phil and now I'm trying to keep out of mischief."

Vi smiled and turned to Joan.

They counted all the drugs to make sure the narcotic count was correct. They turned on all the lights, because as soon as they started the count the first patients arrived.

Standing there I could see them entering the PAR: a baby in a tiny heated crib, an old lady with a fractured hip all strung up in traction and with so much equipment that her bed could not even fit through the door; a young woman having her tubes tied—no more babies for her; and in the next little room another young woman coming in for a laporascopic look into her belly (belly button surgery) to see why she couldn't have children, a child having his tonsils out, a junkie having an abscess lanced, an elderly yellow-looking man coming in for exploratory surgery to see what was causing his obstructive jaundice, a fellow who caught his hand in a meat grinder having reconstructive surgery, a lady with a mass on her neck. One by one they were wheeled into the PAR and placed in one of the little rooms. Some were sleeping, some looked around fearfully, some were oblivious because of coma or illness. For a while they lay there waiting. The only sounds were of the two anesthetists counting the drugs, the weeping of a child, the coughing of the old man in the corner, the old lady with the hip banging on the siderails yelling "Help me, help me!"

At 7:00 the student anesthetists came in. Mid City General was a teaching hospital with a school of nurse anesthesia. The students came to work early; they needed to set up for big cases: "meaningful learning experiences," they called them. They had the choice of the interesting cases each day, selected for them by their faculty at first, and later on by the students themselves. Each of them went into one of the little rooms to see his or her patient.

"Do you remember me? I visited you last night."

"Where is my doctor?"

"When was the last time you had anything to eat or to drink?"

"My husband is coming to see me before my surgery. Can he come in here?"

The questions were answered. The anesthesia plan of care was shown to the instructor. The student set up the patient. The instructor read from the plan. Later they would discuss it.

By 7:15 we staff anesthetists had come into the P.A.R.

"My name is Joan Smith. I'll be your anesthetist."

"You're not going to give me another needle, are you?"

"Hi, I'm Benita Torres, from the anesthesia department."

"You're not the one I saw last night. Who are you?"

"Good morning. I'm Barrie Evans. I'm going to put you to sleep for your operation. Have you ever had anesthesia before?"

"Sí."

"Habla inglés, señora?"

161

"*Un poco.*"

"*Bueno. Operacion en su ojo, no?*"

"*Sí.*"

"*El ojo derecho?*"

"*Sí,*" pointing to her right eye.

"Ah, yes, you speaking Spanish good, mees."

"Hello, I'm your anesthetist, Maureen O'Dwyer."

"Anesthetist? I'm having a local."

By 7:20 the anesthesiologists had come in. They had visited each patient the night before. They had ordered the premedication and any last-minute lab work.

"Hi, there. How was your night?"

"Thanks to you I slept well."

"What are you planning on using on her?"

"I thought I'd do nitrous curare with a little morphine."

"What's the potassium?"

"It's up now—three point four."

"Great, we can go ahead."

At 7:25 attending physicians arrived to greet their patients, check last minute X rays, lab findings, medical consultations.

"Good morning, sir. Sorry to keep you waiting. Which knee is it?"

"Don't you know? It's my left knee."

"Good morning, Mrs. Johnson. Hope you had a good night."

"Everything's okay—now that you're here, Doctor."

They came into the PAR in street clothes, in business suits with blue striped ties, in sport coats with bow ties, in warm-up suits with no ties, in saris. But when they came out of the surgeons' lounge, they were all dressed alike in formless green pants, formless green tops, white shoes or clogs, and masks. The only individuality was in their hats. Some wore helmets to cover long hair or beards; some wore little hats like the army caps of World War II, some, shapeless white blobs like shower caps, and some caps sewn lovingly to order with stripes, flowers, or other individual designs.

While the attending surgeons were visiting their patients, the anesthetists were busy too, but not with patients—with narcotics.

"Good morning. Is the store open yet?"

"Yes, what can I do for you?"

"Give me ten morphines and five Valiums. I'm in the heart room."

"Let me have, let's see, let me have three Demerol and two Sublimaze. No, let me have two Demerol and three Sublimaze. Psst—what do you think my instructor will . . ."

"What are you getting there?" the instructor interrupted. "I thought we were going to do morphine Valium today."

"Yes, yes—let me have two Valium and three morphine."

"Is that your final decision?"

"Yes—I'm sorry."

"Bill?"

"A box of Demerol and five Valium. I'm in TOP City."

"Joan?"

"Nothing, thanks."

"Why not?"

"I'm covering OB."

"Benita?"

"A box of Sublimaze. I'm doing Innovar today." (She was going to do a combined technique using a short-acting narcotic and a major tranquilizer.)

"Barrie?"

"Let's see, a cataract, a circ . . . Make it three morphine and two Valium."

While the attendings were getting changed, the house staff, interns, and residents came into the PAR. On private patients they would assist the attendings; on ward cases the attendings would assist them.

It was 7:29. The tension was rising. Everyone was psyching himself up in his own way. The residents were milling around in the hall waiting for anesthesia to complete the last details. Attendings were consulting with one another, with the residents, with the anesthesiologists. Anesthetists were completing last notations on the charts. Students were checking with instructors for last-minute details. Patients were ready: hooked up, psyched up, and doped up.

7:30 A.M.

"Are you ready, Maureen?"

"Let's go."

"Are you ready, Benita?"

"Yes, sir. Where are your residents?"

"Never mind them—you and I can take the patient down."

"Are you ready, miss?"

"No, sir. I'm waiting for my instructor. She said . . ."

"Never mind what she said. Let's get started."

"Are you ready, Bill?"

"As ready as I'll ever be."
"Are you ready, Barrie?"
"Vamanos."

It was a simple cataract extraction. The patient was eighty-five years old and in good health. She'd never been operated on—had never even been in the hospital. She lived in the neighborhood and had come to the eye clinic. She knew she had a cataract and looked forward to its removal.

In MCG cataract surgery is done under local standby—we do not put these elderly patients to sleep. I had started her IV in the PAR and given her some Mannitol to decrease the pressure in the eye and also to make her urinate. I had put on her blood pressure cuff and the leads for her EKG.

The attending eye surgeon was early—early and restless. He prowled up and down outside the PAR like a caged animal.

"I'm ready," I told him.

"Let's go, then," he replied.

And although the room was nowhere near ready, we went in. The scrub technician scowled but said nothing. The attending got the blanket, and together we moved the little old lady to the O.R. table. She looked all around—frightened but ready. *"No sé preocupe.* Don't worry, Mrs. Rivera. I'm going to give you something so you can sleep now." I gave a minute dose of Valium and in a few moments she was snoring. She was so sedated that every few minutes I had to encourage her to take deep breaths.

Everyone was already working when the resident

arrived. He looked nervous. I knew it was the first case he'd be doing himself.

I was giving oxygen through a tube placed in the patient's nostrils, since her face would be covered with sterile towels. The attending was adjusting the teaching microscope so that he, too, could see what the resident was doing. The technician was setting out the delicate instruments and extra-fine sutures needed for eye surgery. The circulating nurse was giving him the last-minute things he needed.

The resident stood in the doorway of the operating room. He looked in and seemed to be psyching himself, as if setting himself for the ordeal that lay ahead. He looked at everyone working and hesitated as though making up his mind whether to join us or not. Then he took a deep breath and came into the room. "Go and scrub," the attending said.

The resident went out to the scrub area and started to wash his hands. Soon the attending joined him. The attending tried to talk to him, to make small talk. The resident did not answer, just continued to scrub his hands. He glanced into the room.

The attending finished scrubbing. "Let's go," he said. "I think that's enough of a scrub."

The resident came into the room, his arms held high, water dripping. He was shaking. He tried to control it but he was shaking so much he couldn't stop. The attending said he'd do the prep. The resident got into his gown and gloves. Usually doctors put on their own gloves. He was shaking too much; the technician did it for him.

Local anesthesia is always given by the surgeons. It

is one of the older forms of anesthesia and had remained the responsibility of the surgeon.

It was time to inject the local anesthetic now. The resident took the first syringe. His eyes were wide; sweat started on his brow. He contaminated the syringe. The attending asked for another.

"I'll start the local," he said. Quickly and deftly the attending put in the initial superficial dose. When he finished, he nodded to the technician to give the second syringe to the resident. He quietly told him what he wanted him to do and showed him how. The resident took the syringe. "Now, Mrs. Rivera," he said in a quavering voice. Mrs. Rivera snored.

Together they injected all the anesthetic where they wanted it. They now wanted to place the microscope in proper position so they could both see and work through it. The resident had the control pedal. He moved the microscope up and down. He tilted the lens from side to side; focused in and focused out. He turned the light on and off. "Okay, son," the attending said. "That's enough of that—let's go! Stitch please." The technician tried to hand the suture to the attending. The attending shook his head and motioned that he should give it to the resident. The case began.

Silence descended on the room. Eye surgery is very delicate. The doors to the operating room—the side ones which lead to the scrub room—were kept closed. The only sound was the beep beep beep of the EKG monitor. This morning the beeping was irregular. Mrs. Rivera had some premature atrial beats—nothing to worry about but enough to add further stress.

"Is she okay?" the surgeon asked me. "She's fine," I replied with confidence.

The resident tried not to shake. He tried to hold his elbows close to his body, but then he couldn't operate. He hugged the patient's head to steady himself. It was no use. His cap was soggy now. The sweatband helped keep perspiration out of his eyes. The circulating nurse came over and gave him a wipe. The attending talked him through every instrument, every maneuver. Time marched on.

At one point I looked up because I heard a noise—a welcome hum. The carbon dioxide tank had been turned on. Now they would take a cryoprobe and extract the cataract.

"Now," the attending said, "pull gently and rock the instrument back and forth from left to right."

The resident pulled, he shook; he rocked, he shook; he shook, he shook, he really shook.

"Gently, gently," the attending said in a sharp voice.

Moments later a yellow, gelatinous disc came out—the cataract. "Eureka," we all shouted. Mrs. Rivera snored.

The resident seemed calmer now—not much but a bit. The case continued. Finally it was over.

"Ointment, please," the attending said.

The resident put the eye patch over Mrs. Rivera's eye. We all lifted her into her bed. She seemed quite alert now.

"Su nombre, Doctor?" she asked the resident. "I forget from before."

He told her his name.

"Doctor, *muchas gracias*. I thank you very much," the elderly lady said.

He looked up at me and winked. "Thank you, everyone," he said—and he meant it.

We left the room.

XI

They had another urology case for me. Urology, I had learned early, is a funny specialty. For some reason urologists are looked at, even down at, with faint amusement. They are frequently called the plumbers, and other vaguely derogatory terms are applied to them, but if you get into a situation where you cannot pass your urine, you'll respect them soon enough.

In office practice, urologists see twice as many women as men—lots of "honeymoon cystitis," I guess—but in the hospital the GU (genitourinary) service is definitely a man's world. Men patients outnumber women patients by well over two to one. Why? Because most urology admissions to the hospital are for phimosis (tight foreskin) and BPH (benign prostatic hypertrophy, nonmalignant enlargement of the prostate)—strictly problems of the male sex.

The urologists operate in two different places in the hospital. Operations other than those through the penis or urethra are done in the regular O.R. Those operations which *are* done through the penis are done in the cystoscopy department: a cystoscopy itself (looking into the bladder with an instrument), a stone basket (trying to catch a stone in a ureter) a TURP (transurethral resection of the prostate to ream out excessive prostatic tissue) or a TURBT (a transurethral resection of a bladder tumor). Women can have cystoscopies, TURBTs, or stone baskets, but the TURP is strictly for men only—usually older men. In *my* experience, the youngest patient to have his prostate resected was forty-four, the oldest ninety-seven.

The two types of anesthesia offered urology patients are regional or general. But for many older patients—particularly smokers and patients with low pain thresholds—regional anesthesia is preferred. Many times we have our hearts in our throats putting the older, sicker patients in this group to sleep. Prostate surgery takes its toll on these older fellows. Recovery is not pleasant: many have spasms of their bladder caused by blood clots. To provide pain relief in the immediate postoperative period, we may use either spinal or epidural to block out sensation below the waist.

General anesthesia is a tricky business with older patients, who may have many other complications. We must intubate because the procedure takes at least an hour in most cases; since many patients in the age group we are dealing with do not have their own teeth, it is difficult to maintain an airway with a mask. Our teeth form a good part of our facial structure. Without them the cheeks become hollow, causing the leaking of gases around the mask. As I have said, our problem is not in putting the tube in as much as in getting it out. We do not want to use a lot of narcotics or tranquilizers: older people are sensitive to them and may not breathe well once the stimulation of surgery is over. We could use an inhalation agent, but if the patient is dehydrated prior to surgery (and many people are from tests performed on them before surgery, improper nutrition in general, stress, or their condition itself), when they receive the inhalation agent the "bottom drops out." The inhalation agent dilates the blood vessels, and if the patient is dehydrated, the blood pressure drops rapidly and we must fill up the patient with fluids. But the heart of an older person cannot always manage a lot of fluids, and heart failure may result. Frequently, to be on the safe side, we leave the tube in at the end of the case unless the patient is alert and breathing well.

One of the things that the urology resident usually includes in the initial work-up on the patient's chart is whether or not the patient is still active sexually. This is important, because some of the operations the urologists perform may cause impotence, and others cause sterility. If the patient is sexually active, he must be told of the possible postop complications prior to surgery.

Some of us anesthetists love the little old men; others try to steer clear of them. I like them, but this time I wasn't expecting one.

I entered the preanesthesia room looking for a young man. I looked all around but the only two patients I saw were a child with her hand in a cast and an old, old man. That can't be my patient, I thought to myself. He's older than God: he can't be having a circumcision. I went into his cubicle, but he was asleep. I took a look at the chart and found that he was eighty-one years old. I looked at his diagnosis and yes, there is was, phimosis—tightened foreskin. Before I woke him up his doctor came in. "Is this a joke?" I asked the doctor. "You're really going to circumcise an eighty-one-year-old man?"

"Yes, I am. He's a healthy man for his age," he explained. "He's been my patient for ten years. He's an active man. Until last year he went to business every day. But over the last six months or so he's been bothered with this problem. He and his wife have discussed it and feel that if an operation can take care of it, and we all know it can, then they want to have it done. He wants to be comfortable. Just because he's old, why should we deny him comfort?"

I went over to speak to the patient. "Dudley," I called.

Snores greeted me. He'd had a light premedication; it was working very well. I shook him gently; he stirred a little and opened his eyes. "Dudley," I repeated, "I'm Barrie, your anesthetist. I'm going to be putting you to sleep for your operation."

"Do you mean to tell me, young woman, that you woke me up to tell me you're going to put me to sleep?"

"I'm sorry, but there are some questions I have to ask you. It's really for your safety."

"Well, miss," he replied, "I'm sure you know best."

I set him up and asked him all the usual questions. He did indeed seem to be in good health and presented no problems. I was standing in a corner writing up his chart when Dudley called out "Miss, miss" in a somewhat hesitant voice. I returned to his bedside. "Uh, miss, uh. I want to ask you a question.

Miss, uh, I am eighty-one years old and uh, I uh, well, uh ... Miss, I am ..."

I could not imagine what the problem was. I waited and smiled encouragingly.

"Miss, I am uh, eighty-one years old, and I can't, uh, I can't, uh, I can't do it any more. Do you know what I mean?"

"Yes, I do," I replied.

"As a matter of fact, I haven't been able to do it for a couple of years. Do you think this operation will help me to do it again? My wife and I, we'd be so happy."

I didn't know what to say, but I tried. "Dudley, the operation you are having today is because you have a tightened foreskin and it hurts you. That really has nothing to do with sex. However, people say that sex is 90 percent above the neck and only 10 percent below. Who knows, Dudley. Miracles do happen." Dudley went to sleep with a smile on his face.

Dudley had no problems with either surgery or anesthesia. The entire procedure took less than an hour.

I went into the lounge for coffee. "How are things in your room?" asked Benita. The anesthesia department was a small but closed shop. Everyone liked to know what was going on everywhere. And I was no different. "We did a circ on an eighty-one-year-old. Can you believe it? Eighty-one years he had the damn thing and now his doctor decides to operate."

Benita was shaking her head. "I could tell you a circumcision story."

I had time to hear it.

She settled down and began her tale. "The guy was

thirty-one years old, gorgeous but a retard—not badly retarded, just sort of simple. We took him into the O.R. and I was putting him to sleep. He was going under without a problem—I was using ethrane, and as you know, it takes a few moments until the fat tissues are all saturated and no more is being absorbed by the body. Have you met Paul, the GU resident?"

"Yeah, he worked with us on the circ."

"Have any problems with him?"

"No, he seemed anxious to get moving, but he didn't do anything till I gave the okay."

"I suspect you have me—me and this case, to thank for that. Anyway, I was just putting the guy to sleep when Paul started to prep the patient. I yelled for him to wait, but it was too late. The minute he touched the patient's penis, bang. There was the largest—and I do mean largest—erection I've ever seen.

" 'Damn you, Paul,' I said, 'I told you to wait. You're always so damn anxious to get started. Now sit on it, why don't you, maybe it'll go down.' "

We always try to avoid erection prior to circumcision, because the penis is a vascular organ. The whole principle of erection is that the penis becomes engorged with venous blood. That's great for sex— bad for surgery. So much blood in the area may cause excessive bleeding. Besides, the most important thing in anesthetizing for circumcision is to have the level of anesthesia deep enough.

"Anyway, the attending came in just as I was asking the nurse to call for the anesthesiologist. We couldn't proceed until the erection went down.

" 'What's happened here?' he asked.

" 'Well, sir,' Paul said, 'I guess it's my fault. I was in a hurry, and of course anesthesia wasn't ready.' He waved his arm in my direction.

" 'You mean I asked you to wait and you didn't listen, don't you?' I said angrily. 'I am trying to deepen his level, sir, but I'm afraid you'll just have to wait now.'

" 'It's all right,' the attending said, 'I just won't scrub yet. Call me. I'll be in the lounge.'

"The anesthesiologist came in. He looked at my end of the table first. I was increasing the concentration of Ethrane and hyperventilating the patient—breathing for him very rapidly. Then the anesthesiologist looked down at the other end.

" 'Oh, no,' he muttered. 'Your fault, Benita? Didn't you have him deep enough when they started?'

" 'No, it's not that—Paul just started to prep before I was ready.'

"The Ethrane was now turned on to as high a concentration as I could safely give. The erection remained. We gave the guy some Ketamine. The erection remained. We gave some morphine. The erection remained. We had done all we could do. His blood pressure started to fall. We increased his fluids to try to raise it. It was no use. He'd had so much anesthesia, sedation, and muscle relaxants that the only way we could get his blood pressure up again was to cut our agents. I looked at the anesthesiologist. 'Well?' I asked. 'Beats me,' he said. That was before we started using a nitroglycerine drip to dilate the veins in the penis to get rid of erections that way. But that wouldn't have worked anyway. By that time the

176

guy's pressure was so low we'd have killed him with a nitro drip.

"The attending came in and Paul tried once again to blame it on us, but the attending knew better. And he was pissed that the case was canceled. We had to keep the patient on the table for almost twenty minutes before we could take him to recovery. I'm glad to hear Paul didn't rush you today. Maybe he learned something after all."

"Don't remind me of circumcision," one of the nurses said. "My husband had one two years ago. He hurt so bad, he came in and had it done. When he went home, the doctor told him no sex until he checked him again in his office. But my husband was not about to wait for that. He waited three days, but on the fourth he couldn't wait no more. We were going at it when all of a sudden he gave this cry. I thought he was coming and everything did feel wet. It wasn't that though: it was blood. His damn stitches had broken and he was bleeding like a pig. He had to come back to the hospital. The doctor fixed him up. I'm not quite sure what he did. All I know is that this time he didn't do a thing until the doctor gave his okay."

Vi came into the lounge. "Are your rooms finished, you two?" Benita and I nodded. "Okay, you can go home."

We jumped up and started changing our clothes.

XII

On Wednesdays we have our weekly conference. We file in, in a predictable fashion. The seating arrangement is preset. The faculty and students sit on one side of the room, the staff anesthetists and anesthesiologists on the other. It's one of those unwritten rules. Sometimes I go over to the other side just to be devilish. Sometimes we have a guest speaker, sometimes it's a case presentation. We can learn a great deal from the experiences of others—both good and bad. In a case presentation, the anesthetist and anesthesiologist involved talk to the rest of the group. Today one of the anesthesiologists is telling us about a conference he attended in Montreal. He gives us an overview and lets us know of new developments in our field. It is one way for us to keep abreast of the explosion of knowledge. There are new drugs, new techniques, and new theories. In anesthesia we have mandatory continuing education. Each of us must attend a certain number of conferences a year. In this way we not only acquire new knowledge but share that knowledge with the rest of the group.

It is good to start the day with a little intellectual stimulation. We also enjoy the coffee and doughnuts at these meetings. When the meeting is over we all go to the preanesthesia room together. We never know who or what will greet us. Think positively, I tell myself. I'm going to have a good day.

On my way back to the O.R. one Wednesday I decided to take a detour by way of the I.C.U. I wanted to see what had been happening with Tammy—the girl from the bike accident. I went in and bed three was empty. Oh, no, don't tell me she died, I said to myself. I was just about to ask the clerk when I saw Tammy lying in the corner. Her bed had been changed to move her away from the nurses' station. The most acute cases must be placed next to it.

She looked as though she were simply sleeping. She had not come out of her coma. The family and boyfriend were still in constant attendance every day. She was breathing on her own—they had performed a tracheostomy on her. They had also done a feeding gastrostomy: put a tube into her stomach. This enabled them to give her pureed foods.

I asked the head nurse for news. No news. Yes, there was still a chance she might wake up. How much chance? Very little. How long? Who knew?

I went to the bedside. "Tammy," I called in a loud voice. Her eyes started to open. They were unfocused and quickly shut again. Was it a sign? Of course not.

I sighed and left.

I was assigned to the plastics room. I couldn't tell from the way the procedure was booked what the surgeon planned to do. I could wait and ask him, but since it was early and he had not arrived yet, I decided to approach the patient first.

I checked the name tag attached to the foot of the bed and said, "Cindy, that's you?"

She nodded and we were off. I started with some general conversation. We had a good rapport immediately, so by the time I asked "What are we going to do for you this morning, Cindy?" I got a torrent of words in reply.

"I've always been fixated on my bust," she admitted. "Other people look in store windows at dresses, boots, or sweaters. Not me. I look at bras. It's always been my ambition to wear pretty bras, but in my size, 40E, there's not much choice. You get a bra that holds you up and that's about it. I hate being like this. When I walk in the street the construction guys all whistle and make remarks. Who needs it? I've dreamed for years of having my breasts fixed, of getting one of those reduction jobs, but first of all I never had the money. Secondly my husband wouldn't let me. He loves them the way they are, he keeps telling me. It's his playground.

"Then about a month ago we were making love and my husband noticed that I had a lump in my breast. I couldn't deal with it at all at first, but finally, last week, I went to the doctor. He booked me for immediate surgery. If it is cancer I will have the breast removed. The ironic thing is that even if it is benign the lump is so big that after they remove it I'll have to have the other side reduced to match—just what I've always wanted. I'm going crazy trying to imagine how I'll look—either with one large breast or two small ones.

"Anyway, that's why I have two doctors: the plastic

surgeon and my regular surgeon—just in case it's not cancer. If it is cancer, I'll only need one surgeon.

"My husband has been great about it. I hear some guys leave their wives over stuff like this. But I still can't face it. Could you knock me out now, do you suppose?"

"Just let me get the IV in." I put in a large line. This could be a bloody procedure, and I might have to transfuse Cindy. As soon as the line was in, I started giving her tranquilizers. She drifted off to sleep quickly. I completed my preparations as gently as I could. I wanted her to have as little trauma as possible. When I was finished I pulled the curtain shut so no one would disturb her and went out to read her chart. The anesthesiologist had written a note indicating she was in perfect health except for the lump. When he came to see me I told him she was napping. The premedication he'd ordered, plus the tranquilizers I'd given, were working well.

We took her into the O.R. as soon as her surgeon arrived and I put her to sleep. She would have to be intubated since this was going to be a long procedure. They washed all over Cindy's chest, both sides, with the iodine solution. They covered the left side with sterile drapes, leaving the right side, the side with the lump, exposed. The general surgeon would work first; the plastic surgeon had gone upstairs to make rounds. At this point we didn't know if we'd need him.

The surgery took quite a while. The lump was large, and breast tissue usually bleeds a lot. As the specimen was almost ready to come off, the circulating nurse pushed the button. "Pathologist, please," she said, as the call bell was answered. When the specimen came off and was placed in a towel, the pathologist was waiting. The surgeon thought it was benign; he was seldom wrong. I hoped that this would not be one of the times.

The pathologist returned. "It's a fibroadenoma, Ray," he told the surgeon. A benign tumor. "It's a big one. I've made several cuts but it's benign throughout."

We called for the plastic surgeon over the intercom. He came and did a reduction on the other side. Bleeding was well controlled and Cindy did not need to be transfused. I lightened up the anesthesia. I wanted to see her awake at the end. They put on the dressings, and we took her to the recovery room. On the way she opened her eyes. "One or two?" she mumbled sleepily.

"Two, Cindy, and they look great."

She smiled and went back to sleep.

It had been a good morning's work.

I returned to the desk with my papers, half of the anesthesia record; the other half accompanied Cindy's chart. "Go eat," said my boss. "Your second case has been delayed."

I was happy as I went to lunch. And happier yet when I stopped off in the recovery room on my way back to the O.R. Cindy was sleeping peacefully—a smile on her face.

But I couldn't smile over what was waiting for me that afternoon in the PAR. A mountainous woman was lying in a bed. It had to be Dora back again. I'd heard all about her.

Dora, once called Big Mama (to me she still looked huge), had been to our O.R. many times. She had had all the "routine" plastic work done: her eyelids fixed, her nose straightened, and her face lifted. She'd had some exotic stuff done too: her belly tightened, her breasts and thighs reduced. Today she was here for a reduction of her upper arms. She was turning into a bionic woman—nothing seemed to be the way it was ten years before. She was a whole new person. Since I didn't know her, I couldn't really tell how much improvement there had been.

I'd heard Dora's history from the other anesthetists. Dora had a short, fat neck; she was a three-pack-a-day smoker and also had chronic bronchitis. She'd been a very difficult patient to intubate and had, in the past, posed many an anesthetic challenge. I hoped today would be an exception. I walked over to her.

She grinned. "You've heard about me, haven't you, honey? Well, I've survived eight other times. I'll get by. Don't worry now."

I certainly hope so, I told myself.

Everyone knew Dora's story. She was a landlady from Brooklyn, a widow. She had started buying up old houses from the city with her small savings. She began with one house and rented it out. It proved to be very lucrative, and soon she was able to buy another and another until today she was a wealthy woman. A year and a half before, she had gone to her surgeon and told him she wanted to be beautiful. She had a young lover and wanted to keep up with him, so she'd planned this complete overhaul. He really liked her the way she was, but Dora was not to be deterred. It was the dream of a lifetime coming true for her.

I was in luck today. My anesthesiologist for this afternoon was Raj. I had a feeling I was going to need him. He was known as a skilled technician as well as an academician. It was said about Raj that he could intubate a snake and, what's more, make the snake love it.

When he came in—his turban hidden under the extra large scrub cap one of the nurses had made for him—I asked him why Dora's surgery had been delayed. He told me that she had not received medical clearance earlier, but she had it now.

"I'm almost sorry," I said. I wasn't anxious to do her anesthesia.

"I know what you mean, but hopefully we can avoid the lung problems from her smoking and her bronchitis."

We were waiting for Dora's attending now. I was getting more and more nervous. I needed some distraction. The tension building in me was nonproductive. Raj and I had seldom talked seriously. Why not now?

"What brings a guy like you into anesthesia, Raj?"

"Barrie, anesthesiology attracts many doctors from other countries. It is hard for us as foreign-educated physicians to break into the system. Many hospitals just use us for service. They hire us as residents to fill the gaps but care little about us when our training is complete. In the metropolitan area it's hard to establish yourself; the competition is too great in areas like general surgery or internal medicine. We'd have to go out to rural areas to set up a practice. Anesthesia, since it is unpopular with American graduates, provides a specialty for us. My first love is ophthalmology, but that's a tough residency even for an American. I don't want to live in the sticks, Barrie—I want to be where the action is. So it's anesthesia for me. I had lots of choices as to where to go. I like MCG—I like the people, I like the way that we do anesthesia here, I like the hours, and I like the money. They'd have to come up with a pretty good offer to tempt me to leave. Barrie," he interrupted himself. "I just saw the plastic boys go by—let's take her in."

We went into the room with Dora. It was not Dr. Palmer on this case but another plastic surgeon, one we called Buzz. Buzz had a last name but no one ever used it. He was either Buzz or Dr. Buzz to everyone from the porter to the chief of surgery.

Buzz was a young fellow from the Midwest only about five years out of his residency. He did his residency in Seattle. He was a great big athletic fellow; he looked like a lumberjack, but he was as sweet as he could be—until he was crossed. He believed that his word was the last word on everything. We tried not to cross him—he liked nurse anesthetists as long as we did what he wanted.

Dora had had a lot of experience with the routine—she was ready and waiting for the oxygen mask. Raj and I decided to cut in a little Halothane with the oxygen after the Pentothal to help keep Dora's airway as clear as possible. We had in readiness a few different laryngoscope blades—some straight and some curved—and endotracheal tubes in

185

smaller sizes. We wanted the full assortment lined up on the anesthesia machine.

We were ready to go. I had pretreated Dora, given her a small dose of a muscle relaxant so that she would not have muscle spasms when the short-acting one was given right after the Pentothal. I gave her an entire syringe full of Pentothal, because Dora was still pretty big and we wanted to make sure she was deep. Light anesthesia in a patient with respiratory problems can be very dangerous: it may cause laryngospasm.

I ventilated her and then gave the muscle relaxant. I continued to ventilate her until her jaw was relaxed. I took my laryngoscope and placed it in her mouth and looked in. Her larynx was very anterior; I couldn't see the vocal cords at all. I pulled up on my laryngoscope with all my might but to no avail; there were no cords to be seen.

I came out and put a larger blade on my laryngoscope handle and looked in once again. Nothing. I had to ventilate her. She couldn't be too long without oxygen. I slipped a plastic airway into her mouth, pulling up on her lower jaw, and started to ventilate her. Nothing. I couldn't get through. I was not able to expand her chest.

Raj and I tried it together. I held the chin up and pressed the mask in place while he squeezed the bag. Nothing. Dora was in spasm from the stimulation of the laryngoscope and her bronchitis. Raj nodded as I picked up the syringe and gave some more muscle relaxant.

The airway was okay now. I was able to ventilate

her. But I had looked twice and seen nothing. I was not about to put Dora at risk by continuing to try.

"Switch with me, Raj," I asked. "You give it a try."

I changed places with him, and once again we tried to ventilate her. No dice. Raj gave still more muscle relaxant. The airway opened up. He used a curved blade—I used the straight one. It's all a matter of training which blade you use. I had already put on the blade he liked.

We had to suction out Dora's mouth. With stimulation secretions form, and we did not want anything to go into Dora's lungs. Raj sucked her out and slipped in his blade. He couldn't see anything either. "I'll try it blind," he said. He slipped in the tube and tried to ventilate Dora. The tube was not in the trachea. He removed it and we started over again. It was a nightmare. He tried every blade, then a smaller-sized tube—Dora spasmed several times, her pulse slowed, and there were occasional irregular beats on the EKG screen: Dora was not getting enough oxygen. We were ventilating her only intermittently.

The room was quiet. Buzz and his assistants were sitting on stools—their hands folded into sterile towels. Luckily, they were not bothering us. Sometimes the surgeons get nervous when there is difficulty with anesthesia and try to get into the act. That doesn't help. I glanced up at the clock. We had been at this for twenty minutes; it seemed like forever. We still could not intubate Dora. We had deepened the Halothane now and gotten Dora to start breathing on her own once again. "Take over," Raj said to me and went to the corner where Buzz was sitting.

He told Buzz what he already knew—that Dora was

a bad risk right from the start, and that we'd not been able to intubate her. It was elective surgery. Raj was canceling the case. I waited for the screaming and yelling from Buzz: none came. He knew we were doing the only safe thing.

Raj told him that when he rescheduled Dora we would do an awake intubation. I turned off the Halothane and started waking Dora up. We'd called ahead to the recovery room for an EKG monitor and heated humidified oxygen. Dora was going to have a gigantic sore throat. Many people who are intubated without trauma have sore throats, but in Dora's case there'd been a lot of manipulation. Swelling might take place; the heated humidity would help it. I felt bad as I brought her in to the recovery room. We had worked for an hour and accomplished nothing. I tried to look on the bright side: she was alive and seemed okay. I was worried about her brain: did we leave her without oxygen too long?

Dora opened her eyes. "Hi, honey—I made it."

Yes, I guess she did.

I came back from the recovery room and tossed my papers on the shelf in the office. Everyone had heard about our trouble. They were asking Raj and me for details. We hashed it all out. Vi came by. "Go home," she said to me. She knew how much a tough case can take out of you.

The next morning I was in early. Again for some reason I just couldn't sleep. I kept thinking about Dora and the trouble we had had with her.

I was in plastics again. The first case was booked as

a laparoscopic tubal ligation—tying the tubes. The room had been booked by GYN for the first case. Plastics would take over later. I set up my room and came out to see my patient. Let it be anyone but a fat patient, I said to myself.

My patient was lying in her cubicle staring into space. "Good morning," I announced cheerfully and told her who I was. She didn't seem the least bit interested. Oh, no, I thought, not one of those hostile ones. I'm not up to it.

Linda was a woman whose age was difficult to determine. She looked thirty-five going on ninety. She immediately wanted to know about the IV—was I going to start one? "Of course," I answered. "We can't put you to sleep unless we have a good line in. It is your lifeline—the only way we can give medication, if we need to." She seemed totally unimpressed by this. I put the tourniquet on her arm and started looking for a vein. All I saw were scarred tracks up and down her arm. I tried the other side and got the same picture. Linda was watching me now for my reaction.

"How long have you been doing drugs?" I asked.

"About six years."

"And are you clean now?"

"Yup."

"For how long?"

"About a year now."

"And are you in a methadone program?"

"Yup."

"Our program here at the hospital?"

"Nope."

"What program?"

"Oh, I go to a private one."

189

"How much do you take?"

"Eighty." Eighty milligrams a day of methadone.

"Okay, hope you don't mind all the questions," I told her, "but I'm trying to find out about you so I can take the best care of you. You understand?"

"And it doesn't bother you that I'm a junkie?"

"Why should it bother me? I'm here to care for you and I mean to do it the best way I know how."

This seemed to clear the air.

"Listen, Linda, do you have any veins left?" I asked. Junkies usually know this very well.

"Don't know. I haven't had a reason to look for a while now. When I quit I didn't have any. I was doing between my fingers and toes and behind my knees. I used them all. I guess that's why I really quit. I knew I couldn't go on."

"Well, I don't see a thing. I'm going to have to go to your neck."

"If there's no other place okay, but why don't you look some more first?"

I put tourniquets on her legs to see if there was anything there.

I saw nothing. I put the head of the bed down and the feet up so that the blood vessels in her neck would fill. The neck veins looked great and in no time at all I had a line in.

"You really *don't* care that I'm a junkie, do you?" she asked. "Some of the others give me a hot time. They treat me like shit. It makes me so mad. I'm trying to clean up my act. Some people don't even give you a chance. I had my breast removed last year. It was cancer, and believe me I thought it was the end. I was tempted to start doing drugs again. I figured I

O.R.

had nothing to live for. Then I met Willie. He's black, and my family sure didn't like that, but then, they don't like anything I do. I gave them enough trouble, so maybe they're right. Who knows? Well, anyhow, Willie and I are together now. He's the only one who cares. My family kicked me out years ago. I was definitely not a Jewish princess. We're not planning a family of our own. That's why I'm having my tubes tied. If you come to see me after this is over, you'll meet Willie. You'll like him.

"Listen, about my anesthesia, don't give me any dope, hear? I'm trying to stay straight, so give me just the methadone and nothing else. I'm afraid of anything else. I don't want any tranquilizers either. Can you do that?"

"Certainly. I'll just divide up the methadone dose you usually take. We give two-thirds the dose you take by mouth when we give it to you by needle. You'll get half of that now before we go into the operating room and the other half when you're in the recovery room. When you wake up you may have pain. Methadone's not much help."

"That's okay. I can take pain. God knows I've had enough in my day. It's more important to me not to mess up—you dig?"

I dug.

As soon as we got Linda to the O.R. I put her to sleep. She'd had no premedication except the methadone and a drying agent. Once she was well relaxed and anesthetized I nodded to the resident to go ahead. He made a small elliptical incision under her navel and inserted an instrument by slowly and carefully screwing it in. He did not want to jam it

191

in—he might hit bowel. Once it was in place he connected a small hose and an electrical connector to it. I tilted the table so Linda's head was down and feet up. I did not have it tilted enough.

"More Trendelenberg, please," said the resident.

"Okay, Jack." I leaned under the table and touched one control with my right foot, the other with my left hand.

"Good, good—that's enough, Barrie," Jack said. He wanted her in this position so her bowel and abdominal organs would be out of his way. The circulating nurse flipped two switches on a machine at the resident's side, and CO_2 started to flow into Linda's belly. When the abdomen was well distended he nodded and the nurse flipped a switch. Now the scrub technician handed him a long thin instrument with a periscope on the end. He inserted it through the instrument in Linda's belly. He could now see inside. He and the attending looked all around, examining Linda's uterus, fallopian tubes, and ovaries. Everything looked normal.

Jack made a second small incision, a nick really, in Linda's abdomen through which he inserted an instrument with a cautery tip. He looked in again and picked up Linda's right tube—he was now ready to coagulate. He wanted the attending to check to make sure he was coagulating the right thing—her tubes, not the round ligament. The attending looked in. "Go ahead, Jack," he advised. The resident stepped on a pedal next to his foot and current came through the instrument. Linda's right tube was coagulated. He looked again to make certain there was no bleeding and then repeated the procedure for the left tube.

The periscope part of the laparoscope was removed and the CO_2 released from Linda's abdomen.

"Straighten her out now, Barrie," Jack requested. A few skin sutures were all that remained. I lightened her so that by the end of the case she was breathing spontaneously. I took out her tube, and Linda woke up promptly. She was feeling well and left the recovery room within the hour.

It was 11:30. The next patient was waiting. Another anesthetist had set her up, so all was ready for me. But I had to review her chart and make certain that all was ready in the room. Her name was Anne, and she had come from the west coast to see Dr. Palmer. People come to Dr. Palmer (and to most plastic surgeons) from all over the world.

Anne was a nutritionist at a family health spa in California. She had been referred by her sister in New York, who had had her nose fixed by Dr. Palmer. She was very apprehensive and had a very hostile attitude. It was hard to get close to her; she tried to put me off. "I'm in the field," she said whenever I showed her anything. "I know all that."

I was confused, because according to her chart she hadn't had surgery before—she just seemed to have a very active denial system.

I was not able to relate to her at all. After she told me that she was in perfect health—had never been sick, took no medications, had no allergies—she asked, "Can't you just leave me alone?"

The anesthesiologist told me he'd gotten the same routine.

We got Anne into the room as soon as we could: Dr. Palmer does not like to be kept waiting. She lay on the table quietly with her eyes closed; she obviously did not want to see anything or anyone.

The ritual began and all was as usual. She was having a facelift with Brevital anesthesia. I gave the first dose. Dr. Palmer injected the local anesthetic and surgery began.

I watched Anne carefully. Patients who deny as a defense mechanism are, for me, the most difficult ones to deal with. They don't seem to do as well as "normal" patients, those who admit and deal with their fears. For this reason and for some unexplained sixth sense (to make up for the missing other five) I usually watch these patients a bit more closely.

The first side was almost finished now. I had still not established good rapport with Anne, but she was tolerating me. Suddenly I saw her becoming restless; her blood pressure and pulse were dropping without apparent reason. I took her wrist to feel the quality of her pulse. Her hand felt cool and sweaty. I looked up to see what Dr. Palmer was doing. He was just putting the last stitch in.

I asked her how she felt; she seemed hesitant to reply. A moment later I heard her give a grunt. I looked up at the EKG monitor and grabbed for her wrist again. The wave on the screen did not look good: it had changed from what I had been watching for one and a half hours. I asked Dr. Palmer to give me access to the head so I could give oxygen. I put the mask gently on Anne's face. Dr. Palmer looked at me but said nothing. I asked the circulating nurse to call for the anesthesiologist—stat.

He came immediately. It was a good thing. Anne

was now finally admitting the fact that she was having crushing left-sided chest pain.

I called out once again, this time asking for an EKG machine. Our monitor was not as comprehensive as the EKG machine with its many different parameters. As luck would have it, an EKG technician with her machine was waiting for the elevator just outside the O.R. suite. Quickly she threw on a yellow gown over her uniform, and the O.R. nurse handed her a cap and mask.

The anesthesiologist was speaking to Anne now and doing a thorough exam. Dr. Palmer, quietly pacing up and down, was forgotten. No one went near him; we were all busy with Anne. We gave some medication to ease the pain a bit, but her symptoms persisted.

The anesthesiologist called Dr. Palmer into a corner for a consultation. "You can't go on, Bob," I heard him say. "We're not sure, but we think she might have had an MI"—a myocardial infarction—in plain English, heart attack. "We've got to get her worked up," he continued. "If she gets cleared, it's one thing, but I think at this point you've got to quit."

"Boy, Doug, of all people to have this happen to— she came all the way from the Coast. And she's not easy to deal with, in fact she's a swift pain . . . Christ, how am I ever going to tell her?"

"I'll tell her myself," said the anesthesiologist.

I whispered to the O.R. nurse to tell the recovery room to have oxygen and an EKG monitor ready for our patient. I watched Doug approach Anne. I did not envy him his job. This lady was one tough cookie.

He went through the whole situation with her, explaining that she had had changes in her cardiogram as well as pulse and blood pressure. He told her that it would be extremely dangerous to proceed with surgery now.

Anne became hysterical. "God damn it, I came all the way across the country to have this done and I'm having it. How do you know my life is in danger? You're not even sure I *had* a heart attack. It's *my* life—I'll decide what to do with it. How can I go back with half my face lifted? They'll all laugh at me. You must go on!"

By now we had taken off all the drapes and put away everything except the oxygen, the IV, and the EKG monitor. We were ready to transfer her.

"Dr. Palmer, please," she shouted.

He was shaking now. "It's all in his hands," he said, pointing to the anesthesiologist. "If he says no, it's definitely no."

"Then what happens to my bill? If you do it later on, will you bill me twice? How much additional will I have to pay? And when is the earliest it can be done?"

The questions came faster than he could answer them.

Finally, Dr. Palmer said, "The main thing now is to assess what is happening. All else will have to wait."

We took the weeping, frightened woman to the recovery room. The head nurse had everything ready for us. I informed her of Anne's attitude. It was not going to be easy to care for her.

The cardiologist called in to see her was not sure whether she had had an MI. He recommended transfer to the coronary care unit for at least twenty-four hours so they could run some tests.

Anne was transported by stretcher to the C.C.U.: the resident, transport oxygen, and the EKG monitor went along with her—just in case.

Three days later Anne's name was on the schedule once again. All tests were negative; she had been cleared.

When Anne came back to the O.R., she seemed a lot more reasonable. She'd had a bad scare (as had we all), and she must have reevaluated her priorities.

All went without incident during her second procedure, though I couldn't relax until it was over. She was a patient at risk now. Before she left the O.R. she admitted that we had done the right thing. Somehow the whole ordeal seemed to have made a more mature, likable person out of her—as though she'd gotten more than a facelift out of it.

XIII

I had not been in touch with my friends from my former hospital in some time. Except for Marty Stevenson and a couple of nurses who lived in my neighborhood, my contacts with my old hospital were nil.

It was therefore with surprise and pleasure one evening that I heard the voice of one of my old friends, a former employer (I had worked briefly in his office) and fellow exercise fiend, Ricky Lawrence, M.D. Actually, Ricky was a fitness bug primarily because of *my* influence. We both loved to eat and drink. In the old days when I worked for him and he had a patient in labor, we would finish up office hours and go out for a great dinner. It was with Ricky that I visited many elegant, understated, wonderful restaurants. Ricky hated to eat alone. Through the years when he had a patient in labor, time on his hands, and hunger in his belly he would call me. He knew I loved to eat, lived in town—he lived in Connecticut—and could be counted upon to make plans on the spur of the moment.

When the current craze for physical fitness reached its zenith, Ricky Lawrence decided his time had come. No longer could he dip into the Salzburger Nockerl, the zuppa inglese, the baklava, or the hot fudge sundaes with abandon. If he was to cater to his sweet tooth, and that he certainly was to do, he would have to do something physical. I had been a health club nut for some three years, so when he asked me I was able to give him the name of a good health spa around the corner from his office. He invited me to his club and I reciprocated. These visits were always followed by a luscious meal, but then, who's perfect?

Since the children were now in college, Bev and Ricky had sold the mansion in Connecticut and moved back to the city. One of my fellow anesthetists, Bill, was friendly with Ricky's brother, and he sort of kept me informed.

It was 11:09 P.M. when the phone rang and the familiar voice of Ricky Lawrence sounded in my ear. "Barrie, we're having an open house on Saturday and you're definitely on our list. Can you make it? It will be between five and eight, and Bev and I would love to see you."

"Damn, Ricky, I'm on call Saturday. But maybe I can get someone to cover for me for an hour."

"Try, Barrie. A lot of the old crowd from uptown will be there, and we'd love to see you. Do try to make it."

"I surely will, and thanks for thinking of me."

I'd try to make it, but how? Call at MCG was always busy, what with auto accidents, fights, drunks who fell down and hurt themselves, and the usual contingent of miscarriages, fractured hips, and what have you. Still, I wanted to go to that open house. It would be great to see Bev and Ricky and the old crowd. I drifted off to sleep thinking about the old

Barrie Evans

gang. I knew everyone, and everyone would try to be there. Ricky was a genial host.

What to wear—just in case I could get away. I decided on a simple gray wool pantsuit (it would show how much weight I had lost) and my suede coat.

When I left the house at 6:30 A.M., the streets were deserted. Those people who remained in Fun City for the weekend remained in their beds. There was not one car, not one bus, not even a taxi on the street. Finally a cab came by and I was off to work.

The corridors of MCG were empty too. No one passed me on my way to the lounge. The cafeteria was deserted. The normally bustling place had only one old man sitting in a corner, two cops, two nurses, and me. I grabbed my coffee and went upstairs. I changed my clothes and reported in with the operator. I wished Maureen, who was going off, a nice weekend. I took out the breakfast I had brought from home and started to eat. How would these interminable twenty-four hours pass? I looked at the clock. Only twenty-three hours and forty minutes to go. What a drag.

After breakfast I set up and checked my rooms. As I did so I thought of the many dramas which had been played out in these rooms. Some had happy endings; some were sad. Who would come in here today and lie on these O.R. tables? I certainly hoped no one would. Ah, well, time would tell. I turned up the thermostats in the rooms. At least let them be warm. The thermometer read 55°. I started to leave and glanced up at the big clock. Only twenty-two hours and fifteen minutes to go.

When I returned to the lounge, a few people were

200

gathered. We sat and talked, drank coffee, read the paper, knitted, and smoked cigarettes. I really should go over to my call room and catch some sleep, I thought to myself. I may be up all night. Negative thinking, I said to myself; I will go to Ricky's party and sleep all night.

I had asked the other anesthetist to cover for an hour and he agreed. "No problem," he had said. "Sign out with the operator and call me when you go. Have a good time, and call me when you get back."

I was happy. Now if this damn day would just pass.

Time dragged. I looked over at the digital clock. Nineteen hours and thirty-five minutes to go. I walked to the recovery room and chatted with the nurses. They were glad I only came over to talk. Usually when they saw anesthesia on weekends or holidays it meant a case. I left recovery and walked slowly to the cafeteria.

I waited on line in the crowded cafeteria. All the employees who had to work today seemed to be at lunch now. I sat down with my tray and started to eat. I hoped it would be an uninterrupted meal. It was not.

Just as I got ready to eat my turkey wing, a shadow loomed over me. "Mind if I join you, Barrie?" a familiar voice said in my ear.

"Marty, what are you doing here on a Saturday?"

"What do you think? A patient in labor."

"Sit down, Marty."

"Barrie, I just came over to ask whether you're going to Ricky Lawrence's party."

"I'm hoping to, but I'm on call. Anything can happen, even though I have someone to cover for me."

201

"Well, I'm going. Why don't we go together? I could pick you up and bring you back provided all the patients—yours and mine—cooperate. What do you say? I've been wanting to get together with you for some time. As a matter of fact, I called you at home a couple of times but all I got was some damn machine singing 'Leave a message for me.' What in hell makes you think you can sing, Barrie? Each time I heard the damn thing I started to laugh and hung up."

"So they were you, the hang-ups? Most people are provoked into leaving some messages."

"Okay, Barrie, the next time I will. Listen," he said, taking a last bite of his sandwich, "I've got to get upstairs. Let's say I'll pick you up here at 6:30 and we'll go over to Ricky's for an hour or so. It'll be great seeing all the guys again. I think Stan Franklin will be there. Do you remember him?"

"I sure do. Remember that night he and I raced the chairs backwards down the hall?"

"Yes, and he fell over and almost broke his skull."

"That was us. Marty, let's leave it like that for now. Page me at 6:30 if I'm not here in the cafeteria. We'll go to Ricky's and have a ball. I'm really looking forward to it. Hope that lady delivers by then."

"Don't worry about her. She's five CM now and a multip. She should go within the hour. À bientôt."

"Mmm—see you soon, Marty." I tried not to get too excited. This was going to be a great day—if I could ever make the afternoon pass. Marty Stevenson. I'd had my eye on him for some time—hell, who hadn't? He was so attractive and so nice. When he walked into Ricky's this evening . . . Calm down, calm down, I tried to tell myself, but it was no use.

I went upstairs so I could gather my things together. As I passed the O.R. office one of the nurses on duty stopped me. "Barrie, did you hear anything from Pete about a case?"

"Pete? No, what kind of a case?"

"Some kind of vascular one. He just ran by and told me he's working up a lady in the E.R."

"Well, I'll be in the call room. Give me a buzz if you hear anything."

"Will do. I hope they do it now, not in the middle of the night."

"Yeah, me too. I hope they do it now and not this evening. I want to get out for an hour later on." I hoped—I fervently hoped!

I walked through the empty corridors to the call room. Once there I tried to relax. I tried to read the paper. I tried to knit. I tried to watch TV. I tried to take a nap. Somehow the time passed. I opened one eye and looked at the tiny travel clock which sat on the night table. Pleasant surprise, it was almost six o'clock.

I jumped up. A little over half an hour until Marty was coming.

When I returned to the O.R., I was all dressed for the festivities at Ricky's. I called the other anesthetist to let him know I was leaving. I called the operator to sign out for an hour. I threw my coat over my shoulder. I was ready to go to the cafeteria to wait for Marty.

I stopped at the O.R. office for one last check. I

said to the O.R. nurse, "I'm going to leave now, and . . ."

"Oh, no, you're not," she replied. "Pete's on the phone, booking that vascular case. The lady's over in X ray now having an arteriogram. They'll be bringing her over soon, he says."

"Let me speak to him." Anxiously, I picked up the phone. "What's up, Pete?"

"Well, we're going to do this lady as soon as they're through over here."

"What time will that be?"

"Well let's see—it's 6:15 now. Probably about 7:30."

"Couldn't make it 8:30, huh?"

"Barrie, the lady has an embolism. She could lose her leg. For Christ's sake, we've been sitting on her all afternoon. We can't wait any longer."

"Why in hell didn't you do her earlier? I heard about this case hours ago."

"They couldn't locate the X-ray technician."

"Hell, we could have been done by now. And where's your attending?"

"Don't worry about him. He's sitting at home, just waiting for my call. I'm booking the case for 7:30. It will be local standby. See you later."

What to do now? It was 6:20 P.M. Seven thirty did not mean anything. They had to send for the patient from her floor, which usually took fifteen or twenty minutes on a normal day; on a Saturday, it could take thirty minutes. The floors were short-staffed because of the weekend. Half of the elevators were shut down to conserve electricity. Hell, if the knife fell, if the incision was made by nine o'clock, we'd be going some. I could probably go to Ricky's and be back in plenty of time. And, if worse came to worse, the other anesthetist could start for me. It was only a standby, I wasn't putting the patient to sleep.

But then I thought, what if they do get her down here on time? What if the attending gets in early? What if the other anesthetist gets tied up with something else? What if I can't get back right away? What if—

Ah, shit, I said to myself, I just can't do it. I won't have a peaceful moment at Ricky's party. I'll just worry myself sick; it doesn't pay. I can't go. But Marty—my big chance. What to do? I opened the cafeteria door. Marty was sitting at a table for two. He stood and came toward me. He took one look at my face.

"What is it, Barrie, a case?"

"Yes, it's a case—a local standby embolectomy, of all things. Pete just booked it for 7:30—it could go on all night."

"Ah, that's a real bummer. Listen, Barrie, why don't we grab a bite here in the neighborhood and then you can do your case."

"I'm disappointed, Marty. I've really been looking forward to Ricky's party." And to you, I thought to myself. "Ah, well, let's make the best of a bad situation, Marty, and thanks."

"Let's go. We can eat now and you'll be back in plenty of time."

We went out. It was raining. We were in a hurry now. The only place we could get a fast meal was the Cuban-Chinese place on the corner. We were the only customers. The chefs and waiters were playing a game of cards when we came in. It was too early for their customers.

Might as well make the best of it, I thought to myself. Enjoy what little time we have together. We ordered our food and waited. The conversation was light and friendly. Marty was so easy to be with. We finished a spicy meal with steaming cups of espresso.

Why did this damned case have to come up and spoil our evening? Why did it have to be now? All day I'd sat around, hung around waiting. The only time I wanted to be free they had to book this case.

Marty walked me back to the front door.

"Okay, Barrie, I guess I'll leave you here. How about a rain check on this evening, what do you say?"

"I say yes indeed, Marty. Listen, give Ricky my best and make my excuses. And Marty, when I go home, I'll try to change the message on my machine."

"Try to make it more sexy, Barrie, and don't sing."

"You can bet on it, Marty. Have fun."

I ran to the O.R. and found the patient already waiting in the hall. The radiologist was with her. She had had the arteriogram and he was pressing her groin with all his might.

The femoral artery is a very large vessel, and by doing the arteriogram—injecting dye to outline the arterial circulation for the involved area—the radiologist had made a large puncture site. He did not want this to continue to bleed and form a hematoma; a collection of blood. So he maintained pressure and compression to make sure the bleeding had stopped. This hurt quite a bit. The scene that greeted me was of a little bundle of misery moaning constantly, while the radiologist towered over her. It did not look encouraging.

This case would be done under local standby. The cooperation of the patient would be necessary.

I verified her name with her patient tag. "Martha Silver, is that you?"

"Yes, I am Martha Silver."

And so we began. I didn't expect much from this history. She was ninety-seven, in acute distress, and in strange surroundings. Any information I could get would be a plus.

"When did you eat last?"

"At 6:45 A.M."

"And what did you eat?"

"Well, let me see—I had an orange, two slices of toast, and yes, and a cup of coffee."

She was as clear as a bell, Martha Silver. She answered all my questions promptly, clearly, and concisely. I was pleased. It's always a great help to get a good history. I started to relax. Maybe it wouldn't be just hours of moaning.

The resident came by.

"What have you got here, Pete?" I asked.

"Not too bad. It's a superficial femoral occlusion. Should be fast."

Another plus. The clot was located in a superficial artery, not a deep one. Access should be fairly easy. We wouldn't have to struggle for hours and hours.

The attending came. We'd been waiting for him.

"Okay, gang, let's go."

I looked for Pete, but he had gone into the surgeons' lounge. As soon as he came out we could go in.

Idly I glanced through the chart, looking to see

Barrie Evans

whether I had missed something. I looked at her address.

"Hey," I turned to her, "I see you live at 203. I used to live right across the street from you. You know, over the candy store. I haven't lived there for many years, but that makes us neighbors, doesn't it?"

"Yes, indeed. And what did you say your name was?"

"Barrie Evans."

"Oh, yes. Well, Miss Evans, I am comforted to know that a neighbor will be caring for me. It makes a bond, doesn't it?"

And it did. I started to warm to the little old lady—to get protective. I tucked her blanket around her neck to make sure that she was not chilled. She looked up at me and smiled.

"I'm glad you're here, Miss Evans," she whispered.

And I started to be glad too.

Pete and the attending came out of the lounge. "Let's go, Barrie, time's a-wasting."

"Only waiting for you. We're ready. Say, do you know Mrs. Silver and I are neighbors?"

"Yes, yes," the attending muttered. "Let's go."

We were moving into the room. We gently lifted Mrs. Silver to the O.R. table. One leg looked pink and normal; the other looked blue and cold, lifeless. We had no time to spare. She might lose the leg.

"I'm cold, Miss Evans," she said loudly, and well she should be: she was lying on the table exposed from the waist down.

"Yes, I know," I replied. "In a moment you'll be even colder. They're going to wash you off with an iodine solution."

"Yes?"

"And then after that you'll be covered with sterile sheets and towels. That will warm you up."

I was happy I at least had warmed up the room this morning. That should help her a bit.

The resident prepped her, and the scrub nurse and resident draped her, while the attending gowned and gloved.

Soon they were ready. The attending picked up a syringe.

"Mrs. Silver, I'm going to give you the local anesthesia now."

"Yes, Doctor."

"You'll feel a stick and then a sting."

"Yes, Doctor."

"You'll feel touch and pressure but no pain."

"Yes, Doctor. Oh, Miss Evans, I'm so glad you are here. I'm getting scared now."

"Don't be afraid," I reassured her. "I'll be here with you as long as you're in the operating room."

"And then?"

"And then you'll go to the recovery room overnight and tomorrow you'll go to your own room."

"And you won't be there?"

"No, I only work here in the operating room."

"But you'll come and visit?"

"Oh, yes, I'll visit you in the recovery room first thing in the morning before I go home."

"Why do I have to stay there all night? I mean in the recovery room?"

"Because they will want someone to check the circulation in your leg. You know, the bad one, the one they're operating on now."

"Oh," she said loudly, "are they operating on me now?"

"Yes, they are."

"Barrie," said the attending, "do you think you could hold it down? Pete and I are operating here."

"Don't you think I know that? It's either drug the hell out of her, which I don't want to do with a ninety-seven-year-old, or talk. I vote for talk."

"You're right," he sighed, "but could you lower your volume?"

"She's hard of hearing."

"Oh, shit, Barrie, do the best you can."

"Okay. Will do."

For a few moments all was peaceful. Mrs. Silver was napping. I stood up and peeked at the operative field. All seemed to be going well.

"Miss Evans," our patient said loudly, "do you know Mrs. Stein?"

"Mrs. Stein?"

"From the house. She lives in 15B. Mrs. Stein."

"Oh, yes, I know her."

"She is my friend. She had a cataract operation last year. Did you know that?"

"Well, no, I didn't."

"Yes, she did. And she's fine now."

The attending peered at me over his mask. I shrugged my shoulders helplessly and rolled my eyes. He got back to the operative field.

A few moments of silence.

"So Miss Evans, who else do you know from the house?"

"Well, I haven't lived there in a long time. Ten years."

"You call ten years a long time? Huh."

"Well, let me see. I knew the Robinsons. You know, the ones who had the black poodle?"

"Mitzi?"

"Mitzi—yes, I guess that was its name. Mitzi."

"Sure, I know them. And Mitzi too, Mitzi died, you know. Kidney failure."

"Oh, I didn't know. Did they get another dog?"

"No, they were heartbroken over Mitzi. Maybe they will, though. Mitzi was like a child to them."

The attending cleared his throat. I looked at him and started to say something.

"I know, I know," he said wearily.

"Do you remember Mrs. Hamilton? She owned the boutique up the block from the newsstand."

"Why, yes. A blond woman?"

"Yes, well she moved out west. Denver, I think. Her sister is there."

"Oh, how nice for her."

"Yes."

Once again silence descended on the room. Good thing it was quiet now; the delicate part of the operation was in progress. Small tubes with balloons on the end were passed inside the artery with the blockage. They were passed one at a time, the smallest first and then gradually increasing in size. When the tube went up the artery the balloon was not inflated; once past the point of occlusion, the balloon was inflated and the tube gently pulled out. Clinging to the balloon were pieces of the blood clot that caused the occlusion of the artery. They increased the size of the tubes until they felt the vessel wall and knew the clot had come out. They had to be sure pieces did not break off and go to the other parts of the body and create an occlusion there.

I was hoping Mrs. Silver would remain quiet during this phase of the surgery. Thankfully, she did. They irrigated the artery with a weak solution of heparin and were preparing to close it.

"Miss Evans," she called loudly, "is my poor doctor working down there all alone?"

"No. He has an assistant and the nurse who is passing him the instruments."

"Oh, thank God he has some help. I know the hospital is an awful place to be in over a weekend. I'm glad he has some assistance."

"There is a full team here in the operating room today as there is at all times in case of emergency. Don't worry, you're in good hands. You've got the A team."

"I don't know about any A team. I've got my doctor and I've got you. I'm lucky."

She drifted back off to sleep. This time it was the attending who rolled his eyes.

The artery was closed and blood flowed through once again. Now they would close the rest of the wound. It was tedious work and anticlimactic.

"So tell me, Miss Evans, do you know the Prices? He's a retired attorney."

"Yes, yes, the Prices. They lived on our floor. Sure, I know the Prices. How are they?"

"Well, Mr. Price is very sick. She has to have an aide come in for him every day."

"What's wrong?"

"Oh, he had a stroke. He's all right mentally but he can't do for himself anymore."

"Oh, I'm very sorry to hear that. He used to be so independent. It must be hard for them both."

"Yes, yes. What's going on down there now, Miss Evans? I'm getting a bit tired of the whole thing."

"They're finishing up. We should be out of here within the half hour."

"Good. Now what about my clothing?"

"Clothing?"

"Yes, they took it away from me downstairs. I'll be needing it again if I go home."

"If?"

"You mean I really will go home again?"

"Absolutely. They fixed your leg; you should be fine."

"I hope so. I really do."

"Mrs. Silver?"

"Yes, Doctor."

"Does your leg feel like it's waking up again?"

"Yes, Doctor."

"Can you wiggle your toes?"

"Yes, Doctor."

"Does the leg feel numb now?"

"No, Doctor."

"Well, good. You'll be spending the night in the recovery room. I'll see you in the morning."

He peeled off his gloves and tossed them into a waste bucket. He peeled off his paper gown and threw it aside. He stretched. This had been precise, exacting, and tedious work.

The resident was putting on the dressing. The attending turned to go. "Thanks, Pete," he said to the resident.

"What about a little thank you for the rest of the

team?" I complained. "We work hard as a matter of course, but a little thank you goes a long way."

"Oh. Of course. Thanks, Barrie. Thank you one and all."

Once the dressing was in place we lifted Mrs. Silver back into her bed and took her to the recovery room. She listened intently as I gave the report to the nurse.

"I'll come and visit you the first thing in the morning."

"I'll be waiting for you. It's been such a comfort having you here, Miss Evans. It's made a hard time much easier."

"Thanks. Have a good night."

"God bless you, Miss Evans."

When I came in the next morning Mrs. Silver was confused, the nurse told me. I was upset. I knew she'd had major surgery, was ninety-seven years old and was in a strange environment. Any or all of these factors can cause confusion, but I was upset nonetheless.

"Do you have a next of kin on her?" I asked the nurse.

"No. There's no one listed on the chart."

I brooded a moment. I'd grown to love the little old lady, a perfect stranger only a day ago. "Listen," I started.

"Yeah?"

Should I get involved? After all . . . I was ashamed of myself for even doubting. "Listen," I said positively to the nurse, "I'm putting down my phone number. I want to be called in case anything happens. Okay?"

"Is she a relative?"

"No."

"Friend?"

"Yes. Yes, she is."

"Okay, so put your number down on the chart."

I felt good as I put my number down. I returned to my patient. She did not know me. I reached down and planted a little kiss on her forehead. "Have a good day," I whispered.

I dressed and left the hospital. I felt good.

XIV

I was still my own worst enemy in the heart room. I could not get used to it. I never wanted to. Vi knew, hell everybody knew, how I felt.

Whenever possible Vi tried to accommodate us, and so for almost eight weeks now my name had not appeared on the heart room schedule. Strictly speaking this was unfair. We were all supposed to do hearts in rotation. I made up for it, though. Many staff members didn't do TOPs; I did them about once a week. Many staff members hated to do pediatrics; I loved it. Others shuddered at the thought of neurosurgical anesthesia; I adored it. It was a great challenge, especially when they operated on the brain. There were so many things to be aware of, to do, to try to keep stable.

Still, the morning came when I walked into the office for a paper clip and saw my name on the heart room schedule for the day after next. I froze—the paper clip forgotten. I just stood there looking at the piece of paper. My name wouldn't go away.

Stew, our new anesthesiologist, walked by. "Barrie, I see we're working together day after tomorrow. I look forward to that."

"Don't be too sure, Stew. The heart room and I are not friends. In fact, it's worse than that. They consider me a jinx around there. Sometimes I can hardly gear myself up to go in there."

"Listen, Barrie, most places wouldn't even touch some of the patients they operate on here for open heart. It's not you—it's the patient selection. I've done open heart anesthesia for a good while—first down in Texas and then in the Midwest. When we had good patients, we got good results. MCG takes them on as a do-or-die effort. You've got to expect that many of them will die."

"Thanks, Stew. I know what you're saying is right. It's just . . ." I shrugged. "Anyway, I'll be there on Wednesday."

As I left the office, I could feel the old sad feeling starting to well up inside me. I would meet my patient. I would establish rapport. I would care for him, put him to sleep—and the way I imagined it he'd never wake up.

The case was booked for the day after tomorrow. I had to put it out of my mind until then.

The next afternoon as soon as I finished my cases I started gathering all the forms I needed for the heart room: the special anesthesia form—twice as big as the usual form—the many slips to do blood gases, to check the oxygenation of the blood, request forms for fresh frozen plasma in readiness to promote blood clotting after the patient was off the pump, labels for bloods to be taken, specimens to be sent. All the forms were prepared in advance. When I went to visit my patient, I stamped each slip, form, and label with the patient's plastic identification card—a plastic card something like a credit card.

As I was assembling all my forms, I saw Jeremy, the chief resident, who would be scrubbing tomorrow. Jeremy and I had always gotten along—had mutual respect for one another. One of the reasons was that we both cared about patients. Some residents seem to care more about the procedure than the person who is having it. They want to operate, all else is unimportant. Some residents just want to get the work done. Some we see really do not seem interested in much of anything. Jeremy was never like any of these. As a young resident, the girls told me, he was eager, pleasant, and on time, and he worked hard. The older surgeons liked him and taught him, as did the O.R. nurses, the anesthetists, the aides and orderlies and clerks. A hospital is a funny place; everyone is an expert in something, and if you let them, they will share their expertise with you. Jeremy let them, and so he learned a lot more than just how to tie a surgeon's knot.

"Doing the heart with us, Barrie?" Jeremy asked. "I'm so glad it's you. We always work well together, you and I."

"Thanks for the compliment, Jer, but you know me and the heart room," I muttered.

"I don't pay any attention to that. The reason I'm glad to have you," he continued, "is that this guy is one sick number. He's so bad that we moved him off fifteen during the night. He's in C.C.U. now. It will be a long, tough case. It's a reop. He was done five years ago, Barrie, but now he's barely functional. He's a young guy, too. Too bad. Oh, well—see you, Barrie."

Yeah, yeah, you'll see me, I thought to myself. Maybe I could call in sick. But what good would that do? They'd just find another one and make me do it. It was no use—there was no way out. One thing I could do, though, was omit meeting the patient.

Many of my coworkers never saw the open-heart patients preoperatively. They merely visited the chart. I had never done that. After all—I would be an integral part of the patient's care. I knew how frightening it was to go to the O.R. for any surgery—to say nothing of open-heart. I had always felt that if I could establish rapport, then the patient would see a familiar face the next morning—feel a little easier. I had told myself it was a copout not to see my open-heart patients.

This time, however, I decided I would take the easy way—I would visit the chart. Maybe my colleagues were right. Maybe that was why they handled death better than I did; they didn't let it get too close.

I didn't even want to visit the chart, but I knew I had to get going. When I entered the C.C.U. I looked neither left nor right. I went immediately to the nurses' station. An English nurse was the only one at the desk. She was checking the afternoon lab results that had just come up. "May I help you?" she asked.

"I'm Barrie Evans—anesthesia. Mr. Donovan is booked for tomorrow?"

"Yes."

"May I see his chart, please?"

"Really, I don't know where it is. Maybe the doctors have it."

"Oh."

Barrie Evans

"You could go to the conference room and see if it's there. But never mind all that. There's Mr. Donovan himself." She pointed to a very pale, tired-looking man sitting bolt upright in the bed, just across the way. "Mr. Donovan, here's Miss Evans, anesthesia, come to see you. Isn't that nice?" He nodded weakly.

Oh, no, I thought. "I'll be over to see you in a while, Mr. Donovan. I want to look at your chart first."

"Ha, here it is," the English nurse exclaimed. "It was just under these papers." She handed me the chart.

I sat down to read it. What I read did nothing to lift my spirits. Mr. Donovan *was* one sick fellow. I dawdled over the chart for as long as I could. I stamped all the forms. Then I forced myself to go over to Mr. Donovan.

"Mr. Donovan, I'm Barrie Evans. I'll be your anesthetist tomorrow."

"Happy to know you, miss. Won't you sit down."

We started to talk. He was a builder. He had a wife and four sons: three of them married with children of their own. One son was in the business with him—the youngest. He'd done well following the surgery five years ago—done well until about six months ago.

"Yes, I was in the hospital up home two months ago. The ticker gave out, they said. Fluid, you know. I got better, but they said I needed this operation. I can't do a thing anymore. Can't hardly walk a block. Thank God for Jim junior—he's doing it all now."

We spoke about the anesthesia. I explained everything I could—the IV, the premedication, the arterial line, the endotracheal tube, postop respiratory sup-

220

port—all of it. I explained it simply and he listened carefully. When I finished, I asked, "Any questions?"

"No miss, I understand what you said. It's in God's hands now—God's—and all of yours."

"Have a good night, Mr. Donovan. I'll see you early in the morning." I turned to go. He waved weakly.

"Everything AOK?" asked the English nurse.

"Oh, sure, AOK. Thanks."

I came in early the next morning. I couldn't sleep. It's ironic, the night I need sleep most, it evades me totally. I went into the locker room: it was deserted. I put on my uniform and of course my support stockings, the heavy white ones, which I always wear in the heart room. Slowly I pulled them up. One of the students came into the lounge. "What's up, Barrie, leg cramps?"

"Nah—just prophylactic. I'm doing the heart today and you know you *never* get to sit down in there."

I went outside. I was ready now—as ready as I'd ever be. I had a cup of coffee. It was early yet.

As I came around the corner, Jeremy was coming toward me.

"Morning, Jeremy."

"Morning, Barrie." He seemed to hesitate a little. "Barrie, uh, we, uh, well, we're not going to do, I mean, we're doing another patient today. Not the one originally booked."

"What do you mean, Jeremy? You're not doing Mr. Donovan?"

"No."

"Why not?"

"Well ..."

"Jeremy, tell me! Why not?" I looked up at Jeremy. He looked so pale, so tired, so sad. "Jeremy, he died? Did Mr. Donovan die during the night?"

"I was up all night with him, Barrie. Up the whole fucking night—and he died. Shit!"

"And now we're doing another heart patient?"

"Yes, Barrie, and believe it or not, it's someone sicker than Mr. Donovan. It will be a shorter case—it's only an aneurysm—if that's any consolation. See you later."

I went into the office. Vi was preparing the schedule adjusting last-minute things. She looked up when I entered the room. "Barrie, what can I say? It's uncanny—and they say the guy they're doing is even sicker than the one who died. By the way, how did it work out—just visiting the chart? Did it help?"

"I couldn't even do it. Thanks to one of the C.C.U. nurses, I *had* to see the patient. He was a nice guy, too."

Stew came into the office. "Heard the news, Barrie?" he asked.

I nodded.

"Oh, well, it's better for us than losing him on the table, isn't it?"

"Yes, but Stew, they're doing another guy this morning they say is even sicker. How can that be? The first one is dead."

"Beats me. Barrie, are we still the team doing the case?"

"Yes and Stew, I have a favor to ask."

"Yes?"

"Would you do it? I'm too unstrung at this point about the other guy, Jim. I don't think I can get myself together in time. I'll help you with whatever you need, but *you* do him, okay?"

"Great. I love to keep my hand in."

When we had everything set up in the room, Stew and I, Jeremy and his intern and one of the nurses from the open-heart intensive care unit brought the patient over. Stew and I read his chart, and was he ever sick. Mr. Macintosh was hardly responsive at all; the consent had been signed by his son, the next of kin.

Stew raised his eyebrows.

"Boy, they *do* pick them, don't they?" he whispered. "This one looks dead now." I was happy that Stew would be doing Mr. Macintosh for me.

We had set up the most extensive support systems we could. He was already on an intra-aortic balloon, a device to help a failing heart. He had lines coming out from everywhere. He looked like a bionic man. Without all these things he'd have been a dead man.

We went through the corridors and arrived in the O.R. Everyone glanced at us as we passed—glanced and thanked their lucky stars that it was *us* and not them, with this patient.

We no sooner had him on the table than he lost his blood pressure and his heart stopped. Everyone started to yell. "Let's get him on the pump. Quick!"

Stew slipped an endotracheal tube down. We gave no medication: he was almost gone. But we had to paralyze him: he had a lot of muscle tone. We gave only oxygen and within moments he was on the pump.

He'd had a huge amount of blood and fluid in the sac around his heart, his pericardium. The fluid had built up so much that it had acted as a vise around the heart, a cardiac tamponade.

Well, Mr. Macintosh had pneumonia; he had diabetes; he had emphysema, he had bronchitis, he had anemia; he had a hole between his ventricles; he had an aneurysm of one of his ventricles. Poor soul, he had it all. He hadn't wanted the surgery. He didn't want to live. His wife had died three months earlier, and he was horribly depressed. When he had slipped into the coma, the son had signed the consent.

Now, miracle of miracles, he came off the pump. He came off the table. He came off the balloon. In two days the endotracheal tube came out as did all the lines except one IV.

He was still bitter. He had wanted to die. We didn't let him.

XV

It was Friday morning. It had been a long week. Any day I spent in the heart room made the whole week longer, tested my endurance, made my legs achy. Friday is a day unlike any other in the operating room of MCG—and I guess other hospitals. Patients are eager to have their surgery before the hospital goes into its weekend slowdown. Attendings are anxious to push in any case they can, since the weekend is for emergencies only. House staff is divided into two groups: one half planning to sign out early to start weekend plans, the other half dreading the start of a long siege. Many of these young men and women will be on duty until Monday afternoon at 5:00. They are praying for a light weekend so they'll have time to eat and sleep and survive until the next weekend, when they will be planning to leave early.

Large gleaming carts full of sterile equipment come to the O.R. from the central sterile-supply department. The technician must bring up enough supplies for the entire weekend. Other carts come from the laundry department carrying sheets, blankets, nightgowns, booties, and towels. These must last through Monday afternoon—the next delivery will be on

Tuesday morning. Salesmen and personnel from purchasing and receiving crowd into the small office of the supply coordinator making sure that all special instruments, sutures and whatever other equipment has been ordered have arrived. The O.R. is really cooking on a Friday.

For me, Friday is the best day of the week. I savor thoughts of the weekend ahead. I think of my friends and the things we will do together—the plays, the ballets, the concerts, the street fairs, the shopping, the restaurants. Working under such great tension, such responsibility, such precision, constantly looking, listening, checking, calculating, regrouping, can wear you down. We all recover in our own way. Some of us sleep away our weekends, some booze them away, some spend them on sex. Each of us comes down in an individualized manner. We replenish ourselves to start all over again on Monday morning.

I am always "up" on Friday. No matter how hard, how long, how difficult, how tiring the day, I am charged with energy. I am so high, so happy. I try to restrain myself. After all, I am dealing with sick, frightened people facing a crisis in their lives. I must try to maintain a level appearance, try to be cool and professional.

My room was set up. I prepared my equipment in the PAR and watched the patients come in. It was always the same. When I was early and all ready, my patient was late. When I was late or needed some extra equipment or anything, it all went wrong and my patient was the first one to arrive. I paced back and forth. I hummed a tune I had heard on the radio before I left the house. I looked all around.

Everyone was working. Maureen had a child today. She was showing him a mask and trying it on for size. Benita had a deaf old man: I could hear her yelling from across the room. Where was my patient? I was getting impatient now. In ten minutes the doctor would arrive and expect me to be ready. Only one space remained—the one for my patient. I looked at the door for the fifth time. At last the orderly was coming with my patient. I had to work quickly now. We had several cases in my room. I did not want to delay.

I looked at my patient. The schedule said she was Carmen Delgado, scheduled for a hysterectomy. "Carmen?" I said with a smile. She smiled back. I started to introduce myself; "My name is Barrie . . ." Hold it, I told myself. "Carmen, do you speak English?"

She shook her head "No."

"A little bit? *Un poco*?" I asked.

She nodded.

I was relieved.

I picked up her chart to check the name tag on her wrist against her chart and her bed (and also the patient herself). Attached to the chart was a five-by-eight index card with a message written on it in bold red lettering: DO NOT DISCUSS THIS PATIENT'S SURGERY WITH HUSBAND OR ANYONE ELSE! This was a bit weird. Who was this message meant for? The surgeon? Me? I'd find out soon enough.

Some of my questions she understood.

"Did you eat or drink anything today?"

She shook her head.

"Do you smoke cigarettes?"

227

Another "no."

When we got into allergies, previous anesthetics and false teeth, I had to use Spanish, since she made it quite clear she hadn't a clue to what I was talking about.

"Tiene usted problemas con sus pulmones?" (Do you have any problems with your lungs?) brought yet another no and another smile.

I completed my history. I listened to her heart and lungs. I inspected her teeth. I started her I.V. I did all the things I needed to do to get her ready. I still had time to spare. None of the doctors had arrived. But I still did not know what the note meant. My Spanish was too limited. We couldn't really converse. I saw tears starting to well up in her eyes.

"Carmen, are you okay? Is something wrong?" I asked. I hope I can handle this, I thought to myself.

"I gotta too nervous," she told me. "My doctor. *Donde está?"* Where is he?

"Your doctor is coming," I told her. "We will not take you to the other room until he comes. *Entiende?"* Do you understand?

"Sí."

"I am going to give you some medicine now. Medicine—to relax you—*para descansar—entiende?"*

"Para dormir?" To go to sleep?

"No, solamente para descansar." I gave her some Valium. I told her she would feel a cold sensation or some burning. I pointed to her wrist where the IV was in place. I ran my finger up her arm.

"Lo siente?" Do you feel it?

"Sí." She pointed to the arm. *"Frio,"* she said.

"Sí—es normal," I reassured her.

She smiled weakly. The tears were falling now. What could I do? I didn't really know what the problem was. I looked around for someone who spoke Spanish well. I didn't see anyone. Suddenly her attending came in.

"Carmen, good morning."

"Ah, Doctor," she said. She started babbling very rapidly in Spanish. Neither one of us understood her.

"Take her in, Barrie," he said. "I'm going to change my clothes."

The resident came in. "Let's take her down now, Lynn," I told her. "By the way, do you know what her problem is? I don't seem to be getting through to her."

"Beats me, Barrie. I don't know the patient. I was off last night. I didn't work her up."

We started down the hall. We went into the O.R. The nurses were waiting for us.

"You're late today, Barrie," one told me. "What's up?"

"The attending was late."

Lynn went to the heater closet to get a warm blanket for Carmen. She motioned to Carmen to hold the blanket. She peeled down Carmen's sheet and spread.

"Carmen," I said gently, "move over here to the table." I patted the O.R. table.

She shook her head no. I thought maybe she didn't understand me. *"Mueva se par derecho"*—Move over to your right— *"Carmen, por favor."*

She shook her head. She was sobbing now.

Everyone was ready. Thelma, the anesthesiologist, the two nurses, two residents, two medical students and I. No one knew what the problem was.

Carmen hugged the blanket close and sobbed.

"Go and get the attending," Thelma ordered Lynn.

"He's changing his clothes," she replied.

"Tell him we can't get his patient on the O.R. table. Maybe he'll hurry."

Lynn left the room. Moments later she and the attending appeared.

"What's wrong here?" the attending asked.

"We don't know," the anesthesiologist said. "Your patient refuses to get on the O.R. table."

"Carmen," he ordered, "*mueva se*"—move over.

She started to move and then seemed to hesitate.

"Doctor," she started and sobbed wildly, "you don't forget? You promise, yes? My husband, *mi esposo*, you don't forget?"

"I know, I know. I promised you I'll take care of it, didn't I?" he answered brusquely. "Move over here this minute," he commanded.

Carmen moved onto the O.R. table.

"If it's okay with you," I said to the anesthesiologist, "I'll put her to sleep right now."

Thelma nodded vigorously.

"Carmen," I said to the hysterical woman, "I'm putting you to sleep—*Dormir ahora*."

Quickly I administered the sodium pentothal, the muscle relaxant, and intubated Carmen. Thelma checked the chest and let me know that the breath sounds were good and equal.

The attending and two residents came in from the scrub area, their hands held high, dripping water. The scrub nurse handed each one a towel.

One of the medical students came over. "Excuse

me, sir," he said, "what was wrong with your patient? She seemed to just fall apart. What was the matter?"

We all listened attentively.

"Well, son," said the attending, "we do a lot of hysterectomies here at MCG. We do them for leiomyomata—fibroids to you—and we do them for cancer too. By and large, patients accept their surgery well. They are happy to be rid of their symptoms: their cramps, their bleeding or backache. Generally by the time they come to surgery they have been having these symptoms for a good little while. Of course they have feelings about their loss of womanhood, their continued attraction to the men in their lives, their inability to have children. All women think of these things and some discuss them with us prior to surgery. It's good if a patient can get it out of her system before surgery. Once it's open and out on the table she can deal with it and we can help her. But some women—quite a few, I guess, even in this enlightened day and age—do not discuss how they feel. I see them in my office and make the diagnosis, and they seem to accept it. They come to the hospital, have their surgery, and accept it. I visit them every day in the postoperative period, I take out the catheter, I change the dressing, I take out the clips, and they seem to accept it. Then, after they are home, sometimes a weepy phone call, sometimes a distraught husband or lover lets me know that they have not accepted it at all. I have an associate—she works as a sex therapist primarily, helps me with my infertility patients—I refer these patients to her. She works with them either alone or with their partner. She does a great job. . . ."

As the attending was talking, Lynn had prepped
and draped the patient. Her legs were up in the stirrups—she was ready for the D&C, the dilatation and
curettage. The attending, the two residents, and the
two students examined Carmen after I put her to
sleep. EUA (examination under anesthesia) is the
first part of almost every gynecological operation.
When the patient and her tissues are relaxed—thanks
to the anesthetic—a much more comprehensive exam
can be done than in the doctor's office. It will reas-
sure the attending that his diagnosis was correct and
his plan of action a good one. On occasion after an
EUA, his plan may change. As his patient is more
relaxed, he may encounter different findings from the
ones he felt in his office.

Lynn had the patient ready. The attending did the
D&C. The circulating nurse pressed the intercom and
asked for the pathologist. He took the tissue to the
laboratory and examined it.

While we were awaiting the pathologist's report,
time hung heavy. Carmen was lying flat on her back
on the O.R. table covered by a blanket. I had her at
a fairly light level of anesthesia until we heard the report. I did not want to have her deeply anesthetized
and ready for a major surgical procedure only to hear
the words "Wake her up!"

I could wait. As long as she was sleeping, I could
deepen her at any time.

"So, sir," began the medical student once again,
"you were going to, you know, uh—you were going to
tell us, you know, about Mrs. Delgado's—about her
problem. We're still waiting to hear, sir."

The attending looked at Carmen sleeping quietly

and shook his head. "It's a long story. You know that here at MCG, at most voluntary hospitals in the city, we have a large Spanish-speaking population. And many of my colleagues call these women HPRs."

"HPRs, sir? What are they?"

"HPRs are hysterical Puerto Ricans. But here at MCG we have patients from Cuba, Costa Rica, Panama, Santo Domingo, and El Salvador in addition to Puerto Rico. Besides, calling them HPRs does not solve the problem. We must understand what makes them tick. The uterus, *"la matriz,"* is the center of their womanhood, literally and figuratively. Without it, they are nothing, neuter. They have been told this by their mothers and their mother's mothers right down the line. Hispanic men do not want women who do not have a uterus. It would make them less a man, less macho to screw a barren woman. It makes no difference what you tell them—that they'll be sexually attractive, sexually active (perhaps more than before), sexually free. They look at you as though you're crazy or shake their heads knowingly. To a hispanic woman, particularly a young one, a hysterectomy means the end—the end of womanhood, of love, and in some cases even of life.

"When I was a young practitioner I didn't know any of this. I had to learn it on my own. I've had some sad experiences. The worst thing is, there's nothing you can do. Carmen came to me a year ago complaining of urinary frequency and urgency; she had to get up to urinate six or seven times a night. Her periods had become longer and longer and heavier and heavier—and very painful. Usually she had to remain in bed for two or three days each time.

I made the diagnosis of fibroids and about six months ago convinced her to have a D and C. From the onset, I told Carmen that she would probably wind up with a hyst. She didn't want to hear it. She was forty-nine years old, had four grown children—two in Santo Domingo, her home, and two here. She certainly does not plan to have more babies. Her husband is the manager of a supermarket—a nice guy. She brought him to my office once but wouldn't let me talk to him at all. He came in, and said 'Hi,' and left—just like that.

"Now she is having this operation and he's totally unaware of the nature of her surgery. It's the only way she'd have it done."

"But what does he think Carmen is having?"

"Woman trouble."

"And what are you supposed to be doing about it?"

"Fixing it."

"Well, what if he comes right out and asks you what you did?"

"I'll be vague."

"And lie to him?"

"Well, not lie—I'll just be evasive."

"But that's dishonest."

"Look, son, my doctor—patient relationship is with Carmen—not her husband."

"But what if something happened to her? Doesn't he have a right to know?"

"Son, I promised this patient that I would not discuss her operation with her husband—or anyone. I guess I really shouldn't be discussing it with you but *you're* a doctor, almost. Anyway, I'll keep my promise to Carmen."

The medical student shook his head and sighed, deeply. He didn't seem to agree with that promise.

The pathologist returned. The specimen was negative—no cancer. The attending could go ahead. He made his incision. He and Lynn clamped bleeders, tied them off, cut sutures, and proceeded. The medical students stood by silently, watching every step. When he got to the uterus it was the size of a football: full of fibroids everywhere. Quickly, and with minimal blood loss, the specimen came out. It lay in a rectangular metal pan on a small table near the door, awaiting the pathologist. It was pink and gleaming, an inert piece of tissue, home for Carmen's children, symbol of her womanhood for the husband who waited anxiously and unknowingly for Carmen in her room. She could never be the same. We all looked at it lying there in the pan. We had seen many a uterus but this one had special meaning.

Time moved slowly now. "Kellys, please," said the attending. "Let's close now."

XVI

The weekend had whipped by. Before I knew it it was over. Monday morning, when I came into the anesthesia office, I checked the assignment sheet as I did each day. I could not find my name anywhere. Oh, no, I thought to myself, don't tell me I'm supposed to be off today. I grabbed the time book from the shelf and quickly checked. No, I was definitely on today. Then why wasn't I given an assignment? Vi was fixing a ventilator out in the hall when I approached.

"Vi, I can't find my name on the assignment sheet. Did you forget me?"

"No, Barrie, you're doing ECT this morning."

"ECT? I thought shock therapy went out twenty years ago when all the psychotropic drugs came in."

"You mean to tell me you've been here since May and you haven't done ECT yet? In that case I'll have to send someone over with you. I'll send Joan. She has a second case, so she's free now. You'll observe her today, but the next time it's scheduled—on Wednesday—you'll be on your own. Go find her, Barrie. She'll go over the setup with you."

Joan was having coffee in the lounge. I gave her

O.R.

Vi's message. "Sit down for a few minutes, Barrie. We
have plenty of time. Whatever time we get over there
to psych, they won't be ready anyway."

"Joan, how come they're still doing ECT here?"

"They say that for some cases of depression they
haven't found any drug as effective."

"Electro convulsive therapy. God, I'll never forget.
I got a good taste of it when I was on my psych affiliation in nursing school. We had to spend twelve
weeks at one of the state hospitals.

"They did it three times a week in those days.
Early in the morning they would catch all the patients—about thirty each time. And when I say catch,
that's just what I mean. They never gave any drugs
then, and the patients were scared to death. They
caught them and locked them up in a big room.

"Once the doctor was ready, an aide would open
the door and grab a patient. Two big aides or orderlies were always assigned. They would force the patient onto the table, the doctor would put the
electrodes on either side of the head, and I, the
student, would have to push the button. After the
treatment, when the patient was unconscious, the two
orderlies would take him and dump him on a
mattress down the hall. One aide was assigned to
watch the thirty patients. It was a miracle that nothing seemed to happen to them. I hated every minute
of it."

"Barrie, nothing like that happens now. That's why
they want us over there. We give Brevital followed by
Sux—and preoxygenate and are ready to intubate if
we have a problem. No, it's nothing like what you
described."

"And who gets these treatments, Joan?"

"Mostly older women who are depressed. I don't know why, but it seems to work."

"Well, I'm still unconvinced, but I'll be interested to see."

"We've got to check all our equipment here. They can't help us over there. They're only interested in the patient's psyche—nothing else."

We made sure that both oxygen tanks on the small, portable machine we were taking were full, checked that the laryngoscope worked, that we had endotracheal tubes of varying sizes, airways, suction catheters, the drugs we would need, butterflies (small needles with a length of plastic tubing attached) of various sizes, a tourniquet, alcohol sponges. We had it all. We were ready to go. But I still had those memories of pushing the button on those poor patients.

"Let's go, Barrie. We don't want to be late."

Together we started over to the psych building. Joan was wheeling the portable anesthesia machine. We went via the overpass. Psychiatry is located across the street.

Once we got into the area we had to push a button to enter. The units are open—patients are not locked in—but the elevator is kept locked. Too many patients have escaped over the years—eloping, they call it. An orderly peeked out at us and let us in.

We were in a cheery-looking unit now. All the patients were in single or double rooms. Each room was furnished in a different color scheme. The furniture was modern. It didn't look like a hospital at all—sort of like a Holiday Inn. Not like the old days, I thought to myself.

The staff was all dressed in street clothes. It was impossible for me to decide which ones were patients and which staff, except for the people in bathrobes. It was early yet—many patients were not dressed. But the others . . . Unconsciously, I found myself moving closer to Joan.

We went into a large, spacious nurses' station. There was a big rolling cart with medicines. As on the other units, each patient had his own drawer. They gave plenty of drugs up here.

Joan showed me our patient's chart. The previous anesthetist had written

> Brevital 40 mg
> Succinylcholine 40 mg
> Good seizure, rapid recovery.

"Exactly what they want," Joan said. "We'll use the same dose today. Sometimes it takes a few attempts to get just what they want, Barrie. I guess when they did it in the old days the seizures that patients had were violent."

"Violent—they sure were. Sometimes they even fractured bones with them."

"Well, now all they're looking for is a slight trembling of the extremities. *That* pleases them—the 'rapid recovery' pleases us."

"Boy, Joan—I feel like I'm starting from scratch here."

"That's why I'm with you."

We went in to visit the patient.

An older, ungroomed, unkempt woman was lying in bed, staring into space. An aide was with her.

"Gracie?" Joan started.

"Uh?"

"We're from the anesthesia department. We're going to put you to sleep for a few moments so you can have your treatment."

"Uh."

"Gracie, did you have anything to eat or drink yet today?"

"No."

"Did you have your shot?"

"Yes."

"Do you remember about breathing the oxygen?"

"Uh."

"Okay. We'll be back when the doctor comes."

We left our anesthesia machine in the nurses' station so that no one could fool with it. As we passed by there, a patient was lighting a cigarette from a lighter attached by a string right outside the station. Patients were not permitted to have their own matches or lighters.

We were waiting for the doctor now. "We're going to get coffee," Joan told the nurse. "Come get us when you're ready."

It was a huge kitchen-dining area. Patients had access at all times. There was coffee, tea, soda, fruit, cookies, potato chips, Danish, toast, peanut butter, and jelly. I was impressed. We poured ourselves coffee and went out to the sitting room to drink it.

"You don't mind, do you, Barrie?" Joan asked.

"No, no, I love psych, always did. It's just the ECT that makes me nervous."

O.R.

The sitting room was a large, spacious room with many magazines, books, games, puzzles, and the daily newspaper. There was a large color TV on the wall in the corner of the room.

A couple of patients looked up as we came in: an older woman in a bathrobe and a sullen-looking, young black man.

"Good morning," I said as I sat down.

They looked at me inquisitively.

"Good morning," they replied hesitantly.

The TV was on. The story was about a murder trial featured prominently in all the newscasts. "What do you think about the trial?" I asked the young man. "Think he did it?"

"What do you think?" he asked me in return.

"Well, I figure he did it but certainly with good reason."

"Hey, that's what I think, too."

The woman in the bathrobe joined in now. "Well, I feel he should be punished and I believe in capital punishment. Maybe there wouldn't be so many murders if they made an example of him."

Soon we were all three talking animatedly. Joan sipped her coffee and said nothing.

"Where do you come from?" the woman asked. "You're from outside, aren't you?"

"We're from anesthesia. We're here to help with Gracie's treatment."

"Can I tell you something, dear?"

"Sure."

"You're like a breath of spring. You know how they talk to you here on this floor? Well, they never talk to you. They just repeat what you're saying back to you.

It's enough to make you crazy—if you're not already. Me, I'm just depressed. You've made me feel so much better. Thanks for talking to us."

"Yeah, I hear you," said the young man. "Thanks —you know, we do get tired of the shit they . . ."

"Ladies—we are ready for you now," the nurse called from the hall. Joan stopped off in the nurses' station to pick up the anesthesia machine. A bunch of people in street clothes were inside the glass-enclosed station looking out: the staff. A bunch of people in street clothes were outside the glass-enclosed station looking in: the patients. They were lined up waiting to receive their morning medication.

We returned to Gracie's room. Nothing had changed. Gracie stared, the aide sat. With us now were the nurse assigned to the ECT and the psychiatrist. Joan started to check the suction. One of the few things they provided: the suctions in the O.R. were attached to the wall. If Gracie should vomit for any reason we would need it. Many psychiatric patients develop excess secretions, especially due to some of their medications. These secretions may effect their airway, so we must be able to suck them away.

"I already checked that suction," the nurse said truculently.

"It is for my use," Joan said. "I will check it myself. May I have a BP cuff?"

"Her pressure was 120/80 this morning."

"So what? You know we always take a BP before and after the treatment. Why don't you just go and get it?"

"Go get her a cuff," the nurse told the aide.

While waiting, Joan listened to Gracie's heart and

lungs. All was well. She preoxygenated Gracie, asking her to breathe normally. When the aide came, Joan checked Gracie's blood pressure, then put the tourniquet on her arm. "I'm going to wash you off with a little alcohol now and then give you the medicine to put you to sleep, Gracie," she said.

Quickly she found the vein, secured the butterfly, and started to inject the Brevital.

Gracie's eyes closed. Joan was able to ventilate her with ease. She gave the Sux, and as soon as Gracie stopped twitching from it, the psychiatrist gave her the treatment.

For a brief period she had a seizure, and then her muscles relaxed.

Joan took out the rubber airway the nurse had put in to prevent Gracie from biting her tongue. She replaced it with a plastic airway and breathed for Gracie. In a moment Gracie was breathing on her own.

Joan left the oxygen on for another minute and rechecked Gracie's blood pressure. She asked the nurse and aide to turn Gracie on her side.

We went to the nursing station to fill out the chart. I felt more and more anxious. Today there were two of us, but after this first demonstration I'd be on my own.

"See you day after tomorrow?" asked the psychiatrist. "You'll be doing the treatment again, Miss Smith?"

"No, I won't, Doctor. Miss Evans will be your anesthetist."

I looked at Joan and nodded brightly. "See you

Wednesday," I said cheerfully. We took our equipment and left.

Wednesday morning I went over to psych with all my equipment. The same nurse was there, but this time all was in readiness. I knew Gracie, and I knew her drug dosages. I'd been at MCG a long time, I told myself. It was only here in psychiatry that I felt like a novice.

The psychiatrist watched me carefully as I repeated everything that Joan had done on Monday. All went well—I, too, would be able to write "Good seizure, rapid recovery" on Gracie's chart.

"See you the day after tomorrow?" the psychiatrist asked.

"You bet," I replied. He felt confident in me now. I did too.

XVII

The next afternoon when I came into the office there was a message for me. That was unusual. We are not permitted to have phone calls at work, so a message usually means bad news—of one sort or another. I grabbed the slip of paper. "Call Mr. Thomas, ext. 9898."

"Mr. Thomas." I mumbled to myself. "Oh, yes, Allan."

Allan was a friend who lived in my apartment house. We always walked our dogs together, I, my dachshund and he, his schnauzer. I'd promised to do his anesthesia and help him get settled in the hospital. He was a physical therapist in one of the VA hospitals, but he'd never been a patient before. He was married, had grandchildren, and was still active sexually. A couple of months ago he had noted bloody urine. He was getting up to pass his urine about four or five times a night. Each time he had difficulty in starting his stream and never seemed to feel that his bladder was empty.

He felt pretty sure he knew what it was—he had enough friends with enlarged prostates.

Allan couldn't believe it when his doctor told him

he'd need surgery. He had expected some form of conservative therapy—pills or something. His father had suffered from urinary retention and always carried what he called "a hollow tube" (probably a catheter) in his hat. When he was unable to void, he'd put the tube in and empty his bladder. Allan was certain that when he got older he'd have retention too. It was this fear that finally convinced Allan he should have the surgery.

I dialed the number and asked to speak to Mr. Thomas.

"Barrie, it's Allan. Allan Thomas. I'm here in the hospital, in the admitting office. . . . Barrie, I'm booked for surgery tomorrow and there are no private beds. The fellow here is telling me to take semiprivate. Barrie, I can't be in a room with anyone else, I need to be alone, with Margot."

"Allan," I said quickly, "I'll be right down."

I got off the elevator and headed for the admitting office. There, sitting on a sofa in a corner of the waiting room, was Allan. His blond hair, usually combed in neat well-set waves, was all disheveled. He kept running his fingers through it and shaking his head. When he saw me he jumped up. "I'm so glad you're here, Barrie. I'm not used to being a patient. I'm nervous—and I don't like it."

"Let me see what I can do, okay? I'll try to make it as easy as I can for you."

I went into the admitting office itself. It is a well-lit cheerful place with colorful wallpaper. Athough it is a long narrow room, each admitting clerk has his own desk with a small chair for himself and another for the patient. As you come in you can see the board and the Xerox machines. The board is the most important part of the place: that's where all room numbers and patients are listed. That's how beds are assigned.

I looked around to see if I could find the clerk handling Allan. As luck would have it it was Don, the only clerk I knew. Don told me that Allan had better take a semiprivate bed—there were no private beds now. As soon as one became available, Allan would be transferred.

I went outside to Allan and explained the situation to him.

He was quite peeved. "I made the reservation in advance. I work in a hospital. Doesn't that count for anything? Margot and I need to be by ourselves."

"Allan, your operation will be tomorrow morning. Please take the bed."

Finally he agreed. Together we went back into the admitting office and told the volunteer that he was ready for Don. Don came and asked us in. There wasn't room for me in the little cubicle so I told Allan I'd wait outside.

As I left I heard him say to Don, "How can this be? I made all the arrangements. Margot . . ." Quickly Don completed the paperwork and sent Allan outside.

We sat down in the waiting room and had some coffee. In a few moments a volunteer came to take us to the preadmission lab so that all the tests could be done before Allan got to his room. When we arrived at preadmissions, the clerk nodded to Allan. "Sit down, sir. Your turn will come soon." She smiled. "Can you give us a urine specimen now? If you can, go down the hall to the left to the men's room and pick up a jar. When you are finished, put this slip around the jar and use this rubber band. Leave the specimen in the box marked 'Urine.' "

Soon a technician came to take Allan into another room. "I'm going to draw your blood now, Mr. Thomas," she told him.

They went off and returned again in a few moments. "Just sit down here, now, Mr. Thomas," she told him. "The volunteer will come to take you to X ray. After that it's off to the EKG lab; that's to have your cardiogram, you know."

"Yes, of course I know. I work in a hospital too," he muttered.

Another volunteer arrived.

"Mr. Thomas? Come with me." She had two other patients to collect, and all of us followed her to the X-ray department.

The technician gave all three patients long white gowns to put on. "Each of you go into one of those rooms, take off all your clothes and put on these gowns. They tie in the back. Do not leave any money or valuables in the cubicle. Take them with you. When you are ready, come on out and have a seat in the waiting room."

I waited for Allan in the waiting room. The other patients were already there. When Allan came out, he was still wearing his trousers. I decided not to intervene. When the technician came into the waiting room she saw Allan. "Sir," she said, "you'll have to take those pants off."

"You're only taking an X ray of my chest."

"Sir, you'll have to take those pants off. If you're

not completely undressed, we won't take the X ray. It's very simple—your choice."

Allan sighed and returned to the dressing room.

Finally his X ray was completed, and then it was off to EKG. By the time we arrived it was after 5:00 P.M.; the department was closed. Allan started to carry on, but the volunteer, a young man this time, just looked at him. "Sir," he said, "if you're having your operation tomorrow they will come to your room after dinner and do any tests you couldn't get done now. Calm down, mister, you'll live longer."

We waited for the elevator to go upstairs to Allan's room.

We got off and approached the desk. "Got an admission for you, Jeannie," the volunteer addressed the unit clerk. "Thomas for room 1562."

The clerk took the chart from the volunteer and glanced at it. "Mr. Thomas," she said, "come with me. I'll show you to your room." We walked down a long corridor almost to the end of the hall.

"Mr. Thomas," she announced, "this is your room, and this is your roommate, Ronnie Lee."

Allan looked aghast.

Ronnie was lying in bed with nothing on except a pair of very short cut-off dungaree shorts. A big bandage was wrapped around his head. Surrounding him were his visitors—six of them. Everyone was smoking cigarettes. The music was on full blast, playing the latest Kenny Rogers hit. They all seemed to be having a ball.

"Howdy," said Ronny Lee. "Glad to know ya. These are my friends. Say 'Hi' to my new roommate. What's your name, anyhow, fella?"

"I am Mr. Thomas."

"And what's your first name?"

"Young man, my name is Mr. Thomas, and that's what I'd like to be called."

"Don't get all bent out of shape over it, Mac. What's in a name anyhow? What are you in here for, huh?"

"I'd prefer not to discuss it, young man," Allan said, as he started to busy himself with getting settled.

An aide came in to take his temperature and orient him to his environment. "This is your call bell, sir. If you need anything, ring it and we will answer it over the intercom. Someone will say 'May I help you?' Then you just say whatever it is you need and we'll get it for you. Don't be afraid—just say what you want. Over here in the middle of the bed are the controls. You can go higher or lower, lift up the head or foot of the bed. You can do all that yourself. You don't need to call out for those things. Here is your water pitcher. At twelve midnight we will take it away because they don't want you to eat or drink anything after that. Do you have any questions now, honey?"

"No, no questions." Allan sounded exhausted now. He was seeing the health care system from a consumer's viewpoint and not liking what he saw.

I'd done my part for now—I'd gotten him settled. I told him that I was going home. "You might as well try to get some rest, Allan. Before the night is out you'll be seeing a few more people."

"Oh, no," he cried. "I can't take much more of this. Who else is coming?"

"Well, first of all, a resident is coming to take your

history. Then your own doctor, of course. And the fellow from the prep team—I don't remember whether or not you get shaved for this surgery. The dietician will be by to review any food problems you may have. And last but not least, your anesthesiologist. I'll wait till morning for my questions. I'm leaving now."

"Wait, Barrie, don't leave me. I have some more questions. What about television and a newspaper? How will I get them?"

"A man comes around twice a day with newspapers, and as for the TV, Ronnie Lee obviously has already ordered it, because it's on now. You'll have to work out an arrangement with him on that."

"You're not suggesting that I'm staying in this room with *him*, are you? What about my reservations? What about Margot?"

I interrupted him. "Allan, you are in the hospital now and you are part of the system. The system will not adapt to you—you must adapt to it. Meals are served when *they* want, medications are given when *they* administer them, rooms are changed when *they* get to it. Here in the hospital we tend to treat people less like individuals than we should. You remember how it is in your department? Well, you're a part of the system now."

"Okay, Barrie, I'll try to fit in. But I'll see you tomorrow in the O.R., won't I? You haven't forgotten your promise to put me to sleep have you?"

"Of course I'll put you to sleep, Allan. You know that. Look, here comes Margot. You'll be happy now."

I was relieved. I knew she'd take over. This was Al-

Ian's second marriage and Margot's first. They had
met in France during World War II. Allan had been
a patient in a field hospital. Margot had been there
as a hospital librarian. Their love affair was overwhelming and long-lasting.

Margot was not a pretty woman physically. She was
tall and awkward in appearance. The love that she
felt for Allan, however, shone through and made her
beautiful. They spent every possible moment together. They seemed very young indeed when they
were together. They quite literally lived for each
other.

I had asked beforehand to do Allan's anesthesia.
Now I wasn't quite as certain as I had been when he
asked me originally. Allan in the hospital was not the
Allan I knew. I realized that his behavior was due to
his own feelings of fear, helplessness, and frustra-
tion—feelings that all patients have but which were
greater in his case because he knew a little bit about
hospitals. Little of his knowledge would help him to
cope with the trauma of his *own* hospitalization.

When I'd originally requested to do so, Vi had
asked me to think about it carefully. "It's not easy to
do, Barrie, or even smart. Anesthesia's tough. You
can't help but get emotional if your patient is your
friend. If you think you can handle it, go ahead. You
know the situation much better than I do."

Now I was really facing the situation for the first
time. I was not at all sure I'd made the right decision,
but I was too stubborn and too proud to admit it to
anyone but myself.

The evening was not a pleasant one for me. Every
so often Allan and Margot would come into my

thoughts and I'd battle back and forth mentally. The battle did not end at bedtime. All night long I slept in fits and starts. When I slept I had nightmares—of cardiac arrests, of aspiration, of a disconnect in the anesthesia circuit. When I was awake, and that was a good part of the night, I thought of my two friends and wondered was it an ego trip on my part. By morning I was exhausted.

The anesthesiologist had ordered a heavy premed for Allan. When he arrived at the preanesthesia room, he was quite drowsy. Margot was at his side. I asked her to wait outside while I got him ready but told her that later she could put a yellow gown on over her clothes and stay with him until it was time for his surgery to begin.

Allan had great veins and it was a good thing—I felt my hand tremble as I started his IV. I hope this is not a preview of what is to come, I thought to myself.

I reviewed his chart. I looked at all lab values and the EKG. Allan seemed to be in perfect health. Everything seemed "within normal limits." We mark this down on the chart with the abbreviation WNL: one of our guys said jokingly one day that it meant "We Never Look, We Never Listen."

I asked Margot to come in and gave her a metal stool to sit on. Routinely, visitors are not permitted in the preanesthesia room, except for parents of a child coming into surgery, but we do make an exception with health care personnel. Allan was being treated like a V.I.P.—but he was too sleepy to notice. He was just happy to know that Margot was with him. In a few moments Dr. Kaye, his doctor, arrived and looked in on him. When he saw Allan was asleep he put his hand up and motioned that he did not want to disturb him. He went to the surgeon's lounge to change his clothes, and it was time to go.

Margot stood up quietly and planted a gentle kiss on Allan's forehead. "I'll be upstairs in his room," she told me. "Please ask Dr. Kaye to let me know when it's over. Barrie, I don't have to tell you what Allan means to me. He is my life, literally." Tears were starting to form in her eyes. I turned aside. I didn't want her to see what was happening to mine.

"Margot," I said firmly, "I am going to take care of Allan. He's healthy, this is not a major operation and he should do well. I'll remind the doctor to give you a call."

The resident came in and we wheeled Allan off to the O.R. The case was booked as a general anesthetic. As we started into the room, Allan looked up and said "Is it time now?" and then returned to sleep. He moved onto the table with quite a bit of help. He was very groggy.

I gave him some oxygen to breathe. The anesthesiologist today was Doug. He had come some years ago and stayed to become a senior member of the anesthesiology staff. He's very bright, well-read and also competent technically. I like and respect him, and for this reason I had asked that he work with me on Allan's anesthesia. Usually it is just the luck of the draw which anesthetist and anesthesiologist a patient gets. Anyone, however, may make a special request. Thus Allan had requested me and I had requested the anesthesiologist.

Doug was in early. I had asked him to help me and he wanted to be available.

O.R.

We were ready to go now. I'd practically worn out the batteries on my laryngoscope—opening it and closing it time and time again to make sure the light was okay. Allan was breathing quietly taking the oxygen. When I gave the drugs I said nothing. There was no point in waking him up just to put him to sleep. In another moment his jaw was relaxed and I put in the laryngoscope.

I could not see his cords. I could not even see the arytenoids, the little cartilages at the base of the trachea. The anesthesiologist asked me "Pressure?" He meant did I want him to press down on the neck so I could see better whether the larynx was anterior. "Yes, please," I replied.

He pressed down. I still saw nothing.

"Try it anyway," he advised. "He looks very anterior."

I passed the tube in gently. I did not think it was in the trachea. We hooked up the breathing circuit and gave him a breath. His chest did not rise, no breath sounds were heard. The tube was in the esophagus. I quickly pulled it out and inserted a plastic airway. Ordinarily I would look again after ventilating the patient, but this was not ordinary—this was Allan. "Switch with me," I said. "You do it, Doug."

"You don't want to try again? I know you can do it. You're just nervous," he said.

"Please. Just go ahead." I was ventilating him by mask now.

Quickly we switched places; my hand was shaking. I felt I was not breathing at all. The anesthesiologist asked for a smaller size endotracheal tube. While I set it up, he ventilated Allan. I cut off an inch and a half on the end of the tube, inserted a stylette so it would not bend on insertion, and tested the balloon to make sure there was no leak in it. I moved suction up to where we could reach it, since many times the stimulus of the larynoscope causes increased secretions in the mouth. He took a look and slipped in the tube. No sweat! I was grateful. A part of me wanted to try again, but I had made myself step aside: I knew it was best for Allan.

I hooked up the anesthesia circuit and put Allan on the respirator. I gave him the medication I like—a little morphine and a muscle relaxant. I wanted him to be comfortable when he woke up. I could feel that I was starting to relax now. Allan was no longer Allan. He was just my patient, and I needed to watch not only him but the surgeon too. When doing a TURP the surgeon must be reminded of the time every fifteen minutes he is cutting or resecting. It is important that he not cut for more than an hour. With these reminders he can set his pace. The reason for limiting the time he's permitted to cut is that all the time he's working, an irrigating solution called glycine is going into and out of the patient's urinary tract. This is to keep the small pieces of prostatic tissue, called chips, moving to the outside and to keep good visibility for the surgeon, who is doing the procedure under direct vision through a resectoscope. If too much glycine is absorbed by the patient, it starts to deplete the body of sodium, a vital mineral. Without adequate sodium levels, the heart will not function; indeed, the patient may arrest.

Allan's prostate was not too big. He'd gotten it taken care of within a normal time span. After forty minutes of cutting, Dr. Kaye looked up. "I'm finished now. Just give me a few minutes to control bleeding, and then we'll go home."

I took Allan off the respirator and started to get him back breathing on his own. As soon as the doctor put an indwelling catheter in, I switched off the nitrous oxide and reversed the muscle relaxant. I suctioned Allan and took out the tube.

Allan's legs had been up in stirrups for the operation, causing the blood from the legs to flow into his trunk. As soon as circulation was restored, I had to recheck his blood pressure. Some patients become shocky when the legs are put down, either from insufficient fluids or excess bleeding without adequate replacement. It's safer to know and correct this immediately than to take an unstable patient into the recovery room.

Allan's blood pressure was fine—Dr. Kaye had waited for me to take it before going upstairs to see Margot.

"Let her know she can come down to recovery in about half an hour," I told Dr. Kaye. "He'll be fully alert by then."

Allan was opening his eyes and coughing as we wheeled him through the hall. "Margot," he called. I tried talking to him, but it was too early yet. "Margot, Margot," he was calling.

Don't worry, Allan, I thought, nothing could keep her away.

I was completely whipped—mentally. I went into the female lounge for coffee. I was thinking how right Vi was: "Anesthesia is tough. You'll be buying a lot of unnecessary stress." I'll never agree to put a friend to sleep again—it isn't worth it.

I opened the door to the lounge. I guess I must have looked just the way I felt. Joan was waiting for a case. "What's up, kid?" she asked. I told her all about Allan.

"Boy, you better learn early not to do your friends. It's not good for your coronaries."

As she finished speaking, there was a sharp knock on the door. Herb, one of the GYN attendings, stood there, hesitating to come in.

"Ladies, are you decent?" he asked with a smile.

"Yes, damnit," called one of the O.R. nurses. "Come back later, honey. We'll help you out."

"I'm looking for Joan. Is she in here?"

"Yo, Herb. I'm here. They're not quite ready in the room. Sit down. Join us for a cup of coffee."

"Who are you ripping apart this morning, girls? Hope it isn't me." Herb had completed a residency at MCG two years ago so he knew all the gossip—old and new. He poured himself coffee and sat down in the chair next to Joan.

"We're talking about taking care of friends—you know, putting them to sleep, Herb," Joan started.

Herb interrupted immediately. "Friends? How about family? How about a guy who delivered his own kids? This guy had a kind of a God complex. He figured that no one could do it as well as he could, so he delivered his own wife four times. Me, I think it's kind of weird. I took my wife to the best OB guy I know and let him take care of her. I'm too involved to be able to think clearly in a situation like that. Well, to get back to the story. This guy was married to a woman much younger than he was—over twenty years younger. He was quite successful, and she was very beautiful. I think he showed her off like his swimming pool, his Georgian house—you know, the whole thing fit a certain image—a fantasy he had in his mind.

"Well, they had these kids. She worked—she was in advertising—and the governess brought up the kids. The three oldest were girls, and when they finally got the boy, they figured they could quit.

"When his wife was in the hospital having the fourth baby, she met this resident in OB. The husband was thinking of taking him in as a partner. To make a long story short, the wife and the resident ran off together. They're in Arizona now. The husband and the four kids stayed here. He's remarried and living in the same place. Everyone is waiting to see what happens when this wife gets pregnant—to see whether or not he'll deliver her too."

"Joan, they're ready in your room now," the intercom announced. Joan left the room.

Herb got up. "Weird, it's really weird to me. Here we have all these guys—skilled practitioners—and this man up and delivers his own wife. At a time when you need to be really objective, you should stay away from friends and family. You do no favor to your patient and you certainly are putting the screws to yourself."

"Okay, okay, Herb, I get your drift. I don't need convincing after today. I'll keep my friends friends and my patients patients."

The phone rang. "It's for you, Barrie," the O.R. nurse said. "Your next patient is here."

"I'm on my way."

My next patient was waiting for me in the preanesthesia room—both parents at his side. He was sound
asleep.

Craig was a beautiful child, blond. Lying there, he
looked like an angel. His father assured me he was
anything but. The parents gave me the history. He
had been in good health until the night before, when
he went to sleep sort of cranky; he woke up at 5:00
A.M. and vomited once or twice; diarrhea a little
later, temperature 101 degrees, pain in the right
lower abdomen.

"It sounds like a classic case of appendicitis to me,"
I told the parents.

"That's what our doctor said too. He told us to
meet him here at the hospital. We live in the neighborhood."

I looked at Craig and decided to try to "steal"
him—not literally, although he was cute enough for
that. When we talk of "stealing" a child in anesthetic
terminology, we mean anesthetizing the sleeping child
without waking him. This means that the child will
never have to undergo what might prove to be a
frightening experience. The technique requires cooperation, skill, and great coordination by at least three
people—the anesthetist, the anesthesiologist, and the
circulating nurse.

I told Raj, my anesthesiologist, that I was planning
to "steal" Craig. He had no objection.

When Raj came in to see Craig, I introduced him
to the parents. After an exchange of *How do you do*'s
I added that they were lucky to have Raj, that he's
terrific. "He's my brother," I said. They looked con-

fused. "Oh, yes," I continued, "he's definitely the black sheep of the family."

We all laughed. It relaxed them a bit.

I told the parents what we intended to do. "Your little boy will simply continue to sleep just as he is now. He won't feel the mask being placed over his face. He'll never know about starting the IV. It's a great technique for the child. I love it."

The surgeon came and off we went to the O.R. We moved the bed slowly and quietly. We did not want anything to awaken Craig. We got into the room and told the circulating nurse that we planned to "steal" Craig. She was experienced in pediatrics, had helped us before. I checked that all was in readiness. It was. I moved the anesthesia machine close to Craig's bed and turned on the nitrous oxide and oxygen. I gently taped a precordial stethoscope onto his chest: I needed to monitor his heart rate. I slipped my hand with the mask next to his face. He was sleeping peacefully. For a few moments I held the mask near him. Then as his level deepened, I gently turned him on his back. I supported his airway by holding up his chin; he was breathing on his own. Raj was putting on the EKG leads and hooking up the machine. While I was cutting in the Halothane, Raj put on the blood pressure cuff. As soon as Craig was deep enough, Raj started the IV. My intubation equipment was ready. By the time the IV was secured Craig was deep enough to intubate without using a muscle relaxant. I slipped in the tube and we were ready to go.

The intern was starting to prep Craig. I had him at

a good anesthetic level and in another moment his
surgeon would start the operation.

The appendectomy went quickly. I had Craig
breathing throughout the case. The appendix was
indeed inflamed. The closure was speedy and
uneventful. When we were finished and had Craig on
his way to the recovery room, the surgeon called the
parents.

Craig was still sleeping. He looked exactly as he
had in the preanesthesia room. We had placed him
on his side to prevent any possible aspiration.

His parents looked at him fondly. "It's all over, is
it?" they asked the surgeon.

"Yes, it is, and he did really well," he replied.

Craig stirred a bit but still did not wake up. I knew
that when he did he would not know what happened.
He wouldn't experience that awful trauma about
anesthesia that I had had. I came out of the recovery
room smiling. I met Rajah in the hall.

"So we stole another one successfully, huh, Barrie?"

"Yes, Raj, we sure did."

I thought back about another child I had. She was
having tubes put in her ears for recurrent middle-ear
infections. She came from a foundling home. No
parent accompanied her. No one could get near her.
There was no reasoning with her: as soon as someone
approached her she yelled and kicked. We spent almost half an hour trying one approach after the
other. Nothing worked. Finally the resident and the
anesthesiologist grabbed her and held her down. I
gave her a shot of Ketamine and waited until she got
sleepy. It was the only way to get a mask on her. I

thought of the easy way Craig went to sleep compared to the really hard time the little girl had.

Oh, well, I thought, maybe she'll grow up to be a nurse anesthetist.

XVIII

What a good five weeks I'd had, I thought to my-self—no assignment to the heart room, easy calls, nice cases. It was definitely one of my "up" periods. I hated the ups and downs of anesthesia, but it did seem that the up periods were extending in length and the downs had temporarily faded from my memory. I was feeling confident. And God knows, I needed to feel confident today. I was scheduled for a neuro case, and there you need to have everything go-ing for you. I had known about the case for a couple of days now. Louis, one of the neuro residents, had told me all about Glenn.

It was a festive time in the hospital—these weeks before Christmas. Every patient floor, every unit, was busy with decorations. Anyone with talent was pressed into service. Each unit wanted to win the dec-orating contest. The O.R. schedule was very heavy now. All the doctors and patients wanted their sur-gery done before the holiday. Groups of volunteers visited the hospital singing Christmas carols. Dona-tions came too—toys for the children, other gifts for the adults. Vi hung a list for us prior to making up the holiday time schedule. We were asked to volunteer: Christmas Eve and Day and New Year's Eve and Day. If we did not volunteer, we would be assigned. As a new employee I would have to work one of the holidays. I selected Christmas.

Then there were the parties. Each floor had one. The specialty units did too—I.C.U., C.C.U., E.R., O.R., R.R., and anesthesia. So many of the parties were held on the same day you had to select the one you really wanted to go to. Only soft drinks were served at these parties: liquor was not permitted on the hospital premises. But the food—they'd told me about the food. People from other countries cooked the holiday specialty of their native land—curried goat, pansit, calalou, pepper pot, Szechuan chicken.

And in the midst of all this festivity was Glenn. He was a restless young man who could not seem to find his niche. Glenn had been to college and was bored by it. He had worked for his father, and was disgusted by it; he'd hung out with his friends doing nothing— and couldn't handle it; done heavy construction work with other friends—and couldn't handle that either. He was getting fearful that he'd never find himself. His parents were about to write him off. They couldn't relate to him at all. They gave him everything. He gave them nothing. Three weeks ago Glenn had started to black out, black out and have seizures.

His father had gotten upset—had figured Glenn was doing drugs. He had sat down for a man-to-man talk with his son—with no results. His mother had cried and wrung her hands. She had begged and pleaded with him—with no results. His sister had taken him to a doctor, who admitted him to MCG.

All the tests were essentially negative, except the

brain scan. It showed one area which looked somewhat abnormal—nothing definitive—just a problem
area. The doctor spoke to Glenn and his folks and
laid it out to them. Ten years ago no one would have
even discovered the suspicious place: diagnostic tools
were not available. Even now many doctors would be
in favor of just observing him for a while to see what
developed. But Glenn's doctor wanted to operate: he
felt it was either an abscess or a tumor. He asked
Glenn and his parents to think about it: he'd be back
the next day. Glenn was all for the operation. He
hated the seizures. He hated the blackouts. He hated
his life. Maybe the surgery would change his luck, he
felt. His mom cried and wrung her hands. She never
made decisions anyhow. It was up to his dad.

His dad called in consultants, who also felt that
surgery should be done. He decided to let the neurosurgeon go ahead and operate. Glenn was his son—his
only son.

I met Glenn and his folks in the preanesthesia
room. Usually parents are allowed to accompany only
young children. Glenn was twenty-two years old, but
all three of them felt the need to be together at this
time. Now they watched me as I got things ready for
Glenn's anesthesia. In addition to the usual setup we
wanted to have constant blood pressure monitoring
and an accurate measure of fluid balance, so I set up
an arterial and CVP line.

Glenn was a husky young man with plenty of
muscles from that construction work. He had long
blond curls and a heavy beard. "I'm going to look
like a Hare Krishna," he told his mom. "Please," he
asked me, "ask the doctor to shave off *all* of my hair.

I don't want to have hair on one side and look like a freak, okay?"

The resident and I wheeled Glenn into the O.R. He moved to the table with ease and lay quietly napping from the premedication and the additional drugs I had given him. I got everything ready and put him to sleep. He never really had a chance to get frightened. He never saw the huge tables with their awesome-looking instruments. He never saw the headlights, the saws, the razors. He never saw a thing.

Once he was asleep I positioned all my equipment so that I was out of the way of the surgeon and assistant. Glenn had a catheter in his bladder to measure his ouput. He had a needle in his spine to draw off spinal fluid if there was swelling of the brain. He had a tube passed through his mouth to his esophagus so that I could hear breath and heart sounds: his airway would be far away from me. I would have to rely on my eyes, my ears, and my monitoring equipment: the I.V., the arterial line, the CVP, the EKG.

While I was getting everything set, Rick, the neurosurgeon was busy too. First he shaved Glenn's beautiful hair—all of it, I reminded him—with a barber's clipper. That took almost all the hair off. Next he took a long, wicked-looking straight razor and took off the remainder of the hair until Glenn's scalp gleamed. He did indeed look like the Hare Krishnas.

While Louis prepped the head, Rick went out to scrub. When he came back, he and Louis began the draping. Glenn's head rested on a round rubber cushion called a doughnut so that it would not move around as Rick worked. The two doctors placed towels and sheets over and under Glenn's head. The drapes extended the length of Glenn's body and were clipped on tall poles on my side so that I was completely "draped out" of the operating area. The scrub nurse had a special table used only for neurosurgery. After all the draping was completed the circulating team—there were usually two people for craniotomies—moved the large heavy table into place. Except for the open heart room, this was the procedure that required the most instruments. You never knew what you'd find here, so almost every instrument had to be laid out. In other procedures you could keep a majority of the instruments on the "back table" and the scrub nurse would quickly reach back if one were needed. Here, the few seconds that this would take could not be spared.

Rick drew lines on Glenn's skull indicating where the incision would be. Then he made his incision in Glenn's scalp and peeled back one area. It made me think of the days when people were actually scalped. Next, Rick took a saw and cut a window out of Glenn's thick, tough skull bone. Something pinkish-whitish showed through where the bone had been removed. It looked quite swollen.

"Take 50 cc off," Rick said. I reached under the sterile drapes and removed a little less than two ounces of spinal fluid. I went to discard it and a little spilled: it was clear and warm and a little sticky. I shivered.

Rick opened the dura—the covering of the brain—and peeled it aside gently. There it was in front of us: Glenn's brain. Everyone took in a breath.

I looked around. Two medical students, the resident, the anesthesiologist, the circulating nurse,

Rick, and I were all staring at a portion of Glenn's brain. But the only one who knew what he was looking at and could do something about it was Rick.

No one spoke for a few moments. Rick sighed.

"Why are you sighing, Rick?" I asked. "What do you see?"

"Well, Barrie, if you look at this brain, you will see that much of it looks like a bunch of wrinkled worms, with convolutions running this way and that, in a seemingly regular pattern." I went around to the head of the table. The respirator breathed for Glenn. "Now—look at the area right in the front. What do you see?"

"Well, it looks sort of stretched out—tense."

"Very good. So it does."

"And what does it mean, Rick? That something is under there pressing on it to stretch it out?"

"Exactly."

"And what is that something?"

"That's what we're here to find out. It's either a tumor or an abscess, and it does not look like an abscess to me."

I returned to Glenn's side.

"Brain needle, please," Rick asked the scrub nurse. He plunged the needle in and withdrew some fluid. It looked yellowish and thick.

"Smell it," Rick said to the medical student. "Is it foul smelling?"

"No, sir."

"Damn, then it isn't pus. Here, let me smell it. No, it's not pus."

With very delicate instruments he probed Glenn's brain. As he went further, he shook his head. He took a couple of pieces of brain tissue for the pathologist to examine.

When she came to the door, she asked him, "What have you got here, Doctor?"

"I'm not sure. It looks bad to me," he replied. "This is a twenty-two-year-old boy with a three-week onset of seizures. Do a frozen section on it, will you?"

She stayed away a long time. When she returned, she looked glum. "I'm not certain—you'll have to give me more specimen—but I think it's a glioblastoma. I'll wait. Give me some more."

Rick gave her two more bits of tissue. Some bleeding started.

Louis tried to keep a clear field for Rick by suctioning away the blood. He was a little too vigorous.

"Watch what you're doing, God damn it. This is his brain. Can't you be a little more gentle?"

Louis looked up, startled.

"I'm sorry. I'm upset." Rick apologized.

The bleeding was under control now. Rick put little pieces of felt moistened with a salt solution on the exposed area. He did not want the tissue to dry out.

There was nothing to do but wait. No one spoke. The only sounds were the beeping of the EKG monitor and the whooshing of the ventilator. Rick and Louis sat with their arms held high, wrapped in sterile towels to maintain sterility. They were considered "sterile" only from the waist up.

Suddenly Rick jumped up. "I'm going out to see what she's doing. Put out another gown and gloves for me. I'll be back as soon as I find out."

We looked at one another—and waited some more.

O.R.

Finally we heard footsteps in the corridor. Our door was open a few inches. It was so hot in the room. We never could regulate the heat on warmer days. Rick came back into the room. He held out his hands. The circulating nurse helped him peel off his gloves. He ripped off his gown. Silently he regowned and regloved. No one dared to speak.

"The pathologist said it's definitely a glio—highly malignant and very rapid growing," Rick said in a flat tone. "There's not much I can do. We're in his dominant hemisphere. If I go poking around now, I may impair important functions—and for what? It's only a matter of time. We'll try chemo or radio therapy, but at his age . . ."

Rick closed the dura. He held up the section of bone he had removed, drilled some little holes in it for drainage, put the piece of bone back, sewed up the scalp, and put on a big dressing.

I turned off my agents, gave 100 percent oxygen, took the tube out, and moved Glenn to his bed.

He wouldn't have to worry about what to do with his life. It would be over—very soon.

What awful things can happen to the human body—things that with all our skill we cannot fix. This was one of those times. And tonight was Christmas party night. How easy it would be to skip. I usually avoid hospital parties anyway, and I hadn't planned on going to any.

But I needed to get this afternoon out of my head so I did a quick double take. I'd go to the OB-GYN party—the biggest and best of the parties, everyone said.

Maybe Marty Stevenson would be there. I hadn't heard a word from him since the night we'd had dinner. I'd missed one party with him. Maybe I could make up for that tonight.

XIX

The annual OB-GYN Christmas party, held in the residents' quarters right off the OB service, was famous throughout the hospital. An invitation was something to be sought after: outsiders were not permitted. Other parties could be crashed at will, but anyone who tried to get into this one was unceremoniously thrown out, literally or figuratively, by the OB-GYN residents. In addition to the house staff, attendings, nurses, technicians, aides, clerks, and secretaries who worked in the OB-GYN departments and clinics, invited guests included members of the O.R. and anesthesia departments.

No expense was spared by the chief of service. He himself would put in an appearance very early on, they said, but very briefly. He was fully aware of what went on at these parties, had no objection, but did not want to get involved.

Each year the party had a different ethnic theme—since about half of the residents came from other lands. There would be enough food to feed a regiment, and the chief resident, who was on call for the night, would act as bartender, since he was not permitted to drink. If for some reason he was called out, a junior attending would take over the bar.

The party, it seemed, was always held on a Friday night around the middle of December. They wanted as many people as possible to come, and had found by experience that this was the best time to hold it. Each attending obstetrician-gynecologist was assessed twenty-five dollars. Since there were over fifty of them, this created a sizable sum. Any additional expense—and there usually was—was carried by the chief himself. The party was always catered by the best restaurant available, in line with the ethnic theme.

This year the theme was to be Chinese, and the food, I had been told, was coming from my favorite Chinese restaurant, Szechuan Kitchen on First Avenue. I knew it would be sensational.

I decided I'd wear my mink to the party. It was ten years old and had been sitting in my closet entertaining the moths since my days as a nursing administrator. I used to wear it all the time back then. Now there were few occasions on which I felt it was really appropriate. At least one advantage to having mink these days is that you don't have to be dressed to the teeth to wear it. I love that. I'm a casual dresser. Years of having to dress well and be on constant parade had turned me off the dress scene. I wore a pair of tapered black silk pants with a lovely matching red and black tunic top.

The party was given for people associated with the OB-GYN service only. Mates were definitely off limits. I had heard advance reactions to this—some people looked forward to it. Others planned to go early and leave early. But at least everyone knew what he was getting into. I planned to leave early—that is, unless Marty was there. If he were, I'd play it be ear. I was annoyed I hadn't heard from him, but maybe there was a good reason.

The party started at about five to permit people who could not come later in the evening to put in an appearance. Some of the attendings wanted it that way. "Hell, we're paying twenty-five dollars, we might as well get something out of it," was the way one of them put it.

I had walked the dog and worked out at the club before dressing for the festivities, so it was about seven when I arrived.

Because we were not in the hospital proper, we could have liquor—and there was plenty of it. It turned out to be one of the responsibilities of the chief resident to keep it in a special closet, to which only he held the key. There was a full selection of drinks, not just a lethal punch. A large garbage can (clean of course) held an extra large plastic bag filled with ice.

The room was crowded. People congregated in three main areas—the bar, the food, and the music—and in that order. I said "Hi" to Joan and Bill, who were sampling the punch, and Estelle, one of the midwives. I'd always be grateful to Estelle, because whenever I'd been in OB, she'd always been gracious and helpful. Even now she greeted me warmly. "Barrie, welcome. Your first OB-GYN party, huh? Have fun." I felt more at ease. I knew many of the people there, I'd heard a lot about this party, but it was nice to be welcomed just the same.

I looked around for a safe place to put my coat. I was also looking for Marty, but he wasn't there. Ah, well, maybe he'd be along later. My friend Ralph offered to lock the coat in his closet. I began to feel kind of silly for having worn it. If I'd worn my sheepskin coat, I could have hung it anywhere. But I took Ralph's offer.

The party looked very successful as far as I could see. The entire OB staff was there: attendings, residents, midwives, nurses, aides, secretaries, clerks. A few people from GYN were huddled together over in a corner. We from anesthesia tried to mingle: they always accused us of sticking together and talking shop.

I had gone over to get myself a glass of wine and something to eat and was just debating whether to have the chef's special chicken or the shrimp with walnuts, when a quiet deep voice behind me said, "Go ahead, live a little, have them both." I turned around. It was Marty looking very good. He was beautifully dressed in a pair of gray slacks, a light blue turtleneck sweater, and a navy-blue blazer. I looked up at him and felt weak.

I also felt somewhat uncomfortable, though—after all, I hadn't heard from him at all. We started talking about silly things, the food, the music, people we both knew. After a while he started describing an OB-GYN convention he'd been to in San Francisco. "Barrie, it was a lousy conference, but I love the Coast. I took three weeks off after the conference— one week I spent with my folks. The other two weeks

I just relaxed. I really needed it." Thank God he was not giving me some routine about why he hadn't called. He was letting me know in his own quiet way. I was happy. I wanted to have a good time tonight, I wanted it to be with Marty. His very look said "Come with me."

I tried to be cool. Marty sampled some of the food. "Hey, this is good, Barrie." He wolfed it down. I bet he hadn't had anything to eat since breakfast. These OB-GYN guys lived on some rat race, I thought. Who'd ever want to get mixed up with one of them? I would.

They were playing some slow music, for a change. "I'm too old for the disco bit," I told Marty.

"I'm glad to hear you admit that, Barrie. I can't handle it either." He laughed. "Let's try this." He held out his arms. He felt good too—strong, at ease. I moved closer to him.

Soon, there might just as well not have been a party going on for all the attention either of us paid the others. "We should mingle, Marty," I said to him at one point.

"I'm happy the way I am. Damn, I do what *they* want all year long. Tonight I'm not interested in politics or any of the rest of it. Let's you and me mingle, the hell with them," he murmured in my ear.

"Suits me," I sighed, and moved still closer. We really were not dancing at all at this point, merely rubbing up against one another in time to the music.

"Who's home at your house, Barrie?" he whispered in my ear.

A shiver went through me. "Only my dog—and she loves men," I responded.

"Why don't you get your coat, and I'll take you home?" We had drifted over to one of the windows. A heavy snow had started sometime earlier, and from what we could see, a couple of inches were already on the ground. "You don't want to try to get a cab in all this snow, do you? I'm parked right around the corner—in the No Parking zone: you know what MD plates can do. But if this is going to be a blizzard, I want out of that spot."

"I'll get my coat," I replied. I tried to remember where I put it. Ah, yes, I reminded myself, in Ralph's closet. I looked over the entire room. The lights were dim, an aroma of grass hung over the place, people were definitely mellow now. But where was Ralph? I couldn't find him anywhere.

I knew that the only one sure to be sober by now would be the bartender.

"Phil," I asked, "have you seen Ralph lately?"

"Why do you want to know, Barrie?" he countered.

"Well, I had him lock up my coat in his closet, and I'm ready to leave now."

"Barrie, I think you're out of luck. I saw him go into his quarters about a quarter of an hour ago and he was with that nurse from GYN who has the hots for him."

"Phil, I need my coat. It's snowing out, and I want to get home."

"What's your rush? The evening is young. You and Marty seem to have a lot to say to one another. What's your problem?"

"Well . . ." I sort of drifted off. I had no intention of explaining the situation to Phil. He was

278

known as the department gossip, and it was a well-deserved title. He was a good guy, but if I could help it I did not want to be on his agenda the next day.

I drifted back to Marty.

"What's happening?" he asked.

I explained the situation and he listened carefully. "Let's go over to his room and see if we can get it, first. If not, we'll think of something else," he said.

We went around to Ralph's room. Faint music could be heard from within. I knocked softly. "Ralph," I called, "it's Barrie. Could you let me have my coat?" No answer. I rapped loudly and repeated my request. No answer.

"Ralph," Marty said in his quiet, authoritative voice, "this is Marty Stevenson. Please give Barrie the coat, will you?"

No answer. And the music that he heard was no longer audible. Silence—only silence. We looked at one another and started to laugh.

"Hell, you can't blame the son of a bitch, can you, Barrie? Would you come out for a damn coat at a time like this?" he asked.

"I guess not," I replied grumpily, "but what am I supposed to do now?"

"Go powder your nose or something. Then meet me at the elevator in about ten minutes. I'll see what I can come up with. Okay?"

"Great," I replied. Once in the ladies' room I thought what an exceedingly stupid thing I had done to let Ralph lock up that coat. When I returned to the elevator, Marty was waiting.

"Come with me, Barrie. It's all set," he said.

"What's all set, Marty?"

"I borrowed a set of keys to Laurie's room. She's on duty on the labor floor, they told me. The place is popping. She'll never get back to her room tonight. If it quiets at all, she'll sleep over there. We can wait out the storm, make one of our own, and wait for your coat or whatever, there. Is that okay with you, Barrie?"

"Yes, it is," I replied. I told myself the matter was out of my hands now. After all, I couldn't go out into the cold without getting pneumonia.

Laurie was one of the first-year residents. She had a double room, warm and friendly. My poor dog would get no walk tonight. She'd have to use her papers. I'd make it up to her tomorrow. Tonight belonged to me. I'd waited for it long enough.

Marty turned on a small light on one of the night tables. Then he came over and put his arms around me. "It's time we got really acquainted," he said.

He lifted my tunic over my head, then he came up behind me and unhooked my bra. He had his arm around me as he helped me out of my pants. Then he turned me toward him. "How lovely you are," he said. He undressed quickly. I gasped. He was beautiful: slim and muscular. He took me in his arms again and we lay down together. "I've been waiting for you for a good little while now," he told me. He had no idea how long I'd been waiting for him.

He was skillful and gentle, and carried me with him. And when we were both happy, he snuggled closer. I loved it. I loved the togetherness of our lovemaking as much as the actual sex.

O.R.

We fell asleep—I had no idea what time it was and could not care less. I was off the next day. It was still dark when I woke up. For a moment I didn't know where I was. Marty stirred and turned toward me. We held each other. This time we knew a little more of what we each liked. It was slower and better—yes, better than the first time and the first time had been very good.

We sat up after a while. I glanced at Laurie's clock. It was 4:30 A.M. We showered together and dressed. Marty offered to make one more effort to get the damn coat. I was combing my hair when he went out to tackle Ralph again. He returned empty-handed. "No luck," he said, "but don't worry. I'll bring the car around to the ambulance entrance. You'll only have to walk a few steps. Meet me down there in about five minutes."

I went down and tried the emergency door. It was open. I didn't know what I would have done if it hadn't been. Marty brought the car around and I hopped into a maroon Mercedes. What else for a successful OB-GYN man?

He drove slowly. There was almost no traffic. The snow was sticking. "Let's say goodnight now, Marty," I said. "You'll never find a place to park around here. Just leave me off in front of the house." I leaned over to kiss him.

"I'll call you soon, Barrie," he said. "This has been a special Christmas for me."

"For me, too, Marty."

I slammed the door and ran into my lobby. The doorman looked half-asleep but he woke right up when he saw my outfit. "Well, madam," he said. "Good evening, and good night. Looks like it was," he muttered.

It was, it was indeed!

XX

I was still thinking about Marty and the terrific time we'd had on Friday night when I came to work on Monday morning. I was thrilled with my assignment: OB. Maybe I'd get to see him. It would be exciting to exchange glances with him, chat casually, maybe even work together. Watch it, I said to myself, you remember what happened with Greg. Let's not get into that again. I removed the beeper from the drawer and picked up the phone.

"This is Miss Evans, anesthesia. I'm on call for OB. I'm carrying beeper number 43836."

"Hello, Sylvia, Barrie. I'm on call with you today. How are things down there today? You busy? Not too, huh? Okay, try and keep it that way. See you soon."

I had checked in with both the operator and the labor floor. I gathered some equipment that might be needed, a fresh supply of Pentothal, and made my way to OB. Once things were in order down there I could come and go as I pleased. They could reach me on the beeper.

Obstetrical anesthesia had changed quite a bit since the time I had been a nurse on labor and delivery in the heyday of the sedation era. In those days a patient in labor had to be under almost constant observation since she could tell us nothing—she was too sedated. We took a patient to the delivery room when she sounded or looked ready—she was never able to verbalize that the baby was coming. "I want to be awake for conception only; then wake me again when it's toilet-trained" was the wish of many women. Obstetricians complied with their wishes and kept their patients "snowed."

Since there was no way we could get these patients to understand us, there was no way we could get them to push during the second stage of labor—when the cervix is open and the baby descends the birth canal. That did not matter if the labor was strong and the pelvis adequate—and if there had been previous children. Many women, however, needed time to push the head down—especially women who were having their first babies, as they needed to push and stretch out their tissues. Large numbers of forceps deliveries were done.

Although there was natural childbirth back then, it was just becoming popular and only a minority of patients took classes, had their husband in the labor room, or had rooming-in. So anesthesia played a gigantic role on our service. There was an anesthetist and an anesthesiologist assigned to obstetrics each day, with call rooms located right on the labor floor. They were on for a twenty-four hour stint and they worked very hard. In those days we used spinal anesthesia almost exclusively for cesarean sections. For vaginal deliveries we used deep general anesthesia by mask.

O.R.

* * *

I threw away the day-old Pentothal and replaced it with the syringes I had brought from upstairs. I went into the section room and checked all the anesthesia equipment. I went over to the Kreiselman, the crib where the baby would be placed. Although suction and oxygen were part of the machine itself, our emergency equipment was kept on a lower shelf. I pulled it out and checked it. I picked up the laryngoscope with its tiny blade for babies and clicked it open. It lit brightly. I closed it and put it away.

The Kreiselman started me thinking back to my initial introduction to OB, so many years ago. When I had graduated from nursing school I'd requested OB as my first choice. I spent six weeks in the nursery and then was assigned to the labor floor. Even in those days of heavy anesthesia a baby fooled us once in a while. I had been there about a week when we received a call from the clinic: a patient was in active labor. They told me to take a stretcher and go upstairs and get her. She seemed very active, and when I came back the supervisor took one look at the patient and called Tom, the chief resident. We never even got the lady into a bed. Tom examined her on the stretcher and said, "Take her in. No rush. She's a primip." (A primipara is a woman having her first baby.)

I took the lady to the delivery room with the intern. He left us in the room and went to join Tom at the scrub sink. "Miss," said the patient, "I think my baby's coming."

I went out to the scrub area and told Tom.

"Yeah, yeah, I know. Don't worry about it, she's a primip. She has lots of time."

I returned to the patient, put her on the delivery table and placed her legs in stirrups.

"Oh," screamed the patient, "it's coming, it's coming."

Once again I went to the scrub area. This time I did not leave the delivery room. I just poked my head out. "Please hurry," I urged Tom and the intern. "She says it's coming."

"Listen," Tom said, "I am trying to teach this intern how to scrub up for a delivery. If you keep interrupting us, we'll never get done. Go in that room and stay with that patient and do not come out here again. Got it?"

"Got it," I replied.

Another moment passed. "Aggggggggh!" shrieked the patient.

Oh, no, I thought. If I go out there again he'll kill me. I looked down at her perineum. Something black was there—the baby's head was crowning. I knew I couldn't leave her. I didn't dare. I looked out to the scrub area. They were still scrubbing. In another moment the baby's head came out and right after that the rest of the baby. I grabbed it as best I could. I did know to hold it upside down, and that's what I was doing when Tom and the intern came in.

"Damn," Tom said. "Why didn't you let me know?"

So that baby escaped the medications given indiscriminately twenty-five years ago. But since that time the campaign against all medications during

286

pregnancy, labor, and delivery has grown intense—too intense, in my opinion.

I ran into this attitude one night when I was on call. It was 3:00 A.M. and I was sound asleep when the phone rang—it was OB. "We need you," said a commanding voice.

"Coming," I replied. I jumped into my clothes and raced through the hall; it could be anything and two lives were involved.

I entered the delivery room and said "Good morning" to the attending obstetrician. A nurse was over at the Kreiselman getting out some equipment. Another nurse was checking the fetal heart. A technician was gathering up some linens from the floor. A young woman was on the table pushing down with all her might. Her young husband was loaded down with all sorts of things. He had ice chips, a washcloth to wipe her face, a tape recorder, movie camera, and two still cameras. There was no doubt *he* would be very busy here.

"Hi," I said. "My name is Barrie Evans. I'm your anesthetist and I'll be . . ." I was quickly interrupted by the patient. "Anesthetist? I don't want anesthesia! Who called you, anyhow? Get out of here! I'm having my baby naturally."

"My dear," I said when I could get in a word, "let me tell *you* a couple of things. First of all, I was called out of my bed at the request of your physician. I'm here to stand by in case I'm needed to help either you or your baby. Believe me, I'd rather be sleeping than here. That's number one. Secondly, nothing would please me more than just to sit here and not do anything to you. I've been working since 7:00 A.M.

yesterday and I'm not looking for more work. But again, I'm here to help you, your baby, or both—if you need it."

At this point the nurse said, "The fetal heart is 80." Normal is 120–160.

"Outlet forceps, please," the attending requested. "Mary Ann," he said to the patient, "your baby's heart rate is very slow now. You have been pushing for an hour and the head has not made much progress. I'm going to have to do a forceps delivery. Barrie will put you to sleep now—just for a couple of minutes."

"But Doctor!"

"I don't have time to discuss it with you, Mary Ann. Just do as I ask."

Fortunately, Mary Ann already had an IV. Some obstetrical patients refuse to have them—they feel it's unnatural. The reason they need it is first of all to provide adequate fluids at a time when they are working hard and are not permitted to take fluids by mouth. But the main reason for having the IV in, however, is to be prepared in case of fetal distress. If for *any* reason, fetal or maternal, a patient must be put to sleep quickly, having a line in saves time.

Since obstetrical patients are considered to have full stomachs, we use a slightly different technique to put them to sleep: we call it a crash induction. The purpose is to provide as little stimulation as possible, so that the patient will not vomit. I started out by preoxygenating Mary Ann with a mask over her face. I gave a small dose of one muscle relaxant to prevent muscle spasms of the body when I gave the next muscle relaxant (if the patient gets muscle spasm,

288

vomiting may occur). I waited a few minutes for the "pretreatment" to take effect, had suction at hand in case vomiting did occur, then gave the Pentothal and the muscle relaxant and watched the bag until Mary Ann stopped breathing. I removed the mask, positioned the patient, opened her mouth, inserted the laryngoscope, visualized the cords, passed the tube, inflated the cuff, hooked up the tube to the anesthesia circuit, inserted a plastic airway, taped the tube, and ventilated the patient. So Mary Ann kept me busy despite herself.

The doctor needed only about two minutes of anesthesia: the time it took to apply the forceps and pull down and out to deliver the baby's head. After that he wanted his patient awake—and so did I. I used a concentration of nitrous oxide and oxygen, 50 percent of each, in order to give as much oxygen as I could to the baby.

Mary Ann was back breathing within moments, and the doctor told me I could wake her up anytime—he had the head out. I turned off the nitrous, watched her for another minute while giving 100 percent oxygen, and took the tube out. She was alert. "Mary Ann," I said, "your baby is being born now." She tried to focus her eyes on the mirror hanging in front of her. Stuart, her husband, was a whirlwind of activity. He was trying to set up his tape recorder, take movies, and also snap a couple of stills—all at the same time.

There was cord around the baby's neck—the probable cause of the fetal distress—and as the baby came out it was covered by a greenish fluid. Amniotic fluid is clear; the green was caused by meconium: the baby's first stool. When a baby has distress inside the uterus, it responds by opening its rectal sphincter.

In this case the amniotic fluid was only lightly stained, indicating recent distress. When distress is prolonged, the meconium increases, becomes what we call "pea soup" meconium, and is more serious.

We had to make sure that none of the meconium was in the baby's respiratory tract: it can plug an area of a tiny lung and cause pneumonitis.

"I've got some meconium here, Barrie," said the obstetrician. I went over to the heated crib. I set out the laryngoscope with an infant blade, a couple of tiny endotracheal tubes, and an even smaller suction catheter. The obstetrician held the baby upside down to permit drainage of mucus. He had already sucked out the baby's mouth with a bulb syringe. The baby was trying to cry, but it sounded very moist.

I quickly wiped off the baby's face—I wanted to see the color. It was a bit bluish—not too bad. The delivery room nurse put her stethoscope down on the left side of the baby's chest and tapped out the heart rate with her index finger so that as I was working I would know what was happening with the heart rate of the newborn: I inserted the laryngoscope and visualized the cords. They looked okay. I passed the endotracheal tube. I had to be certain no meconium was down there. The baby was breathing—not too well, but adequately. The nurse's tapping slowed in rate. I placed my mouth over the end of the tube and sucked as I withdrew the tube. A small glob of meconium came up through the tube. I oxygenated the baby—it was pinking up now. I went down a second time, passed a sterile suction catheter, and moved it around to make certain I'd gotten everything. The nurse's finger was moving up and down at a rapid rate. It looked like the heart rate was about 160. I sucked once again with my mouth as I was removing the tube. All was clear. I listened to the tiny chest. Both sides were clear—breath sounds were good. The baby was going to be okay. I looked over at Mary Ann and Stuart. They were holding hands and looking toward me anxiously.

"Your baby is okay now," I told them. "Say, what is it anyway?" I asked, uncovering the baby from its blanket. Now that all the excitement was over we could concentrate on happy things. "Boy, that's some son you've got, Mary Ann. You ready to hold him now?" Tears were in Mary Ann's eyes as I put the baby in her arms.

"What's doing with the placenta?" I asked the obstetrician. I didn't want to go back to sleep and get called out again for a retained placenta.

"It's out, no problem. I'm just about finished. Listen, Barrie, thanks a lot."

From the head of the table came a call. "Barrie, can I talk to you a moment before you go?"

"Certainly, Mary Ann. What's up?"

"Barrie, you must think I'm the most stupid person in the world for jumping all over you like that. I feel like a fool. I could have lost my son if you hadn't been here, and here I was yelling at you to go away. I just didn't know any better. Will you forgive me?"

"I will, Mary Ann, because I've run into your attitude before. It doesn't stem from you. It stems from segments of the media and some of the preparation for childbirth programs. They tell you nothing about possible complications. They just stress normality.

"Now, I'm all for normality. If all had been normal with you, I'd be sleeping now. But the reason you go to a doctor, the reason you deliver in a hospital, the reason we cross-match blood and start an I.V., is 'just in case.' And just in case can come up at any time. If that were not so, you could go out and squat under a bush in Central Park or have your baby at home. We are not trying to interfere with your goals. But where you need us, we can help you.

"There is nothing wrong with using anesthesia when it is needed. Sometimes labor is hard and prolonged. A little Demerol is not a sin. If you don't need it, great—but if you do, it doesn't make you a failure.

"Sometimes there is a long, seemingly unending series of back pains caused by the baby's lying posteriorly. Epidural anesthesia can end those pains. If you don't need it, great. If you do, it doesn't make you a failure.

"Sometimes in the second stage of labor, contractions are very severe. Intermittent whiffs of nitrous oxide and oxygen—the anesthesia I just gave you—offer a bit of temporary relief. If you don't need it, great. If you do, it doesn't make you a failure.

"And if, as you have just found out, for some reason you have to go to sleep, that's not a sin either. Mary Ann, we in anesthesia are on your side. Why would we want to do anything to hurt you or your baby? Studies have shown that babies are drowsy for a while after general anesthesia is given to the mother.

Medications do pass the placental barrier. You're sleepy, he's sleepy. But you wake up soon, and so does he. . . . I'm sorry, I'll get off my soapbox. Enjoy your baby."

"Thank you, Barrie. I won't forget what you did."

Everything was ready in the section room. I repeated the check in both delivery rooms. I went outside to "check the board." One entire wall in the doctor's lounge is taken up by a large green blackboard which contains all the information anyone needs to determine what is happening on the labor floor. Starting with the patient's room number, name, and doctor it goes on to indicate how many times the patient has previously been pregnant, which part of the baby is coming first, how low down the baby is lying, a description of the patient's cervix—whether it is long or thinned out and how far open it is—the time of the last examination, and in the last column, any complications. The fastest way you can get an overview of what is happening is to go into the lounge and read.

Of course I had yet another reason for going into the lounge. Maybe I'd see Marty. I didn't see him sitting there. He didn't even have a patient on the board. Damn. A couple of the residents were sitting around reading the paper and chatting.

"Ever get your coat back, Barrie?" Phil inquired.

"Yes." I didn't want to go into any explanation with him. He was always looking for a new tidbit of gossip. "Did you enjoy the party, Phil?"

"As much as I could without drinking, yes. What

293

are you doing up here, Barrie? Someone call you for a problem?"

"Not yet. Just checking. Why, you got one?"

"Not me. We only have one primip and she's almost ready. Kenny's got a postmature primip though. He may have to section her later. We have a third-trimester bleeder on the way in and the midwifing patient is going in now. Not too much."

I sat down and picked up the paper. All the OB-GYN men stopped on the labor floor whenever they were "in the house." Their locker room was there, and even if they had no reason to get into a scrub suit, they'd come and pick up a white coat. Maybe Marty would be coming through. I stopped that thought, put the paper down, stood up and started for the door.

"Where are you going, Barrie? If you're going outside for lunch maybe you could pick up some pizza for me."

"Phil, I'm going to check the patients up here and then I *am* going out. Can you wait about a half hour?"

"Sure. See you later. If I'm not here, page me. Get me two pieces of pepperoni pizza. Here's the money."

"See you later, Phil."

I left the lounge and went outside. I wanted to see each of the patients in labor just to say "Hi" and review their charts. That way, if they needed me, they'd see a familiar face. Joan said I was overdoing it. Her philosophy was "If they need you, they'll call you, otherwise stay away." But OB was in my bones. I loved hanging out on the labor floor. Now, with the added interest, it could get to be a habit. I'd have to watch it.

I decided I'd go out and get lunch now and visit the patients after I ate.

I came back quickly. In OB things could change in one minute and we needed to be available at all times. I brought Phil his pizza and then went to the cafeteria to eat the lunch I had brought for myself—a quart of hot-and-sour soup and an egg roll.

Jeremy was there with a couple of the junior residents. He motioned to me to join them. "Barrie, remember Mr. Macintosh, the aneurysm we did together? Well, he went home. God damn, do you believe it, went home?"

"What about Harry, Jer?"

"Harry, Harry who?"

"The guy with the gunshot wound of the neck."

"Don't know, Barrie. They flew him out to the Coast. His wife wanted him out there. We haven't heard a thing. What are you doing here in the cafeteria, Barrie? You usually eat and run upstairs."

"I'm on call for OB today, Jer. Standing by—what a drag. The time passes so slowly this way."

"Enjoy your breathing time while you've got it."

Jeremy and the boys left, and as soon as I finished my lunch so did I. The board looked just the same when I got upstairs.

I picked up the first chart and entered the patient's room. It was Kenny's patient, Pamela Moore. She was three weeks overdue, having her first baby and not making much progress. A candidate for "section city," I thought to myself.

Two tired-looking people looked up at me as I entered the room. "Pamela Moore?" I inquired. The woman nodded. "Pamela, I'm Barrie Evans. I'm the anesthetist on duty today. I hope you won't be needing my services for anything, but in case you do, I wanted to meet you. How are you doing?"

"Barrie, I'd like you to meet my husband, Jason."

He nodded at me glumly.

"You two seem a little down. Anything I can do?"

Pam and Jason exchanged glances. "I guess this is all anticlimactic to us now. We don't quite know what to do," Pam said weakly.

"Listen, I've done a lot of OB and a fair amount of anesthesia. Why don't you just tell me about it? It might make you feel better."

"Barrie," Pam started, "this has been the longest pregnancy. We tried for three years before I became pregnant and then I must have known the instant I conceived. I've been into maternity clothes for so long now I can hardly remember what I looked like before. I've been having these pains—I know they tell you to say contractions and not pains, but they hurt, no matter what you call them, and I've been having them since 5:00 A.M."

Jason interrupted. "She didn't tell me until seven. I got so excited. I wanted to rush her off to the hospital, but when we called our doctor he said to wait. Hell, I knew the drive to the hospital by heart, we'd done so many practice runs. Pam's suitcase has been packed for weeks."

I smiled. It was a familiar story.

Pam picked up the story. "When I called the doctor back about 8:30 he said to come to the office for a checkup."

Jason interrupted again. "Can you beat that—go to his office for a checkup? Hell, we'd been doing that for weeks and months. It was so routine. God, do I hate to sit in that waiting room with all those pregnant women. Barrie, do you know? Even the brass sculpture on his end table is pregnant."

Pam continued. "After he examined me he told me I was in labor—to come to the hospital. He said it was a good thing my labor had started. He'd have admitted me anyway in another two days to try to induce my labor."

"Maybe I'm missing something, you two. What's making you so low? This all sounds quite normal so far."

"Well, Barrie, when my doctor examined me a little while ago he said I hadn't made progress and he spoke to us about the possibility of a cesarean. That's what's got us down."

"I can understand that. Did he give you any time frame?"

"No, he said he'd come back this evening after his office hours and decide then what to do."

"Barrie," Jason said sheepishly, "we're tired of the whole thing now. I feel like we've been in this hospital forever. We've walked up and down the damned hall till we're sick of it. We've breathed together till we're sick of it. Pam brought a picture from home and concentrated on it while she breathed, like they told us to do in class, and now we're ready to throw darts at the damn thing."

"They won't give me anything but ice chips. I'd love to pour a stiff scotch over them. *That* would be a help—and then they are so short of people here today. Everyone just rushes in and rushes out—except you, of course."

"So, really, you two are in a holding pattern until your doctor comes, aren't you? Try and cool it a bit. Labor is just that. It's hard work. Try to save some of your energy for later, okay?"

"Barrie, I guess it's just that we expected something different. Listen, thanks for stopping by. It's been great to be able to bitch and moan to someone."

"No problem. I'll try to get back to you, if not today, tomorrow. I want to know what you're going to have. Good luck to you both."

I left the labor room and returned to the O.R. lounge. By the time I finished chatting with Pam and Jason the service primip had delivered, the third-trimester bleeder had not yet arrived, and there was only Pam on the board.

Bill was the anesthetist on call for OB for the evening. As soon as he came, I could go home. What a boring day. Finally I saw him coming toward me.

"What's doing in the baby factory, Barrie? Much action on the board?"

"There's only Kenny's primip, postmature with lousy labor. He's coming in later to . . ."

"Stop, Barrie. Let me tell you. He'll get here at about 6:00 or 6:30 after office hours. He'll send her to X ray for pelvimetry, then he'll stimulate her labor with some Pit"—Pitocin—"and long about 2:00 A.M. he'll call me for a section. Is that what you were going to say?"

"Just about. By the way, they also have a third-trimester bleeder on the way in."

"Another possible section, huh, Barrie? That makes two for two. Should be a great night."

"Good luck, Bill—hope you have an easy call."

Vi was waiting for me when I came to work the next morning. "As soon as you've changed, Barrie, go downstairs and relieve Bill. He's doing a section."

I wondered if it was Pam. I arrived downstairs and peeked into the section room. It was empty. I found Bill in the lounge having coffee. "What's up?"

"Barrie, I've been up the whole fucking night. I worked in the O.R. till midnight helping to finish the schedule. As soon as I got to bed they called me from OB—a section—the bleeder. After that there was a premie delivery—I had to stand by for the baby. Everything was okay. I went back to the call room, and I swear it was two minutes later when they called again. Perlman wanted to put on forceps so I dragged myself back for that. He finished about half an hour ago and then they told me Kenny wanted to section his patient. She hadn't made progress and we're waiting for Kenny and Thelma."

"Thelma's on today or was she on call last night?"

"No, she's on today. She'll be here with you. They want an epidural, so I set up for her. Everything's ready. Good night, Barrie."

I went in to see Pam. It was her all right. Thelma had preceded me by two minutes. I could hear her as I entered the room. ". . . your anesthesiologist."

She explained that there are two kinds of anesthe-

Barrie Evans

sia available. One is a general, the kind that puts you to sleep, and the other is epidural. As she started to explain it, Pam interrupted. "I know. We learned about it in preparation for childbirth class. Weren't you the one who came and spoke to us, Doctor?"

She nodded.

"Let me see, you put some sort of needle into my back and put a small tube inside. Then you can give me medication whenever I need it. Is that right?"

"Essentially, yes," Thelma replied.

"What about me?" Jason wanted to know. "I went to class too."

"As soon as the epidural is in, you can come in and remain with your wife," Thelma assured him.

Within a few minutes Jason was all decked out in a green outfit. He looked like one of us now—he whispered to me that he hoped no one mistook him for a doctor. He was going to wait in the lounge while Thelma did the anesthesia. After that, with cap, mask, and even special covers for his shoes, he would come into the operating room. He told me he hoped he could take it.

I assured him I'd be there with them all during the section.

Pam looked grateful.

We wheeled her into the operating room—the labor room nurse and I. I had put leads on her chest and arm for the EKG. I put a blood pressure cuff on her arm and changed the solution in the intravenous bottle, removing the medication which had stimulated her labor. I had Pam sit on the O.R. table with her back to Thelma. I placed her feet on a seat so

300

they would be supported and gave her a pillow to put in her lap. "Push your back out toward the doctor, fold your hands around the pillow, and rest your head on my shoulder," I said.

"You will feel me washing your back now with an iodine solution, and after that you'll feel me touching you. I'll be feeling for landmarks. Next you'll feel a needle stick and a stinging as I put in the local anesthetic," Thelma told her. And that *was* all Pam felt.

After that there was some pressure, and soon they asked her to lie back down. She started to feel heavy in her legs, and pretty soon, wonder of wonders, she could no longer feel her contractions. "Hey, Barrie, this is great. I don't feel a thing. It's like magic."

Kenny and two assistants were scrubbing up at the sinks. One assistant washed Pam's abdomen with iodine after Thelma tested to see that she had the necessary level of anesthesia. Sterile towels and sheets were put in place, and as she looked up, the nurse was leading a pale Jason into the room. "I'm fine now, darling," she told him. He looked relieved. I seated him next to Pam.

"Hey, you two," I whispered, "you're almost there." I was at the head of the table monitoring Pam.

The doctors took their places at the table along with the O.R. nurse who would hand them the instruments. A sheet draped Pam, Jason, and me out of the picture. Thelma and a pediatrician stood off to one side checking equipment at the Kreiselman. For a while all that could be heard was the doctor asking the nurse for instruments. "Second knife, allis, another allis, bandage scissors." In a matter of moments there was a feeling of pressure in her abdomen.

Jason stood up. He couldn't wait any more. Pam was relaxed and tired. She closed her eyes momentarily. Kenny put his hand inside Pam's uterus. "Pressure," he grunted.

The assistant pushed on the top part of the drape. Nothing happened.

Kenny took his hand out and repositioned it. He looked up at the assistant. "Son, when I say push, get your finger out of your asshole and push. Got it?"

"Got it," the assistant said.

The room was still. Now that the uterus was open, the longer it took to get the baby out, the more dangerous it would be for the baby. Having Jason in the room added more pressure to the already pressured obstetrician. One thing we could be happy about was that Pam was not under general anesthesia. Since all the agents used in a general cross the placental barrier, it is important to get the baby out quickly. Here, with an epidural, Kenny had all the time in the world, from an anesthetic point of view.

I stood quietly at the head of the table. Thelma paced up and down like a tiger. The pediatrician clicked the laryngoscope open and shut, open and shut in a nervous rhythm; she was pregnant herself.

Jason turned to me and grabbed my arm. "Barrie, does it always take this long? It seems like forever."

Pam looked up. A tension fell over the room. I could feel everyone waiting for my answer.

"Listen, Jason," I said, "she's made it so comfortable in there, the damn kid doesn't *want* to come out." Everyone laughed, weakly.

"Look up, Pam—you too, Jason," Kenny said. He was holding a pink, slippery infant upside down. The baby was crying lustily. As Kenny held the baby **a** little higher so they could see him, Jason Ennis Moore the third urinated. Tears came to Pam and Jason's eyes. "Our son," they said, and kissed.

XXI

Spring was really in evidence. I had gotten up early and walked to work. I was late, and as always on such occasions, I found myself facing a chart ten inches thick, which I had to digest before putting the patient to sleep, and a patient who seemed to stop me at every turn.

Anyway, I introduced myself and began.

"When did you eat last, Mrs. Martin?"

"Well, now, let's see—when did I eat last? Now that's a good question." I was in trouble. I could see it all coming. "It was about 7:35 P.M.—not true—it was 7:45 P.M. It was somewhere around the middle of ... Well, let's say 7:45 and leave it at that."

"Okay, good. So you ate last at 7:45 last evening and have had nothing to eat or drink today. Is that correct?"

"Nothing to eat or drink today? Well, I did brush my teeth, but I didn't swallow any of the water. And I did have a cigarette. Does that count, a cigarette?"

"Did you eat or drink it?"

"Eat or drink a cigarette? Of course not."

"Then it doesn't count."

"Oh, good. Where were we? Did I eat or drink anything today? Well, dear, I was just wondering whether or not you saw my doctor yet."

"Did you eat or drink anything today?"

"Oh, I really don't know what to say."

"Try yes or no."

"Ha, ha, well I guess in that case it'll be no."

"Have you ever had anesthesia before?"

"Have I ever had anesthesia before? Now that is a joke. This is my fifteenth operation in fifty years. That is, fifteen major ones. I had some minor ones too. One time I had the wart on my foot . . ."

"Could you just bear with me. You say you've had anesthesia before. Now did you have any problems with your previous anesthetics?"

"You bet."

"What does that mean?"

"That means, 'You bet I had problems.' "

"Well, could you tell me what they were?"

"Well, yes, one time they put me to sleep with that mentothal."

"You mean sodium pentothal?"

"Yes, that's what I said, mentothal. Why do you always want to interrupt me?"

"Sorry, do go on."

"Go on? Where was I?"

"Going to sleep with mentothal. Oh my God, you've got me doing it too. Go on, please."

"Anyhow I woke up in the middle."

"In the middle of what?"

"Of the operation. I could hear them talking. I tried to talk too but I couldn't. It was very scary."

"We'll certainly not let that happen again. Any other problems?"

"Oh, yes, one time I got very sick and vomited a lot after the anesthesia."

"Okay, we can give you something for that. Anything else?"

"Yes, one time I didn't wake up for two days."

"Really! Was that before or after the time you woke up in the middle of the operation?"

"Now, how would I remember that, dearie? I've had fifteen operations—that is fifteen major operations."

"Yes, I know, and you've had minor ones too."

"You have a good memory."

"Thanks. Anything else?"

"Once I had a rash when I had a local anesthesia. Oh, yes, and once when I had a spinal I got a headache. One time I couldn't breathe when I was coming out of it. You know, kind of like a choking sensation."

"Anything else?"

"Not that I can think of at the moment."

"Okay, let's go on. Do you take any medications at home regularly?"

"Yes."

"What are they for?"

"Oh, the doctor ordered them."

"Yes, and for what?"

"To make me well."

"You are not well?"

"I told you I have had fifteen operations and you ask me am I well? Of course, I'm not well."

"Do you have any problems with your heart?"

"Yes, I do have them. I get these palpitations. I feel as if my heart is going to jump right out of my

306

mouth. If I open my mouth my heart will jump out. It's very frightening, and then the skipped beats. I get them too; it's a very funny sensation. I get boom, boom, boom and then nothing and then boom, boom, boom and again nothing and then—"

"Do you get them often?"

"What?"

"The skipped beats and the palpitations?"

"No, not often."

"And do you take any medication for them?"

"No, I don't think so."

"That's all—about your heart, I mean?"

"Isn't it enough?"

"It's plenty—let's move on. Do you have any problems with your lungs?"

"You bet I do."

"Yes?"

"Yes!"

"Well, what are they?"

"Well, I have emphysema and I get short of breath. My doctor said it's because I'm too fat. Do you think I'm too fat?"

"Well, let me say this, the body is a machine, and putting extra weight on makes the machine work harder."

"You sound just like my doctor. I used to be able to walk ten blocks. Now I can only walk one or two and then I huff and puff."

"Do you smoke?"

"Yes."

"How much?"

"Well, a lot."

"How much is a lot?"

307

"Just a lot."

"Two packs a day?"

"Probably."

"And how long have you been smoking?"

"I started when I was sixteen."

"And how old are you now?"

"Wouldn't you like to know."

"Look, I'm not asking you these questions for *my* health. I'm asking for yours. How old are you now?"

"I'm sixty-seven."

"So you've been smoking for 51 years, right?"

"Right."

"Two packs a day, yes?"

"Yes. No good, huh?"

"No good. And do you cough up in the morning, Mrs. Martin?"

"You bet I do."

"What color is it?"

"Green—no good, huh?"

"No good. We may have to leave the breathing tube in for a while after the operation. It will help you to breathe and also help us to clear out your lungs. The only thing is, you won't be able to talk while the tube is in."

"Oh, how awful. I love to talk."

"So I've noticed. Let's continue. Any problems with blood pressure, Mrs. Martin?"

"Any problems. Yes, ma'am. Surely, yes."

"High or low?"

"High. No good, huh?"

"No good. Do you take medication?"

"Sometimes."

"What kind?"

"Who knows? It's what the doctor ordered."

"Well, is it a pressure pill or a water pill?"

"I'm not sure."

"Do you take potassium pills or eat oranges and bananas?"

"No. Should I?"

"Well, if you are taking water pills, yes. Maybe you should check with your doctor. Do you have any problems with your liver? Ever had hepatitis—yellow jaundice?"

"Yup, had it twice—once ten years ago and again last year."

"OK, any problems with your kidneys?"

"Kidneys? I only have one kidney. I was born that way. And the one I have is dropped. And I have that burning and itching—and sometimes my urine is bloody."

This cannot go on, I thought to myself. How much can one person have wrong and still function? "Is there anything else you'd like to tell me? Do you have anything false—like your teeth—that comes out?"

"Now, dearie, let's start at the top and work our way down—false or that comes out, you say. Well, I have a wig. I have contact lenses. I had my nose fixed—it's not false but it's not the way God made it. And of course my teeth—you know they are false, a full set of uppers and lowers."

"Have I got all of your history now?"

"Well, you have the medical and surgical part. Do you want to hear the psychiatric end of it?"

"If it's important, of course."

"Well, I've been in and out of hospitals these seven years. Manic depressive, you know. I'm on lithium

309

and it helps. But sometimes I quit taking it and that's when the trouble starts."

"And what are you having today?"

"Having?"

"What operation are they doing today?"

"Oh, I'm not having an operation. It's just an examination. I have some polyps in my intestine. They are going to look and maybe if they can, take them out."

"But that examination, a colonoscopy, is usually done without anesthesia—just a bit of tranquilizer to relax you."

"I know. I'm not planning on having any anesthesia. With all the trouble I've had in the past, I'm planning on 'bite the bullet.' "

" 'Bite the bullet?' I've been talking with you for twenty minutes and you plan not to have anesthesia? Is that right?"

"That's right. Who are you again, miss?"

"I told you when we met. I'm Barrie Evans. I'm a nurse anesthetist."

"Oh—I thought you were the intern. Nice talking to you, miss. See you around, huh?"

I went outside and told my boss. She laughed in sympathy. "Listen, Barrie, you're lucky. What could you use on a patient like that? Hypnosis would be your only safe agent. Why don't you go grab a bite of breakfast? I won't need you for at least half an hour."

A couple of the surgical house staff were in the cafeteria. I sat down to eat with them. They laughed when I told them my tale. "Patients," one said. "If only we could give them a check sheet for the history.

Some places use it but not good old MCG. We're still in the Dark Ages."

The door to the cafeteria opened. A young couple with a baby came in. The baby looked to be about six months old. "Do you remember them?" one of the guys asked. "That baby is alive solely because of our efforts here at MCG. Barrie, did you ever do him? He's had several procedures." He told me the baby's name—it didn't sound familiar. He went on, however, with the baby's history.

"Yes," I interrupted him. "I do know that baby. Wasn't he that premie that Burke and Tim did?"

"Yes, that's the one. He was only three pounds when he had his first operation."

"Boy, I didn't realize he made it. He was so very sick I thought we'd lost him months ago."

The father sat at one of the tables and played with the baby. The mother took a tray and started through the cafeteria line. She smiled shyly at one of the boys sitting with me. "Do you remember me, Doctor?" she asked as she passed our table. "And my son, of course."

"Indeed I do," he replied. "Who could forget such a triumph? We feel as though he's our son, too, you know. With all the time he's spent here at MCG."

"Well, if you want to baby-sit sometimes, he's yours. Otherwise, you'll have a hard time getting him away from his daddy."

We all looked over to the other table. Her husband looked adoringly down at the baby.

"I wonder if she knows what it took to pull that baby through," the resident said. "Looks like it was all worth it, though. I remember one baby we had on our service. She was born here at MCG. She had a lot of congenital anomalies. Some of the things required immediate surgery. Other corrections could only be done when she was older. That kid lived here at the hospital. She knew no other home. We were her family.

"She was three years old by the time all the surgery was over. Three years old and no one wanted her. The mother had vanished long ago. There never was a father on the scene. So we had operated—I think she had at least a dozen procedures done—and when it was all over we sent her to the foundling hospital. Wonder what ever happened to her?"

The door opened again, propelled by a strong hand. The director of nursing stood in the doorway. I really should say filled the doorway, she was so huge. Mrs. Santorini was an imposing-looking woman—large, with black hair, an attitude that was strictly no-nonsense and a chest that could accommodate several rows of medals. I knew her only by sight, by sight and by reputation: they said she was a ball breaker. I had never had contact with her. People said you could hear her before you could see her.

"Do you know Mrs. S?" one of the residents asked.

"I met her here one evening but I really don't know her. They say her husband waits on her hand and foot."

"That's right. Did you ever meet him? He's always bringing food from home. Guido's his name."

"No, I haven't *met* him, but there was a little nervous fellow with her that evening I met her."

"Bald?"

I nodded.

"That's Guido, all right. Don't you report to her? I mean as a nurse anesthetist, isn't she your boss?"

"No, we report to the chief anesthetist, and she in turn to the chairman of the Department of Anesthesiology."

"You are lucky. God help those poor suckers who work for her. Look at them." One had secured a table near the phone, in case one of them got beeped. Mrs. Santorini carried neither a beeper nor a clipboard. They knew where to find her. Another was going through the cafeteria line with Mrs. S. There was no Guido here today. At home or at work, it seemed, she needed someone to wait on her. I did not envy those assistants or supervisors or whoever they were.

As they passed the table at which we were sitting I thought back on my own life and how it had changed over the last few years—changed for the better since I gave up being a nursing administrator.

I had discovered how much easier it was to control myself and my work than six hundred others. In administration when things go well it is expected. You certainly receive no credit. When things go wrong, it's always your fault. After all, you are the boss.

Some thirty outside agencies come to accredit you. You must answer to them all. Life is a series of committee meetings, usually ending in the formation of subcommittees to study something or other. Weeks pass, months pass, years pass. Soon you have forgotten the initial problem.

When I started to do administration I was one of many assistants to a very busy administrator. Every Tuesday she would meet with all of us and all the supervisors. I sat at her right side. As a supervisor raised an issue, she would nod at me and mutter, "Handle this." By the end of the meeting I had quite a list. And I did try to handle those problems. I worked on them all week, and by the next Tuesday I had solved a few. Proudly I spoke up, telling of my efforts—and solutions. The results: more problems. Instead of diminishing, my list grew and grew, and grew some more.

One day one of my fellow assistants called me into her office. "Barrie," she said, "you're making it bad for all of us. No one really wants these problems solved. You're not playing the game."

"What am I supposed to do, then?" I asked.

"You tell them 'I'm working on it.' Just keep telling them that. After a time they'll forget *that* problem and go on to something else."

"But these are things that really need solutions."

"Barrie, that's not our problem."

When I resigned, they hired three assistants to replace me, three assistants who played the game.

In anesthesia we don't wait weeks, months, or years; we don't even wait days or hours; minutes is more like it. A brain which is without oxygen for over four to five minutes is a damaged brain. We must give enough oxygen, enough fluids, enough relaxation, enough . . . After all, two teams—the surgical team and the anesthesia team—are working in harmony over one patient. It sounds crazy, but our goals are different. Theirs is to fix the problem, ours it to wake up the patient again—in a shape as good as when we put him to sleep—or better.

During student days we were taught never to communicate our problems to the surgeon. "Let him do his work and you do yours," was the motto. "But aren't we working on the same patient?" I asked. "Don't argue," was the motto. It was hard to learn these things. I always talk. I always communicate. We must communicate, coexist and cooperate—the surgeons and us.

I remember once a young man came in with a fractured nose. He looked like hell. His nose was bent out of shape and his eyes were black and blue. He came in to have his fracture set. It would be set without cutting—by what is called a closed reduction. In putting it back in place the surgeon would cause bleeding in the back of the throat. In order to maintain a safe airway we had to intubate our patient. It was one of the many situations in which the surgeon and anesthetist competed for the same space. I wanted to maintain an airway; he wanted to set the fractured nose.

I put the boy to sleep—he was only a teen-ager. He got the fracture in a schoolyard fight. A bunch of guys were playing ball when an argument broke out. When it was over . . . here he was, our patient.

I put him to sleep and the surgeons started—one attending and one intern. The older man showed the younger how to do it. They put a nasal speculum—an instrument with two long silver projections—into his nose, one projection in each nostril. Then they pressed the bone in place—molded it, so to speak, over the instrument. They got it back in place. Now the only thing left to do was to put packing in—stuff the nose with a Vaseline-soaked gauze—so the nose would keep its shape, and put a metal mold on the outside. This metal mold would be bent into the shape they wanted the nose to maintain and be taped in place by a couple of strips of adhesive tape.

The case was almost over. I had used an anesthetic technique that kept the patient breathing, enabled him to handle his own airway. It was the best and safest way for this type of procedure. The boy was a smoker. Both the blood from the procedure which would trickle down his throat and the fact he smoked made secretions a problem at the end of the case. I had a soft plastic suction catheter ready to remove his secretions as they accumulated.

The intern was putting the dressing on. The boy was waking up. I had sucked out his secretions. It was time to get the tube out. I deflated the cuff and pulled the tube. I suctioned him again. For a few moments he breathed well and looked pink. Suddenly I heard some noise, a gurgling choking sound: a sound we do not like. I grabbed the suction catheter. I sucked out the secretions. He was hardly breathing at all.

"Move aside," I ordered the intern. I needed access to the whole head. I needed to put the mask on—to make a tight fit, a seal. I needed to pull up on the boy's jaw, his mandible—to stimulate him to breathe. I did not have much time. He was no longer pink, he looked ashen; in another few moments he looked blue.

"Get away from there," the intern screamed. "You're ruining my repair."

"Get out of my way," I yelled and shoved his hand away. Quickly I sucked out the secretions. Quickly I put the mask over the patient's face. Quickly I held up his jaw. Oxygen was flowing in. The boy started to breathe, started to look better, his heart rate came down, his rate of breathing came up and he started to get pink again.

"Listen, I'm sorry," the intern said. "I guess I got carried away. I'm sorry, really."

"And well you should be, honey," I whispered. "A beautiful corpse would please none of us." The boy looked pink now. "He's yours," I said.

He stepped over to the head of the table. He readjusted the metal mold. He reapplied the adhesive tape. "It looks good, Barrie," he told me sheepishly. "Let's put him back in his bed."

Another time a young girl was observing in the emergency room—a physician's daughter. She came home and told her parents what she had seen. "And Daddy," she said, "I saw two cardiac arrests. They got so excited. They all ran. They got so excited."

"And so they should," her father replied. "If that didn't excite them, nothing would."

Yet we can't let everything excite us. We'd be burned out in a month. Some things shock us still—a fifteen-year-old hooker in the hospital with pelvic inflammatory disease having sex in the bathroom with five different guys; a gay guy coming to the O.R. with a ten-inch candle up his ass (he said he'd sat on it— by mistake); a ten-year-old boy with cancer; a girl with a leg amputated from an auto accident, sitting in bed picking pieces of bone fragments off her stump—a vacant look in her eyes; a woman thrown out a window by her lover—smashed to pieces and alive; a baby with no brain, just a brain stem—born alive; a breast cancer growing out of an old lady, greenish and foul smelling (she said she'd had it for a month—we knew it was more like a year or two); a twenty-six-year-old with cancer having her uterus out—and her ovaries, and her tubes—and almost half her insides. And sometimes we are surprised: our Tammy—the bike accident victim—after six months in a coma, sitting in a wheelchair, slurred and confused in speech, with a nonfunctional right side but alive and going to rehabilitation therapy. Under our façade we are caring persons, but we cannot care too much; we cannot involve ourselves too much in each patient, in each story, in each operation, for in so doing we will destroy ourselves. We will cease to be objective. We will cease to use our best judgment. We will use our guts, and use up our guts.

It's not easy to cope with what we see each day, but it's rewarding to put people to sleep gently and wake them up safely; though it's a great responsibility, too, because we bring them as close to death as they will ever be in life.

XXII

As I came out of the surgeon's lounge a beaming Lothar waited for me.

"Barrie, today I come to you with the best news. I have a job as intern in Vermont. It is a small hospital, not so many interns like here. The people are very nice. The hospital is clean. I have my apartment in a building next to the hospital. I will start July first. I have seen it three weeks ago and I have today the letter.

"I can ski just like at home in Germany. I can do many sports—even volleyball. I can learn now many things I will need as a doctor. I will be sorry, leaving you. You have been my first friend in the hospital. I will remember you always. And I think that for me you will always be Dr. Cerna, C.R.N.A."

I walked over to the office to talk to Bill and Maureen.

It was only April, but we were all trying to figure out who would be working the Memorial Day weekend. I was thinking about volunteering because I definitely wanted July Fourth and Labor Day off.

"Anesthesia stat 2020, Anesthesia stat 2020" came over the loudspeaker. It was the emergency room number. A "stat" page for the E.R. meant one of two things: either a cardiac arrest or an intubation. When they called over the public address system rather than using the phone, it usually meant there was a foul-up of some kind.

We had just returned from lunch and were waiting for afternoon cases. My patient had not been called for yet. There was no extra time in a case like this. I jumped up and grabbed the tackle box which held all our emergency equipment and ran out of the office. "Watch for my patient, Maureen," I said.

I ran into the corridor on my way to emergency. As I passed the office I heard one of the rooms calling out over the O.R. intercom. "Send for our next patient." I hoped it wasn't my room. I could only be in one place at a time.

I never would make it if I waited for an elevator. I ran to the stairs and started taking them two at a time. I remembered one time I was making a postop visit on the tenth floor and they called for a cardiac arrest on fifteen. I ran up the five flights of stairs and was sobbing for breath when I arrived. By the time I reached the desk I could hardly talk or breathe. "Where's your code?" I managed to get out.

"Sorry," said the clerk, "it was an error. Someone pushed the emergency button by mistake."

And a damned good thing, I thought to myself. I'd never have been able to function at all as winded as I was.

Thank goodness, there were only two flights of stairs today. As I headed toward the E.R. all seemed to be business as usual. The usual crowd was sitting in the coffee shop. Two elderly ladies stood in front of the gift shop display showing babies' T shirts; they were trying to make up their minds whether to buy one that said "Grandma Loves Me" or the one that said "Spoiled Rotten." The fellow from the receiving department pushed a cart filled with large cartons toward the freight elevator. An old man stood by the cashier's window trying to explain something to the cashier. "But, miss," I heard him say as I flew by. Over by the soda machine a teen-ager with a large transistor radio stood feeding coins to the machine. A young couple stood close to one another next to the public phone speaking quietly in Spanish. A security man was talking into his walkie-talkie. A disheveled-looking woman was trying to get into the men's room while a young man tried to tell her, "No No." An Indian couple, he in a turban and a business suit, she in a sari and sandals, padded softly toward the passenger elevator. A harassed mother slapped her toddler. "How many times did I tell you?" she shouted. "Tell me when you have to make pee pee." A puddle on the floor showed clearly that the baby had *not* told her this time.

It was a weird feeling to me. Sort of like a science fiction story or a movie set. The whole world was moving slowly and I was hurrying along. None of them seemed to even notice. It was as if I were invisible—an apparition gliding through the corridor. I turned the corner. I was close now. What would I find? An old man with chronic obstructive pulmonary disease (a lunger, as we called them)? A lady who swallowed a chicken bone which was obstructing her airway? A man with a bullet wound of the neck? An attempted suicide? A drug overdose? A ruptured cere-

bral aneurysm? A cardiac? What is it the Lung Associ-
ation calls it? "A matter of life and breath."

Whatever and whoever was waiting for me was having some airway difficulty. Even in a cardiac arrest my
responsibility was the airway. My job: solve it. How
many times have I run this route? It seemed ludicrous
not to think back on those first days at MCG—days
when I wondered it I'd ever find my way around.
Hell, I could go this route in my sleep—and sometimes did, when they called me for an intubation in
the small hours of the morning.

I thought of the many times I've run through hospital halls at night and what awaited me—a hooker
pushed out a fourth-floor window by her pimp; a
baby with its lip bitten off by a dog; a motorcycle
gang member rammed by a member of a rival gang,
his leg cut off at mid calf, hanging by a thread of
muscle; a kid who tried to get into a disco from the
garage next door, fell almost sixty feet, and lived to
tell about it; a lady in New York for a church convention, her convention over when she was hit by a
car.

Everyone passed through the doors of MCG's
emergency room: old and young, rich and poor,
black and white, sick and not so sick and very sick.
We got them all. Who would be waiting for me now?
After all these months you'd think I would adjust
and just go see, but no, I still felt that pang each time
they called for a cardiac arrest or intubation.

A life was slipping away and I could do something
to help. I was no longer sitting at my desk wondering
how my budget would be cut and could I live with it.
I was right there on the line.

What would I find when I opened the person's mouth? Vomit in the throat and in the lungs? An aspiration. Blood from who knows where in the throat and in the lungs? Again an aspiration.

A rotten tooth broken off and into a lung? A patient too compromised to breathe and yet too alert to submit to my instrumentation?

Anatomy deviated due to tumor or gunshot or whatever so that I could not see the cords?

I was spooking myself. I had to think positively. A person was in trouble and I was going to help him. I could do it.

I was in the emergency room now. The usual group of interns, residents, nurses, and medical students were huddled around the bed. Two residents were trying to intubate the patient—a youngish dirty-looking woman.

"What is this?" I asked.

"Drug overdose—hardly breathing."

"Step aside, huh, guys," I told the two residents crouched on the floor on their knees at the head of the table.

I ventilated the patient, sucked out secretions and blood, slipped in my laryngoscope, and intubated the patient. I listened to the chest, taped in the tube, hooked her up to some oxygen, and looked around. My work was over. The patient was pink, her airway established.

I was proud of myself. As many times as I do it, as many times as I put someone to sleep safely, as many times as I wake someone up safely, as many times as I establish an airway—and save a life—it's a kick. I get high from it. It gives me a sense of purpose and a sense of pride.

I rang for the elevator and got ready to do my next case. It was booked as "lymph node biopsies."

He looked terrorized as they wheeled him into the preanesthesia room: a thin pale young man with blond hair. I said hello and got no response. I looked at the name tag on his bed and asked him "Andrew?" He nodded glumly and muttered something. I didn't get it. "I beg your pardon?"

"It's Andy, not Andrew," he said, staring at an imaginary point over my head. "Only my old man calls me Andrew. Who are you and what are you going to do to me?"

"I'm Barrie, Andy, and I'm your anesthetist. I'm going to be putting you to sleep for your operation, or should I say your examination. You're having your lymph nodes biopsied, aren't you?"

"If you mean that they are gonna take a piece of tissue from one of my glands and examine it under the microscope, yes. I don't understand all that medical jibbety-jab. I'm a dancer."

"Oh, really—a professional dancer?"

"Well, I'm a waiter, but you wait and see. One day I'll get to the top and then . . . Do you know my situation? Did my doctor speak to you?"

"Not yet, Andy. Why don't you go ahead and tell me."

"Well, as I said, I'm a dancer. I belong to a small company. I'm sure you never heard of us. Anyhow, we had an engagement in Texas, in Houston to be exact. Have you ever been in Houston, Barrie?"

"No."

"Well, it is one hot place. Hot and humid. We had hours and hours of rehearsal every day—it's part of every dancer's life. Anyhow, one day we had a couple of hours off in the afternoon. We got in the car and found a nice lake only about an hour's ride away. We went swimming there for about . . . well, I guess six or seven afternoons. We were due to leave on a Saturday, and Thursday afternoon we went to the lake. I couldn't believe it. All of a sudden there was barbed wire all around the place. Big signs were posted all around saying U.S. Government Property, Do Not Enter. Other signs said Swimming and Fishing Absolutely Forbidden in These Waters. We wondered what had happened to cause all this but there was no one to ask. We tried to ask people in the next town, but they knew nothing. They looked at us sort of funny—we were Yankees and dancers too. They looked like we were Martians or something.

"Anyway, our run in Houston was over and we came home. I started feeling crappy—nothing specific at first, just tired, always tired. I woke up tired and I went to sleep tired and I was tired in between. Rehearsing was an almost impossible effort for me. I kept up for a week, but after that I had to quit. By then I was having other symptoms too. First of all I started to itch on my palms and the soles of my feet. I mean itch like crazy. I could hardly stand it. I wanted to just claw myself. The itch drove me insane. I couldn't sleep, couldn't eat. I lived on some Benadryl capsules my friend gave me. The next thing was the diarrhea. It was unbelievable. I must have spent half of my life in the john. I'd think I was done and come out, sit down to read the paper or watch TV and wham—it would hit me again. I lost eight pounds in a week—and I'm slim to begin with. That was nothing compared to what happened next. My hair started to fall out. Barrie, when I combed my hair whole handfuls came out. I used to have a full head of hair—every one used to tease me about it, say I looked like a wild man. Hell, now I look like an old man. And then I got these lumps in my groin and behind my ears and under my arms and everywhere—big lumps—painful too. And no one knows what's wrong with me, Barrie. They are talking about infectious diseases and malignant diseases. They have scared me right out of my tree."

I didn't blame him for being scared. His blood picture looked weird too, as I examined his chart. He was very anemic and had a very low white blood count. This meant that his body's ability to fight off whatever he had was impaired. He had three specialists caring for him: an internist, who was his primary physician, a surgeon to do the biopsy, and an oncologist, a specialist in malignant diseases. Everyone hoped Andy wouldn't need the oncologist, but who knew at this point?

I was concerned about his anesthesia. He was very weak. He was depleted in fluids because of his diarrhea. His severe anemia meant that his body's ability to transport oxygen—carried by the red blood cells— was diminished. His low white count meant he was very susceptible to infection. Granted, he was young, and youth is always a plus in anesthesia, but as far as I could see, it was his only plus. I discussed his case with Doug, the anesthesiologist assigned to Andy's room.

"I'll use a higher oxygen concentration—40 percent should do it, don't you think?" I asked.

"Sounds good," Doug replied.

"I don't know whether to do him on a mask or tube him. Usually a lymph node biopsy is quick, but it's booked as 'biopsies.' Won't I be safer by tubing him?"

"Ask the attending how long he thinks he'll be," he answered. "I'm inclined to go along with the intubation, though. What are you going to use?"

"Well, if I tube him, I'll paralyze him and use narcotics. If I do him on a mask, Ethrane, with a little narcotic at the end. Okay with you?"

"Absolutely. Call me when you're ready to go in." Doug turned to go.

"Just one more thing, Doug. His IV is not too great. It's okay to put him to sleep with, but once he's asleep I'd like to change it."

"Fine, Barrie. I'll put in a new one as soon as you have him asleep."

"I'd do it now, but he's so tired and so scared, I don't want to bother him."

"No need to, Barrie. As soon as he's under, I'll get you a good line."

"Okay, Doug, I'll check with Dr. Dodd about the length of the surgery and plan accordingly. Don't go too far. The room's almost ready."

"I'll be in the surgeons' lounge, Barrie. Call me."

I had given Andy a small amount of Valium and he was sleeping soundly. I wanted to get going. I was caught up in his story. I wanted to see what he had. I went down to the room. It was the last room in the corridor. I walked quickly, put my mask up, and opened the door. "What do you say, gang?"

"Come on in, Barrie. We're ready for you."

I returned to the PAR and peeked at Andy. He was still sleeping. I went around to the surgeons' lounge to look for the attending. Dr. Dodd was reading the *Times*. He peered over the top of his paper as I came into the room. "Are you with me today, Barrie?"

"You bet I am."

Dr. Dodd was my personal doctor. I always wanted to do an especially good job for him. He never billed me for my care. I was grateful to him and wanted to reciprocate in any way I could.

"Great. Is the room ready?"

"Yes, I just checked."

He put his paper down and stood up. "Let's go then."

"But where is your assistant?" Generally the interns and residents took the patients in with us. Attendings seldom bothered. Dr. Dodd was an exception. He had a very busy practice and always wanted to get going.

"My assistant? I don't know. Let's take the patient down, Barrie, okay?"

"Great."

I nodded at Doug, busy on the phone. He'd be down in another few moments. On the way to get Andy I asked Dr. Dodd how long he thought the surgery would take.

"Don't know, Barrie. We might see what we need to know on the first specimen or we might have to get several. Let's be on the safe side here—tube him."

"Okay, will do."

O.R.

Andy opened his eyes as he saw Dr. Dodd enter the room. He looked at him with a combination of worship and dread. We all knew what he was feeling.

"Okay, young fella," Dr. Dodd said, "let's do it."

We went into the O.R., Andy moved to the table, and I did all the things to get ready. Once he was settled on the O.R. table Andy drifted back to sleep. I murmured that I was going to put an oxygen mask over his face. He nodded sleepily. I wanted him to have an extra reserve of oxygen—he had less than normal due to his anemia.

As Doug came in Dr. Dodd went out to scrub.

"Who's with him today?" asked the circulating nurse.

"Don't know," I replied. She went to the intercom. When they answered she asked them to check for Dr. Dodd's assistant. Andy slept.

"Ready?" Doug asked.

I nodded. I didn't want Andy to wake up just to be put to sleep. I pushed the drugs and intubated him. No problem. Doug checked the chest to make sure the breath sounds were equal. He nodded as he moved toward Andy's right arm to put the new IV in. The door flew open.

"Quick," said the nurse in the next room. "We need you. The student . . ." The door closed as Doug ran out.

I looked up. The assistant came in. "Dr. Dodd . . ." he began.

"Go outside and start scrubbing, Stan," Dr. Dodd said.

By this time Dr. Dodd had prepped and draped

Andy with the help of the scrub technician. He was ready to start.

It was time to give Andy the muscle relaxant. I wiped off the little rubber spot in the IV tubing—the port, we call it—and inserted the needle. I gave the muscle relaxant and pulled the needle out. The rubber port popped out too. The IV solution started coming out of the opening at a rapid rate. The regulator to shut off the flow was below the spot where the solution was leaking. I could not shut if off. And I could not tell how much, if any, of the muscle relaxant had gotten to Andy. Until I could settle him down, I could not put him on the ventilator—I had to breathe for him by hand.

My one hand was busy with the breathing bag, the other was over the leaking port. I somehow drew up another dose of muscle relaxant and inserted it in the second port of the IV while holding the leaking port shut temporarily. I signaled to the nurse.

"What's up?" she asked me.

"Please come over and give me a hand." I showed her where to hold her finger over the port and I opened the IV flow wide. The muscle relaxant went in. In a few moments Andy quieted. Dr. Dodd looked up. "Any problems up there, Barrie?"

"I'm getting it under control. Please go ahead."

Where was Doug? I'd really like to get a good line in. I placed Andy on the ventilator. It would breathe for him now.

I ran around to the side where Andy's arm was. The new IV was waiting.

"You can let go now," I said to the nurse. "I'll get it straightened out as soon as I get the new line in."

She let go and once again solution poured out of the port. There was a large puddle on the floor. I threw down a towel so that no one could get hurt by slipping in it. I started the new IV, hooked it up with new tubing, and removed the defective IV.

I breathed a sigh of relief. His lifeline was okay now. We were safe. I came back around to the head of the table. Had I given him too much muscle relaxant? Would I be able to get him back breathing at the end of the case? Soon his pulse started to go up. He was attempting to swallow. I smiled with satisfaction. I hadn't given him too much—I hadn't given enough! I gave a small additional dose of muscle relaxant and morphine. He had youth on his side. He was metabolizing everything rapidly. I was lucky.

Dr. Dodd could not find an enlarged lymph node. He kept coming up with fragments of dirty yellow-looking fatty stuff.

"What is it?" I asked.

"Damned if I know." He selected another site, made another incision, came up with the same material. Yet another time. Same result. The nurse sent out for the pathologist. He examined all the tissue and returned to the room.

"It's only fatty tissue," he told Dr. Dodd.

"Is that all you can find?"

"That's all," the pathologist replied.

Dr. Dodd was perplexed. "Well at least it's not a malignancy," he said. "This is a mystery. Wonder what he's got. I don't know what happened to you, Barrie, but is the kid okay? I'm through. Are you going to be able to wake him up?"

"No problem," I said bravely. Andy was not yet

breathing, but Dr. Dodd still had the skin sutures to put in: I had a few moments. Wonder of wonders, Andy was breathing. I gave the medication to reverse his muscle relaxant and suction him. I turned off the nitrous oxide and gave him pure oxygen. I took out the tube.

Andy opened his eyes. "What did you find, Doc?" he asked Dr. Dodd.

"Too early to tell yet, son. The pathologist is still doing tests." Dr. Dodd turned to the scrub technician. "Thanks, Al," he said. "Barrie, great anesthesia. Thank you."

I looked at him to see whether he was joking. He wasn't. I felt awful. Here I had pulled the IV apart, flooded the floor, lost the patient's lifeline, and maybe overdosed him and he was thanking me! Oh, well, results are the name of the game.

After taking Andy into the recovery room I went into the lounge for coffee. "Barrie, you look a little green," Maureen said. "Anything wrong?"

"Yeah, this is starting out to be one of those shitty days. The dog ate my clogs, I missed my bus and was almost late for work, and now this case. I was trying to give the curare and the rubber port flew off the IV tubing. The goddamn IV leaked all over the floor. It wasn't even a good IV. I wanted to change it but . . ."

"Barrie, Barrie, did anything happen to the patient?"

"No, Maureen, but then I had to give more because I wasn't . . ."

"Barrie, is the patient okay?"

"Yes."

"You extubated him?"

"Yes."

"And he's in recovery now?"

"Yes."

"So what's your problem?"

"I wanted to do an especially nice job for Dr. Dodd and I . . ."

"And you had an off day just like any of us. Look, Barrie, you recognized the problem and took care of it, right?"

"Yeah."

"So what do you want, perfection?"

"I guess I do."

The lounge door opened. Doug came in.

"Oh, hi, Barrie, did the case go okay?"

"Well—" I started. Maureen glared at me. "Well, yes it did. It did indeed."

A week later I met Dr. Dodd and I asked about Andy.

"Barrie, you'll never believe what the kid has. He's got heavy metal poisoning. It's either zinc or magnesium and an almost lethal dose. It's clearing now."

Thank God the warnings were posted in time—for Andy, just in time.

XXIII

My next on-call day was a Sunday. Wearily, I got up, dressed, assembled all my provisions, and got to work. It was a beautiful day: sunny, clear, and warm. A perfect day for the outdoors—jogging, riding a bike, walking in the park, window shopping—anything but hanging out at Mid City General Hospital waiting for something to happen.

At eight o'clock Jeremy came to tell me about the baby doll. I enjoyed working with Jeremy, no matter what the case, and we had had quite an assortment together. There was the pregnant junkie who was shot in the belly; the baby got a bullet crease in her butt, but mother and child did well. There was the young hooker whose pimp tried to beat her to death and then throw her out the window. Many services and specialists worked on her—she kept the ortho crew busy for months—but she lived too. It was Jeremy who called me at 4:00 A.M. once when a beautiful young thing had swallowed some lye after a lover's quarrel. We worked hard together one night on a professor who came in in shock. He was gay and had picked up someone in a bar; when they got to his place the "number" rammed his fist up the professor's rectum and ruptured his bowel: a "fist fuck" is not unusual for us. The professor was in shock, in pain, frightened to death, worried about his career, a little high. Many young physicians would not have known or cared how to handle this man. Jeremy did, as he did any patient: with skill, compassion, and speed. Steve had a temporary colostomy, and three months later I asked to do the anesthesia when they closed the colostomy. "It's bad enough to go through something like this," Steve confided in me, "but when they treat you like shit in some of the hospitals you could die. Gays are people too, but then you know that."

Yes, I speculated, Jeremy and I had put in some time together in the nine months I'd been here. "Tell me about the baby doll, Jeremy. What's he got?" And Jeremy told me.

The tiny baby was two weeks old. He was the second child for his young parents. He had been born eight or ten weeks early and weighed in at a big three pounds. But he was a feisty little thing and had been doing quite well until early this morning when his abdomen became distended. An X ray seemed to indicate that his intestine might be perforated. If it was, we would have to do immediate surgery. Jeremy was waiting for the pediatric attending to come in and look at the X rays. "Set it up, Barrie," he advised. "It's almost certain we'll do him."

When I say I like pediatric anesthesia I do not mean on three-pound babies. Try to imagine three pounds of butter in human form—it isn't big! Not only is it tiny, but it is very immature. I would have on hand all the monitoring equipment I had. I set the temperature of the room at 80 degrees and put out a temperature probe for the baby. I was planning to use the heating blanket and the humidifier I needed a set of tiny endotracheal tubes and an extra small laryngoscope blade.

Benita, the anesthetist on second call, volunteered to help set up. There was plenty for her to do. Fluids and blood replacement had to be carefully calculated: the smallest amount would make a great difference to such a tiny creature. The baby would come to the O.R. with his IVs on a special pump, set for the number of drops per hour of IV solution the pediatricians wanted. Blood would be administered by a small syringe rather than from the hanging bottles which we were used to. We could not take a blood pressure on such a small infant: there was no cuff small enough. We would place a sensor probe over his heart and rely on heart rate instead.

All drugs would be diluted to one tenth of adult doses. We set up a lot of emergency drugs—I was hoping we wouldn't have to use them.

All seemed ready now. It had taken two of us an hour to set up. I went outside to have a cup of coffee and wait. The news came quickly. "Let's do it," said Jeremy. "We'll get the baby from upstairs in about ten minutes."

Jeremy had discussed with the anesthesiologist, Doug, and me the baby's complete history and lab work. Now we discussed the anesthetic technique. We had to use low concentrations of oxygen, lest the baby develop retrolental fibroplasia: the blindness that premature infants develop from too high oxygen concentration. We would intubate awake—safer in a baby this size. We would have to paralyze the little one: they would be exploring the abdomen and they needed good relaxation. We would maintain the baby on nitrous oxide and oxygen and at the end leave the tube in and hook him up to a respirator. With the perforation, contamination, manipulation, and irrigation it was definitely wise to plan postop respiratory support.

Jeremy and I went up to the nursery to get the baby. It took twenty minutes to get him moved from his heated home to the transport isolette. We did not hurry—safety was our primary concern. Three pediatricians accompanied us on our trip. Everyone who saw us peeked into the isolette. A lady dressed in street clothes shook her head in disbelief. "Is that a real baby?" she asked.

It took us another fifteen minutes to get our patient set up on the O.R. table. Although I dropped the head and foot of the table, he looked lost on the part that remained. The room was hot. We were not going to be comfortable doing this case.

I looked. "Jer, is everyone here? May I start?"

"Please do," he replied. This meant that the attending pediatric surgeon and his intern were all set too. The three pediatricians would watch the surgery and manage the fluids. I would stick to handling the airway.

I started the case. I felt as though I was working on a doll—not a person. The baby was so tiny. Everyone was waiting for me to begin. The baby was quiet. He was struggling for his very life. He didn't even have the energy to cry. I slipped the endotracheal tube in

337

quickly and easily, and gave a minute dose of muscle relaxant.

Jeremy watched. "Ready?" he asked.

"Ready," I answered.

The attending took Jeremy through—advising, consulting, assisting with whatever was necessary—but the case was Jeremy's all the way.

They got in and found the perforation. There were bowel contents spread all over the abdomen.

This was serious: an infection caused by massive contamination could easily kill this baby. They were working with tissue so tiny, it was difficult to identify the different structures. They removed the piece of bowel that was gangrenous, made a temporary access to the outside. If the baby should survive, he would need additional surgery at a later date. They irrigated the abdomen over and over, trying to wash out the contamination. The pediatricians transfused the baby.

Sam, the chief pediatric resident, was here, even though it was his day off. I hadn't seen him since that night in the E.R. when we had the baby with the fever.

Two hours after we started, the operation was over. They put a dressing on the baby but no adhesive tape. His skin was too immature; it would come off with the tape. Once again we moved the baby, the bottles, and all the equipment. The nursery was waiting for us. Jeremy, Sam and I took the baby back upstairs and returned him to his old spot. He was definitely the star: no other baby had nearly as much equipment as our little doll. Jeremy and I looked at one another and sighed. Another good piece of work, we both thought.

O.R.

"Thanks, Barrie," he said. "I'm always glad when you're at the head of the table."

His praise meant a lot to me. I knew it was genuine.

"I wish they'd all come out as well as this one, Jer, but I guess that's just not in the cards."

"Barrie," Sam said, "do you remember that baby I was working on in the E.R.?"

"Do I? I had nightmares over her for weeks. What happened to her, Sam?"

"She died. We worked all night but it was no use. By ten the next morning she was dead. An overwhelming sepsis. We got her too late to help her. Those cases make me so frustrated. Good parents too—really concerned."

Infants are a challenge. There is no reserve at all, no margin for error. A few drops too many in an IV, an increased heart rate ignored for a few moments, a few drops too few of urine, all can spell disaster for the tiny patient in your charge. When you are finished with an infant's anesthesia, you feel like running around, like shouting, like taking a few drinks, anything you can think of to release the terrible tension that has built up inside.

I wondered now how to release the tension I had locked up here. I could eat—bad idea. If I ate every time I felt tense, I wouldn't fit through the door. I could smoke—bad idea. I could find someone to rap with—the best I could do. I walked over to the surgeons' lounge. The people here were here because they had to be: interns and residents here for forty-eight, seventy-two, or sometimes even more hours on a weekend; attending surgeons coming in to make rounds—hanging up suit jackets in their lockers before shrugging into freshly starched white coats; staff on a coffee or cigarette break; and me.

The chief resident in urology was riffling through *The New York Times.* "What are you looking for, Fritz," I asked. "The sports section or are you trying to buy a house?"

"Barrie, I'm just trying to calm down, that's all. I don't even know if I can read at this point."

"I feel the same way. I just got finished doing a three-pound baby. What happened to you?"

"I was called to the E.R. for a big emergency. You know what our urological emergencies are usually, don't you? An old man can't pee or a postop is bleeding. But that wasn't it today. I got down there and they pointed to the room where they needed me. The patient had a cop with him. That's unusual enough on our service. Barrie, you wouldn't believe it. This was a young kid—seventeen years old. When his mom came home after church, he was standing in the kitchen, frying his penis in a frying pan. Yes, you heard me, frying it. She said there was blood all over the floor and there he stood, a space cadet, frying . . ."

"Fritz, stop saying that! What did you do?"

"I examined him. Thank God, there was no active bleeding but he had really done a job on himself. It was cut off, almost to the base. He'll still be able to urinate through it, but that's all. I cleaned it up and admitted him to psych. I can't take this kind of thing. Barrie, when I finish my residency I'm going back to Maine."

"Fritz, let's get a change of scene. Let's go up on the roof and get some sun."

"Okay, anything will be better than hanging around here." Maybe we could bake the tension out of our minds.

Together we took the elevator up to seventeen. There was a little room where the chaise longues were kept. We each got one and dragged them out on the roof after we had given them a good dusting.

Someone had a transistor—it was playing nice quiet music. Fritz closed his eyes. He knew talking about it wouldn't help anymore. In a while I drifted off to sleep.

At about two o'clock my beeper went off. I sat up. I was alone on the roof. I ran to the phone. It was the chest resident. "Set up for an emergency heart. Sick patient, very urgent."

Not again, I thought. I called Benita. She was on for OB and had the right to stay there, but most of us did help each other out when on call. I guess that's why there were always two of us. Time was of the essence here.

We set it up together. I was inside the room doing a final check when the orderly knocked on the door. I went out and asked him, "What's up?"

"The patient has chest pain," was the reply. I wondered how this patient had gotten here without a doctor in attendance.

I went outside and there he was: a middle-aged nondescript, tired-looking man, grimacing with pain. I checked his blood pressure; it was okay. I motioned to the orderly to bring me a tank of oxygen. "Having some chest pain, are you?" I asked.

"Oh, well, yes, but it's not my heart; it's my hiatus hernia. You see, I have this hernia, and when I eat the wrong food I—"

I looked up. He was no longer talking. "Saul," I called to him, quickly applying the oxygen mask to his face. No answer. "Get me help—quickly," I told the orderly. I rechecked his blood pressure. It had fallen drastically; his color was ashen, his skin clammy. As luck would have it, his surgeon was coming down the hall.

"Fred," I said, as calmly as I could, "hurry. Your patient was okay when he came, except for some chest pain. His vital signs were good as he was talking to me. Look at him now. He's unresponsive and shocky."

"Take him in. We need to do him immediately. It's his only chance." We ran into the room, hooked up all the machines, and put him to sleep. As quick as a flash, the surgeon cracked his chest. An entire section of his heart was blue and lifeless. He had had a heart attack there in the hall, an acute MI. He went on pump without delay. We could relax a bit. He had survived the initial insult and now had a chance. Veins were taken from his legs for a coronary artery bypass graft. When he came off pump, the heart looked pink, all of it, including the portion that was previously infarcted.

We all smiled at one another. We had no doubt about this one. He'd have been in the morgue without us.

For once time had flown in the heart room. Usually the time spent on pump seemed interminable: the patient's life is really in limbo as the surgeons work. Today we had hardly been aware of the passage of time. When the surgeon asked for the closing sutures, we were all startled. We were unaware that it was already night.

The closure was slow and tedious. Care taken here was of the essence. Any oozing had to be stopped. Besides, it was all so anticlimactic. The exciting stuff was long over.

When we arrived in I.C.U., they had heard about our patient. "Is he really going to make it? We heard he was almost dead."

"He was—it was a close one."

When it was all over, the cleaning up, the setting up, the rehashing, the relief, Fred took us out to eat—the entire team: residents, pump team, nurses, and me. I'm not supposed to leave the building, but we went to a neighborhood place—right across the street. It was night time now and we were starving.

The waitress came by to take our order. "What are you drinking?" she asked me.

"I'd love one," I said, "but I'll have to take a rain check. Just bring me coffee now." I ordered my dinner and sat sipping my coffee, waiting for the meal.

Isn't it ironic, I thought to myself. The guy is alive now, our patient. He was having an acute MI right in front of our eyes. He's alive because he was in the right place at the right time. If he'd been almost anywhere else when he had his attack, he'd be dead now.

This patient had lived. Could I take the credit? Hell, no, twenty people had worked on him and all together we could not take the credit. Skill, luck, a miracle—I guess it was a little of each. Yet others had died who we thought might live.

What a service. Fraught with tension, with danger, with angst, with sadness—and at times like this, with great satisfaction.

I thought about myself—about all the fears I had had of the heart room. I had convinced myself that I was the jinx. Yet this man, so close to death, was alive at least in part because I was there. The bad feelings, the vibes were not in the heart room—they were in my head. People had told me that right along but it took this case to bring it home to me.

I slept all night. There were no other calls. In the morning I went home—well rested for a change.

Epilogue

Once again my name did not appear on the assignment sheet that May day. I was an old hand now. I had been at MCG just over a year. I could figure out the possibilities. ECT? No, there was none scheduled for today. OB? I saw Benita's name on the board. Could Vi had forgotten about me? I doubted it.

Doug came into the office. "Barrie, Vi's looking for you—you and Chip. She said if I saw either of you to send you to her office. Chip's going over now."

Chip and I had worked together a few times since he'd joined the staff just after Valentine's day. He'd been an anesthetist for a year in one of the large municipal hospitals and was making the adjustment to MCG. He was a thin fellow with a small beard and large black eyes. He was eager to please, a bit on the anxious side—a good anesthetist from what I could assess. We'd been together in TOP City and last week we'd alternated cases in orthopedics. Chip's wife was a nurse in pediatrics. They had moved into MCG housing and were expecting their second child.

What could Vi's call mean? Usually when we got called to the office it was a serious matter. Everyday things were handled on the run. I waited nervously until the secretary announced me.

Chip was sitting in a chair in front of Vi's desk and Vi was sitting next to him. She motioned me to join them. I relaxed. Vi, whether she knew it or not, was a "space broker." I used to do the same thing when I was an administrator. If I sat down next to you, it was a friendly chat. If I sat behind my desk and placed you in front of me in a chair, it was serious, and if I placed you in the corner chair of the six surrounding the conference table you were in trouble. I'd bring my chair closer and closer until you blurted out the information I was trying to elicit. It was great to be on the other side of the desk now—free.

I sat down and gave Chip the high sign. He raised his eyebrows. Obviously the meeting hadn't started.

"Barrie," Vi began, "Chip has been here for three months and I'm going to ask you to help him. I don't know if you can remember last August when you had your orientation to the heart room?"

Are you kidding? I thought to myself.

"At the time it was the height of the vacation period so you did not receive the complete formal orientation."

Oh, no, don't tell me there's something else waiting for me there. I figured I pretty well knew the place by now.

"So what I'm leading up to, Barrie, is that I'm assigning Chip to you just as you were assigned to Maureen last year. You will give him the complete orientation. Go over the procedure book, review the bibliography, show him how to assemble the equipment, set up an actual case and make a preop visit.

By the way, Barrie, I know you still visit the patient as well as the chart. I can't insist that the staff do this. Many people are not comfortable on these preop visits. I'd prefer it, though, if everyone did pay the patient a visit—he deserves it. And then, Barrie, after you've done all that, you'll be Chip's preceptor."

"Preceptor?"

"Yes. You'll do tomorrow's case and Chip will be with you to observe. You'll do Wednesday's heart also while Chip assists you, and on Thursday Chip will do the case and you will assist."

"And on Friday I'll be in bed with phlebitis."

"I know you can do it, Barrie. You're a natural at teaching."

"But, Vi, I don't want . . ."

"I'm not interested at this point in what you want, Barrie. MCG is a teaching hospital, and in our department the more senior staff teaches the newer members. You remember all the help you had?"

I did. I remembered that day Joan and I did ECT. I remembered how helpful Benita had been when we were on call together, but most of all I remembered Maureen and my orientation to the heart room. "Okay, Vi, you're right. Let's go, Chip. Let's get the show on the road."

I wanted Chip to get the help I had had. I wanted to do my best. We went over the bibliography and the procedure manual. We assembled our equipment and set up together. Chip was alert and interested. He picked up information quickly and this encouraged me. We collected the paper work and went upstairs.

Yannis was a Greek seaman—a big fellow, a *bon*

vivant. Three months before, he'd been sidelined with coronary artery disease and severe angina. He was in for a CABG—two vessels. We entered his room and sat down. I sat next to Yannis; Chip hovered in the background. I took his history—we had already reviewed his chart—and we explained to Yannis exactly what we planned to do for him tomorrow morning. He listened closely. "Thanks for coming up, you two," he said. "I feel better now. I'm a strong man—I can take anything. But what I don't know about—*that* scares me."

The next morning Yannis was sleepy when he arrived. He smiled when he saw Thelma. We were his team, his friends; he trusted us.

The anesthesia went smoothly. The surgery went smoothly. It was like a symphony in the heart room: every section of the orchestra played its part well.

We were in the utility room afterwards getting some things to the technician so we'd have them for tomorrow's case.

"Barrie, do you do all the hearts?"

"We all do them in rotation. Why do you ask, Chip?"

"You're so smooth, so sure of yourself, so efficient. Do you think I'll ever get to that point?"

"Chip, you can count on it."

I left work with a sense of fulfillment. How different today had been in the heart room. I could honestly say I wasn't afraid of it anymore.

I remembered those early days at MCG well. I remembered all the things I'd learned. I thought of all the things I had yet to learn.

O.R.

I thought about this thing I do—anesthesia. I thought about the things people say.

"Boring—same old routine every day."

"What do you really do, huh? Put 'em to sleep and wake 'em up?"

"Will you stay around while I'm sleeping or do you go away until it's time for me to wake up again?"

"*You* won't put my patient to sleep? *You* don't think it's safe? Just who do you think *you* are?"

"My surgeon is the boss in the operating room. Just what do you do, miss?"

"Anyone can do anesthesia—just turn on the blue dial until they are blue and then put on the green dial until they are pink."

"While the surgeon assaults patients, you will protect them."

"A life in my hands."

"Going, going—almost gone."

"Ether—or—"

I thought about who I am and decided: I'm just someone to watch over you.

The controversial novel of the world's most fearsome secret!

GENESIS

by W.A. Harbinson

First came the sightings, sighted by nine million Americans. Then came the encounters. Then came the discovery of an awesome plot dedicated to dominate and change the world.

An explosive combination of indisputable fact woven into spellbinding fiction, Genesis will change the way you look at the world—and the universe—forever.

A Dell Book   **$3.50**   **(12832-3)**